*Also by Angie Fox*

### THE SOUTHERN GHOST HUNTER SERIES

Southern Spirits

A Ghostly Gift (short story)

The Skeleton in the Closet

Ghost of a Chance (short story)

The Haunted Heist

Deader Homes & Gardens

Dog Gone Ghost (short story)

Sweet Tea and Spirits

Murder on the Sugarland Express

Pecan Pies and Dead Guys

The Mint Julep Murders

The Ghost of Christmas Past

Southern Bred and Dead

The Haunted Homecoming

Give Up the Ghost

Dread and Buried

Death at the Drive-In

Secrets, Lies and Fireflies

Garters, Ghosts and Wedding Toasts

A Spirited Scandal

### SHORT STORY COLLECTIONS:

Haunted for Christmas: A collection of Southern Ghost Hunter short stories

**THE MONSTER MASH TRILOGY**
The Monster MASH
The Transylvania Twist
Werewolves of London

**THE ACCIDENTAL DEMON SLAYER SERIES**
The Accidental Demon Slayer
The Dangerous Book for Demon Slayers
A Tale of Two Demon Slayers
The Last of the Demon Slayers
My Big Fat Demon Slayer Wedding
Beverly Hills Demon Slayer
Night of the Living Demon Slayer
What To Expect When Your Demon Slayer is Expecting

# Garters, Ghosts & Wedding Toasts

ANGIE FOX

Copyright © 2026 by Angie Fox

All rights reserved.

No part of this book may be reproduced in any form or by any electronic or mechanical means, including information storage and retrieval systems, without written permission from the author, except for the use of brief quotations in a book review.

GARTERS, GHOSTS AND WEDDING TOASTS
ISBN: 978-1-957685-38-0

## Chapter One

Lucy the skunk nosed a ripe red apple across the grass, her double white stripe shimmying as she crouched low, her rear end wiggling. Tail swishing, she batted the fruit like a ball, then darted sideways when it rolled straight at her.

A balmy afternoon breeze rustled through the trees under the cloudless blue sky. From overhead, a second apple broke free and hit the ground next to her with a soft *thunk*.

My little girl shot straight up, spun, and landed a foot away. She glared at the ambushing apple, and I felt a laugh bubble up. Poor thing. Life had a way of throwing curveballs when you least expected them.

"Eyes on the sock," Frankie barked at me.

I turned to find my gangster ghost housemate pointing at the curious contraption I held between two fingers, like it was evidence of a crime. Which, technically, it had been for most of the last century.

"You lost one of your vital ingredients," he groused, as if I were the worst criminal in the world.

I didn't have the heart to tell him moonshining was legal now.

I located the penny on the ground and picked it up, wincing

at what I was about to do to my favorite pink fluffy sock. The one with the polka dots. "Can't I just put the pennies in the sock?"

His eyes bugged out. "If you want to do it the easy way."

I looked past the ghost, to the steaming, shuddering copper contraption that dominated the patch of grass in front of my rosebushes. "Easy went out the window when you made me sing 'Sweet Sue' to that monstrosity."

The moonshine still I'd inherited from my great-great-grandmother gleamed in the afternoon sun, then let out a loud, vibrating belch that made my teeth rattle.

In fact, "easy" went out the window the second I'd accidentally trapped Frankie the German on my property. It had begun innocently enough. I'd simply dumped out what looked like a filthy old vase over my rosebushes. Ashy dirt is great for the roots, or so I'd heard.

Only it wasn't a vase. It was an urn.

And when I hosed Frankie's ashes deep into the soil, I'd grounded the 1920s gangster to my two acres of heaven. I never would have imagined it possible until he went and mustered up the energy to go all scary specter on me. Of course, that was after I'd filled his urn with water and added a nice, fat rose blossom.

Some days I still wasn't sure which of us had gotten the worse end of that deal.

Over the years, we'd made peace. Sort of. The kind of peace where he thought he was in charge, and I let him have his delusion as long as he kept his ghostly poker nights to the porch and his shoot-outs off my lawn.

At least now we were sharing a hobby.

Frankie rubbed a hand down the side of the moonshine still with the reverence most men saved for classic cars. "Attagirl, Betsy Sue."

I took a step back. "She'd better not explode."

"She won't," he said with the confidence of a man who'd already blown himself up several times and considered it character building.

Technically, she was Betsy Sue the Fifth, on account of the first four Frankie-built stills exploding in spectacular fashion. Luckily, those fireworks had gone off on the ghostly plane, where they'd only given Frankie a few temporary holes and an involuntary nap at the bottom of my pond. But this distiller was right here with us in the land of the living, and I had no desire to set the house on fire or explain to the Sugarland Fire Department how my car had gotten launched into a tree.

"All art is a risk," the gangster said, like he was Michaelangelo discussing the Sistine Chapel instead of a dead bootlegger coaxing hooch from a contraption held together with baling wire and hope.

I wondered how many times the gangster had blown himself up after he'd died. Then decided I didn't want to know.

As a ghost, he appeared no worse for wear in his pin-striped suit and cuffed trousers. He wore the same clothes he'd died in. Though he appeared in black and white, I could see through him. Just barely.

Frankie had appointed himself my mentor for illegal backyard moonshine brewing, and I'd conveniently neglected to tell him I'd gotten a permit. He was having too much fun corrupting me.

"You asked for this." He pointed a finger at me, and I could practically see him vibrating with excitement.

Technically, I had. I'd somehow gotten the big idea that we could whip up a batch of my great-great-grandma's legendary Firefly Moonshine to raise money for the new women's center downtown. The recipe had been lost until we'd unearthed it on our last adventure, and Frankie was treating the whole project like a mission from the Almighty.

Or perhaps someone a little farther south.

"Wrap it like you're tying a gag on the mayor," he instructed. "You don't want him screaming, but you don't want to leave visible marks, either."

"Because I do that all the time," I said, sparing him a glance as I folded my doomed sock around the pennies.

Frankie caught my look and lowered his Panama hat over the neat, round bullet hole in the center of his forehead. The one that had killed him.

He was sensitive about it.

"You've got to get it tight, or the pennies will get too hot and start shooting out like firecrackers."

In my yard? Near my skunk? Not on your life. "We'll leave out the pennies."

Frankie snorted. "Fine. Do it. Dump out your great-great-grandma's legacy."

I stopped cold. He knew exactly what buttons to push, and family legacy was a big one. We were brewing up our first batch of hooch—well, my first batch—using the antique still that had been part of my suffragette great-great-grandmother's operations. She'd been ahead of her time, running moonshine to fund the fight for women's suffrage. This distiller was part of her story, and mine.

Just then, it let out a loud, rumbling belch.

"Get the sock in the pipe!" Frankie bellowed. "Before the pressure valve gives and launches that milk can through your kitchen window."

I stuffed my sock into the copper opening while he grabbed a wrench to tighten a pipe on the ghostly side. The moonshine still was a masterpiece of creative engineering—a water heater wrapped in copper squares and secured with baling wire, topped with flattened milk cans sealed with red clay. Copper pipes shot through makeshift holes, and the whole contraption tilted left, feeding into a series of catch basins that ended in a washtub fitted with copper mesh.

It bubbled and hissed, sending up a cloud of steam that smelled like peaches and gasoline.

That couldn't be good.

Frankie's ultra-secret brewing technique called for a dirty sock, but I hadn't been quite willing to manage that, so I'd snuck in a clean one instead.

The sound of tires crackling over the gravel drive along the side of my house made my heart do a little skip. "That's probably Ellis." My handsome deputy sheriff boyfriend had promised me a surprise today, and knowing Ellis, it would probably involve something practical and thoughtful that I didn't know I needed.

Frankie dropped the wrench. It clattered through the still and landed in the grass. "You called the fuzz?"

"He called me. Besides, there's no problem." I might as well admit it. "I have a permit to brew."

Frankie staggered backward as if I'd shot him. "You said you wouldn't go rogue."

He should know me better. "I put the pennies in the sock."

"A clean sock. With polka dots!" He leveled a finger at me. "Don't think I didn't notice." He reeled straight through the stack of wood I'd been using to keep the fire going under Betsy Sue. "I have a reputation to uphold. What next? Are you gonna start payin' taxes on this operation? Filing quarterly reports with the revenuers?" His jaw dropped in horror. "Don't tell me you're going to register with the health department."

That was actually a good idea. "I hadn't thought of that."

A black Ford Focus wheeled to a stop next to my 1978 avocado green Cadillac. The door swung open, and my sister bounded out.

"Melody!" I rushed to greet her.

My baby sister looked a lot like me, with her blonde hair and petite frame. Only she was about an inch taller and had more of a bohemian vibe. This afternoon, she wore a snow-white maxi dress with yellow lace trim and a dazzling smile. And before I knew it, she'd pulled me into a hug that smelled like magnolias.

"I've been trying to call you!" she said, her hair tickling my cheek.

I had no idea where my phone was. I didn't always bother keeping track of it when I wasn't on a case. Truth be told, I kind of liked it that way.

"Big news." Melody flashed a gorgeous round diamond that

caught the afternoon sun and nearly blinded me. "I'm getting married."

"I know." I'd helped rescue that jewel from a buried pirate chest on an earlier adventure.

She drew an uneven breath. "I'm getting married this Saturday."

I wasn't hearing her right. "Today is Thursday."

"I know. We have plenty of time, right?" At my sharp intake of breath, the rest tumbled out of her in a rush. "Just kidding. We have zero time. And I only have $143.50 in my wedding savings account. Alec has saved more, but not as much as we'd need." She shook her head. "But that doesn't matter now because as of"—she checked her watch—"twenty minutes ago, we've booked a historic mansion for free this weekend."

Alec was Melody's fiancé and Ellis's best friend, not to mention my former nemesis. We'd gotten past that, mostly. But this was all happening way too fast.

They'd barely been dating a year. "I thought you were planning for a long engagement." Somebody had to think this through. "You can't possibly get married in less than forty-eight hours. What about the food? The band? The flowers?"

"It's all taken care of. Every last detail." Her cheeks flushed with excitement. "You know Honey Sue Caldwell?"

The event planner. "You know I do." Her younger brother had been my friend Lauralee's first kiss back in seventh grade, a fact that still made Lauralee go pink around the ears.

"She's at the library all the time researching historic venues and checking out regency romance novels. Anyhow, she's been crazy, happy, busy lately, creating custom bridal packages for this new wedding venue. They have a photo shoot set up for the premier package this weekend. They hired models all the way from Nashville, but the bride dropped out at the last minute. Honey Sue was frantic until I told her I could pose. As a joke, you know? But then she said—what if you did more than pose? What if you just got married?" Melody let out a little squeal.

Honey Sue did have a point. And a good eye. It was darned near impossible for my sister to take a bad photo. "So you're going to be a model bride?"

"For the chance to get married? Yes," she gushed. "They're giving us the professional pictures for free, plus the cake, the dinner, the entire package. All they want is a photo spread and video to promote their venue. Honey Sue showed me pictures of the house she took on her phone, and its perfect. In fact, only one thing could make it better." She clasped my hands in hers. "Will you be my maid of honor?"

"Of course." Warmth flooded through me, and I squeezed her hands back. I was delighted, truly touched she was trusting me with her big day.

"I've always wanted a destination wedding," Melody gushed.

I froze. "Wait. We're taking a trip? Where are we going?"

My sister's smile gave a little wobble. "Jackson, Tennessee."

I felt the vapors coming on. She might as well have ordered up a paddleboat to Shangri-La. Jackson was only a half hour away, but it might as well have been another world entirely.

More than that. Our people and theirs... There was no nice way to put it. We didn't get along. Never had. Never would.

We didn't visit. We didn't talk. We didn't even care to hear each other's gossip, which was saying something in the South.

Our towns had been feuding since 1836, when Jackson's founding fathers stole our town seal design. We'd come up with the Greek goddess of agriculture perched on a sugar boat floating down the river. They'd taken the same design, same toga-draped goddess with the hair piled up on top her head, and perched her on a boatload of peaches. Not only was it theft, it was adding insult to injury since everyone from here to Nashville knew Sugarland peaches put Jackson's to shame.

My sister gazed at me expectantly, hope shining in her eyes.

"I haven't been to Jackson in years," I managed. Even if I had, I wouldn't admit it. Not around these parts.

No doubt my sister's wedding was going to be the talk of both towns.

"It'll be worth it," Melody said, sparing a glance at the moonshine still as it gave off a loud rattle. "As soon as I saw the pictures, I felt it in my heart. The Byrne estate is *the* place for my dream wedding. The owners are selling it as the ultimate wedding destination in the Southern house party tradition," she said, steering me away from the still toward safer conversational ground.

"I have a house where we could have a party." Smaller, no doubt. But at least it was in Sugarland.

"This place has bedrooms for the wedding party and parents. It's about having everyone you love right there to keep it personal and lovely, and then there's a ballroom for the reception. Oh, and a little stone chapel just past the backyard garden."

"Please tell me you've done more than look at pictures." I wasn't usually this direct. But this was my *sister*. Leaping before looking. "Please tell me you've visited."

"We saw the outside," she promised. "They're still working on the inside. Renovations and all. But the important parts are done now. The place was closed tight for the past fifty years, so there was a lot of work to do."

"Closed?" I halted.

"After a tragedy. But that's all over now. And Verity." She clasped her hands together like she was praying. "You will just die when you see the chapel."

"Wrong." Frankie finished tightening the bolts on his side of the veil and tossed his wrench on the ground with a *thunk*. "The guy wasn't murdered in the chapel. He died in the garden."

I stared at the gangster, who smirked and began inspecting copper coils.

"Frankie," I prodded. He knew he had me hooked. "Are you serious? There was a murder at the Byrne estate?"

"The heir, the last of the Byrne line," Melody said, slipping into librarian mode. "He fell from the honeymoon suite and onto a spiky fence in the garden below."

I turned to my sister. "You knew?"

She notched up her chin in that stubborn way that meant she'd already made up her mind, and I could either get on board or get left behind. "Of course I knew. The poor man died the night before his wedding. It's part of the history of Jackson. And one of their most famous ghost stories." She waved off my shock. "I know more than you think about the 'town that should not be named.' We even have a book on Jackson. Down in the basement, since no patron of Sugarland has seen fit to go on record and borrow it. But it's there."

Frankie shook his head. "That spiky-fence job was a stroke of genius." He bent to light a cigarette from the fire under the still. "Clean, quick, and everybody thinks it's an accident."

Yes, well, Frankie assumed everything was murder. In his world, nobody ever just fell. They were helped along.

Usually by someone with a grudge and a solid alibi.

"So you aren't bothered by a groom's untimely demise?" I asked my sister.

At her wedding venue.

"In a place that historic, there's bound to be at least one tragedy," Melody reasoned, taking a stroll around the still. "But think of the upside. A grand estate, all that gorgeous architecture, and anyone who really loves us will brave the thirty-minute journey into hostile territory." Her eyes sparkled with mischief. "Consider it an adventure. Like Lewis and Clark, except with better shoes and a premium bar."

Behind her, Betsy Sue let out an ominous gurgle. Steam shot sideways from a joint on the ghostly side that definitely shouldn't be steaming. Frankie jammed his cigarette into the corner of his mouth and scooped his wrench from the ground. Melody and I took a few hasty steps in the other direction.

"I'm heading over to Alec's to celebrate." She gave me a saucy wink.

"Do you think there's time? We still need to find you a dress."

"There's always time," she said with a wiggle of her hips. "And

Honey Sue says I can wear the designer dress they rented for the model. It's spectacular. They're bringing in a seamstress tomorrow, but I doubt we'll need one. The model and I wear the same size."

Of course they did. Melody had always been slim.

"Anyhow, Mom's on her way up from Florida. Just come on by tonight, and we'll get the lay of the land before everything starts tomorrow."

Tomorrow. As in less than twenty-four hours from now.

"Okay, I've got to motor." Melody bounced on her toes, already backing toward her car. "I'll text you the address." She spun in a circle, her white dress flaring out. "Can you believe it? I'm getting married!"

She practically floated to her Ford Focus, pausing at the door. "And Verity? Thank you. For everything. For being my sister and my best friend and—" Her voice caught. "I'm just so happy."

"Me too," I told her, meaning every word.

She blew me a kiss, slid into the driver's seat, and started the engine. "Seven o'clock tonight! Don't be late!" She stuck her hand out the window, wiggling her fingers in a wave as she pulled away, kicking up a small cloud of dust.

I watched her disappear down the drive, my chest tight with a mix of joy, panic, and that particular brand of love that makes you want to wrap someone in bubble wrap and also strangle them at the same time. Two days. I smoothed my hands down the front of my favorite purple flowered sundress. We had two days to pull off a wedding at a haunted mansion in enemy territory.

Yes, it seemed Honey Sue had thought of all the big things. But what about the personal touches? The guest list?

The ghosts?

Behind me, Betsy Sue gave another violent shudder, followed by a withering hiss.

Frankie hit me with a cold spot to the shoulder. "You can't just abandon Betsy Sue!" He stared me down. "She needs to keep a constant temperature or...kablooie! Your catch pan is in your apple tree."

I cringed to say it, but, "We'll have to let the fire go out."

Frankie looked at me like I'd used the *Mona Lisa* for a lunch plate. "You... You do not deserve to brew."

No doubt, it was the ultimate insult.

I took it as a relief.

I was saved from further discussion when a familiar black Jeep rumbled down the side drive. Ellis! My heart did a little happy dance.

"Act natural," Frankie ordered, standing between the deputy sheriff and the moonshine still, like he could somehow block my boyfriend's view of the six-foot copper monstrosity. Should I remind the gangster he was invisible to every living soul but me?

Ellis swung out of the Jeep with his usual easy grace, then headed around to the back. He wore faded jeans and a gray Henley that did wonderful things for his shoulders, and his dark hair was slightly mussed like he'd been running his hands through it. When he glanced up and caught me watching, that devastating dimple appeared in his chin.

Lord have mercy.

"Hey there, beautiful," he called out, hefting a toolbox. "Has Melody made it over here yet?"

"She did," I said, hurrying over to give him a peck on the cheek. He countered with a slow, sweet kiss that had my toes curling in my Keds. He wrapped an arm around my waist and pulled me close. "Alec burst into Roan's Hardware about an hour ago, announcing to everyone in a five-mile radius that he's getting married this Saturday."

"At least he's starting on the guest list." In his own way.

Ellis grinned and shook his head. "I hear you're the maid of honor"—he gave me a squeeze—"which is perfect because I'm the best man."

I nudged him with my hip. "You don't sound surprised by this sudden event."

"Nothing surprises me anymore where you and your sister are concerned." He set down the toolbox and glanced toward the back of his Jeep, then seemed to think the better of it. "Although your present might have to wait until after the wedding."

"Don't you be talking crazy talk," I said, edging around him and sprinting to peek under the tarp.

What I saw, tied with a giant pink ribbon, made me gasp with delight—a gorgeous antique farmhouse sink with a classic white porcelain finish.

"Ellis Wydell, where on earth did you find this?" I breathed, running my fingers along the smooth ceramic edge. It was exactly what I'd been wanting since I'd decided to make grandma's kitchen my own.

"Estate sale over in Franklin," he said, looking pleased with himself. "I pulled up right when they were unloading off the truck. I had to outbid two ladies from Nashville who wanted it for their Airbnb."

"You are a saint."

"Don't let word get around. It'll ruin my reputation." He shot me that dimpled grin that had gotten me into trouble more than once.

Behind us, Frankie made a gagging sound. "Get a room, why don't ya? Some of us are trying to conduct serious business here."

I felt heat creep up my neck and took a step back, but Ellis just chuckled. He'd gotten used to my occasional reactions to thin air.

"So," Ellis said, fighting not to flinch when Betsy Sue belched a cloud of what smelled like sulfur and feet, "I see you've taken up your new hobby."

"More like abandoned it," Frankie said, taking a drag of his cigarette. "Right when she was getting interesting."

"Frankie's not happy about leaving our brewing project this weekend," I translated.

Ellis nodded sagely. "I can understand that," he said, addressing the empty space about two feet to the right of where Frankie hovered.

My boyfriend was getting better at guessing but had a ways to go. "I think Frankie will change his tune once he knows more about the place." Ellis cocked his head. "Built by Lord Thomas Byrne, an Irish nobleman who came to America under questionable circumstances."

Frankie perked up immediately.

"What kind of questionable?" I asked, already knowing this was going to be trouble.

Ellis said it plain. "He was the prime suspect in the theft of the Irish Crown Jewels."

Frankie dropped his cigarette. "Now that's a big-league score."

I'd never heard of it. "The Irish have crown jewels?"

"It's one of Ireland's greatest unsolved mysteries," Ellis said. At my surprise, he added, "I read a book on it a while back. The jewels were stolen from Dublin Castle right before a royal visit in 1907. There were no signs of forced entry, and no evidence was left behind. Just"—he snapped his fingers—"gone."

Yikes. "And they think Lord Byrne did it?"

Ellis lifted a shoulder. "Until the day he died, Lord Byrne claimed he was innocent. But he did flee Ireland right after the theft. And he had enough money to ship his entire manor to Tennessee, stone by stone."

"To Jackson?" I balked.

They'd probably been bragging to themselves for decades about that one.

"Just because he was a lord, it didn't mean he had taste," Ellis reminded me.

"And we're going to go to his house." Frankie straightened to his full height.

I didn't remember inviting the gangster to my sister's wedding.

Then again, it would be unwise to leave him alone at home with the moonshine still.

"It's the trifecta!" Frankie whipped off his hat and spun a

circle. "I've always wanted to case a castle, rob a lord, and wear a crown."

Sweet mercy. "We're going for the wedding," I reminded him.

"Potato, potahto," the gangster said with a flick of the wrist.

Ellis gazed down at me, his man-of-the-law expression sliding into place. "Fair warning, the estate has quite a reputation. Between the mysterious death and all those years sitting empty, locals have some interesting stories about what goes on there."

A chill ran down my spine. "What kind of stories?"

"The kind that usually turn out to be true where you're concerned," Ellis said with a wry smile. "But don't worry. I'll be right there with you."

Thunder rumbled despite the clear sky. I glanced up, squinting against the brightness. Not a cloud in sight.

Betsy Sue gave one final, rattling belch before falling silent.

It would be fine. Melody's wedding would be glorious, magical, her dream come true and then some. I'd make sure of it.

Frankie grinned with the kind of anticipation that made me distinctly uncomfortable. "This is gonna be fun."

## Chapter Two

The wrought-iron gates of the Byrne estate loomed before us like something straight out of a Gothic novel. A pair of ravens perched on top, their beaks tipped with gold leaf. Beyond them, the three-story mansion rose amid the magnolias, its gray limestone walls adorned with carved stone brackets and ornate window casings that spoke of old-world craftsmanship and old-world money.

I let out a low whistle. Melody was right. There was nothing else like it. Not in Jackson, not in Sugarland, probably not in the entire state of Tennessee.

Frankie crowded up on us from the backseat. "Now that's a nice pile of bricks."

"Stones," I corrected as Lucy squirmed in my lap, pressing her little pink nose against the window hard enough to leave a smudge.

The drive curved through a neatly trimmed lawn and hedges shaped into columns. Flower beds burst with late-season blooms in shades of purple and gold. Someone had put in the work to make this place shine.

"She doing okay?" Ellis asked as my skunk escaped my grip to press both paws up against the window like she'd found the promised land.

"She's fine," I said, ruffling the fur on her head. "Impatient."

Her carrier was in the backseat with Frankie, but my little skunk liked to stay as far away from the ghost as possible. He liked her. She didn't even pretend to tolerate him.

Lucy was a Southern girl, and she had her opinions.

Ellis slowed the Jeep, taking in every detail. "Look at those foundation stones, how deep the windows are set. The place is a fortress."

"Bet it's loaded with nooks and crannies," Frankie said, with the reverence he usually saved for discussing armored-car heists. "Perfect for hiding the loot."

"The Irish Crown Jewels could be long gone," I warned, "if they were ever there to begin with."

"I'm going to pretend you didn't say that." A distinct chill smacked me up the side of the head as Frankie's power hit me. The sharp, wet sting of energy radiated through my entire body, seeping over skin and down into my bones like I'd been dunked in an ice bath.

Lucy squirmed out of my lap and onto the floor, shooting me an accusatory look that clearly said, *You just had to bring him.*

"Frankie—" I hissed through chattering teeth. My molars vibrated like I'd been chomping tinfoil.

I could always see my ghostly housemate because my mistake had grounded him to my land. But when Frankie lent me his energy, I could see the ghostly realm the same way he did.

And it wasn't always pleasant.

We'd done it in the past to solve mysteries, but I certainly didn't need to borrow his power now.

"I've gotta be sly while I case the joint," he said. "You tell me if you see any dead Irishmen following me."

"We're not here to rob the place," I insisted. But he was already gone, straight through the car door without so much as a goodbye.

Darn it all.

Ellis shot me a curious look, one hand on the wheel. "Frankie?"

As if I didn't have enough to worry about with the wedding.

"He's a crook on a mission," I said, watching Frankie's translucent form disappear around the back of the house.

At least everything appeared normal. For now.

"Let's hope he doesn't get into trouble," Ellis said, tightening his grip on the wheel.

"Have you met my ghost?" I asked dryly.

Okay, technically Ellis hadn't. But he'd been on enough adventures with me to know Frankie attracted trouble like a puppy to a mud puddle.

We exchanged a look. There was nothing we could do about it now.

The sun had begun its descent behind the towering oak trees as Ellis parked near the front steps. A pair of stone gargoyles flanked the arched entrance, their faces worn smooth by decades of Tennessee weather, their wings tucked tight. Tall, mullioned windows caught the fading light and threw it back at us in shades of amber and gold.

I cracked my door and had to catch my skunk before she leapt out and made a run for it. "Sorry, girl," I said, holding her tight against my chest. Lucy loved exploring new places, but this property was huge, and who knew what was out there.

Ellis had already made it up to the massive green wooden door that looked like it could withstand a battering ram. "Impressive," he said, studying a triple spiral design carved into the stone flanking the entrance with his policeman's eye for detail. "You can see where they've done restoration work, but they've kept the original character."

Meanwhile, I began to get that prickly feeling between my shoulder blades. The one that meant we were being watched.

I stepped back and caught a flicker of movement in a window on the right. Up on the second floor. A pale face, there one second and gone the next.

"Frankie?" I hoped, though I knew better. Frankie didn't do pale and haunting. He did loud and obnoxious.

The figure appeared again, pressing a hand against the glass, its fingers splayed. Then it vanished.

My breath hitched. "Ellis, did you see—"

"There you are!" Melody's voice rang out across the grounds. She and Alec appeared from around the side of the house, her white dress flowing behind her. "We've been exploring the chapel," she said, practically skipping. "It's absolutely perfect! All stone arches and stained-glass windows. There's an antique chandelier above the nave and a little cemetery out front with the most romantic headstones."

Only Melody would find a cemetery romantic.

Alec followed more slowly, carrying Melody's sweater and a thermos that probably contained her favorite chamomile tea. He was tall and steady looking, with the same haircut he'd worn since the Marines. When she shivered slightly in the evening breeze, he draped the sweater around her shoulders without her having to ask.

"The grounds are extensive," he said, nodding to Ellis and me in that formal way he had. Alec wasn't big on small talk. "There's a carriage house in the back, plus the chapel and what looks like an old servants' cottage."

"And the gardens!" Melody added. "They're a bit overgrown, but the cosmos and zinnias are in full bloom, and so are the asters. There's this gorgeous cupid fountain that'll be perfect for photos, and rosebushes are everywhere. Everywhere, Verity."

She knew I loved a good rosebush. "How far back does the property go?"

"The chapel's about a five-minute walk," Alec said, pointing the way. "You follow the stone path past the rose garden, then through a small grove of oak trees. The cemetery starts where the trees end, and the chapel sits just beyond that. Maybe three hundred yards total."

"It feels like another world," Melody added, her voice going dreamy.

"Is the house unlocked?" Ellis asked, ever practical.

"Not yet," Alec said. "The wedding coordinator should be here soon with keys. She got sidetracked stopping into Miss Bee's Boutique to check on the flower order. Mrs. Johnson was having trouble picking up the centerpieces for her best friend's fiftieth-anniversary party, what with her shoulder hurting and not having the budget for delivery, so Honey Sue took over and ended up driving her to the VFW Hall." He checked his watch. "But she promises she'll be here soon."

I sure hoped she'd be there to let us in before dark.

"I can't wait to see the inside," Melody said, linking her arm through mine.

"Me too." Although I wished she'd at least peeked through a window first. This was like the time she quit college to work at the library after volunteering for one afternoon for story time. I mean, it had worked out, but still...

Before she could respond, the front door creaked open, startling the lot of us. A weathered man in work clothes poked his head out.

"You must be the wedding party," he said, wiping his hands on a rag as he nudged the door all the way open. The foyer lay in shadow behind him. "I'm Mort Shackleton, the caretaker. Sorry I didn't hear you drive up. I was down in the basement checking the generator."

Lucy chose that moment to try to leap sideways out of my arms.

"Whoa, little lady," I said, barely hanging on.

Mort's eyebrows shot up. "That a skunk?"

My stomach twisted into a familiar knot. "She's perfectly harmless, I promise," I said quickly, holding my girl a little tighter.

Everyone in Sugarland loved Lucy. But this was Jackson. What if he called animal control? Technically, she was an illegal pet.

"Huh." He tilted his head. "Had a cousin keep a raccoon once. Loved that critter. It'd sit with him on the porch and share his sandwich. Took the pickles right off the top." He gestured to the grounds. "Let her run if you want. It's a safe property. Unless you're afraid of her taking off?"

"Never," I said, struggling to set Lucy down while her legs were churning like tiny pistons. She liked to wander, but she never went far. "Go explore, sweetie."

She took off like a shot, skirting a tight line of miniature yew bushes along the path to the garden before burying her nose into a fat, yellow rose bloom.

That was Lucy, stopping to smell the roses.

I turned to the caretaker and tried to sound casual. "You weren't up on the second floor, by chance?" I ventured, nodding to the house. "Last window on the right side?"

He looked at me like I'd hit my head on a rock. "I came up from the basement."

"Of course." I tried for a smile.

Ellis shot me a curious look. I'd tell him later about the ghost.

"Mr. Shackleton," my sister said, stepping forward with her hand extended and a smile that went on for days, "I'm the bride, Melody Long."

"Soon to be Duranja," Alec added.

Melody's cheeks flushed pink with pleasure. "Honey Sue's been held up. We're so grateful to be getting married here on Saturday."

"Wasn't my doing," he said gruffly, giving her hand a quick shake before dropping it. He ushered us into the foyer and hit the lights.

They flickered. Once, twice. But they came on.

Dark wooden beams stretched across a ceiling that rose at least twelve feet high. A grand staircase swept down from the second floor like something out of Gone with the Wind, its banister polished to a warm gleam. Converted gas fixtures cast a gentle glow over rich wood paneling and oil paintings in gilded frames.

A round mahogany table stood in the center of the space, topped with an arrangement of white roses that had to have cost more than my grocery budget for the month. The whole place smelled of old wood, fresh roses, and a touch of lemon polish.

"Oh my goodness," Melody breathed, pressing her hands to her chest. "Is that..."

Through a pair of arched doors on the left side of the foyer, I could see into what had to be the ballroom. Melody was off like a shot, with me in her wake.

Tables draped in snow-white linens were set with gleaming silverware and champagne-colored china. A wall of windows overlooked the garden featuring a lichen-mottled cupid fountain set in a moat of pink roses.

"They set it all up already?" I asked, following my sister as she lifted a linen napkin tied with an ice blue ribbon and a sprig of rosemary from the nearest table.

"For the photo shoot," Melody said, her voice catching. "And now it's for our wedding." She reached for Alec's hand, and he took it, lacing their fingers together.

They'd make beautiful promotional photos and even better memories.

A hand-drawn calligraphy menu graced each setting. I inspected one, admiring the elegant loops and swirls.

"This is their sample menu," Melody said, reading over my shoulder. "But I love it."

I scanned the delicate script. *Honey-Glazed Ham, Buttermilk Fried Chicken, Collard Greens with Ham Hock, and,* "Oooh, sweet potato casserole," I gasped.

Melody grinned. "With pecan streusel. Plus mac and cheese, hush puppies, and biscuits with honey butter."

"Very Southern," I said approvingly.

"We're still in Tennessee," she reminded me. "Oh, and check out the favors." Darling miniature mason jars graced each place setting. "Handmade local honey from a farm just outside Jackson. Isn't that sweet?"

"Literally," I said, making her laugh.

Through the wall of windows, I could see the rose garden in the fading light, wild and slightly overgrown, but somehow perfect. And right in front of it, framed by the view, stood a towering wedding cake on a small, skirted table.

"The cake!" Melody rushed to see.

Five tiers of pristine white rose up from the base, each layer smaller than the last and topped with delicate piped rosettes.

"That one's just a model," Mort said from the doorway. "For the pictures. They're bringing in a real cake Saturday morning, with the exact same design."

"With buttercream frosting and edible pearl trim." Melody let out a little squeal.

Mort shifted his weight, suddenly very interested in the toolbox he'd left by the door. "Their photographer will give you the pictures of you cutting it, long as they get copies too."

He was going to have to get used to brides.

Melody turned to me, her eyes shining. "Can you believe this? It's like it was meant to be."

"It's a dream come true," I agreed. Her dream. I could see Melody floating down those stairs in her wedding dress, see her and Alec cutting that cake with the sprawling garden behind them, see all their friends and family gathered in this beautiful space to celebrate them.

And for the first time since she'd announced this crazy plan, I understood why she'd fallen head over heels for this place from just a few photos. And why seeing it in person had sealed the deal.

"It's perfect," I declared.

"Minus the deadly balcony," Ellis murmured beside me.

Well, yes. *That.*

I wanted to believe Melody was right, that it was just a tragic accident, one of those awful things that happened once and then never happened again.

Only, I wasn't so sure. I'd seen too much. Been through too much.

The lights flickered.

Mort cleared his throat. "Generator acts up sometimes." He shifted uneasily, his work boots scraping against the polished floor. "Let's head upstairs. I'll show you the rooms."

As we followed him back to the foyer, the temperature dropped. Just a few degrees, but enough that I noticed. Enough that the hair on the back of my neck prickled.

Enough that I knew we weren't alone.

## Chapter Three

Something about the house felt different now. Watchful. Though I couldn't pinpoint why. I scanned the foyer, searching for any sign of movement, for the telltale shimmer of a ghost.

But I saw nothing.

At least not yet.

Mort stopped in front of a portrait near the bottom of the stairs. "These are the ancestors," he said. "Lord Thomas Byrne and his wife, Lady Brigid. They came from Ireland together with their son."

I studied the painting. Thomas was handsome in a brooding, Byronic sort of way, with dark hair swept back from a high forehead and deep blue eyes. He wore a dark suit with an emerald silk tie and starched collar, and his hand rested on the back of a black velvet chair where his wife sat.

"He reminds me of Heathcliff from *Wuthering Heights*," Melody said beside me.

She was right. He had that same dangerous, romantic energy.

Lady Brigid was something else entirely. Her chin tilted just so, her dark hair swept into elaborate coils and studded with diamonds. She wore a silver gown with intricate beading and sapphires at her throat.

"They make a lovely couple," Melody said wistfully, leaning into Alec. "I'll bet they were happy."

Mort's expression darkened. "She took to her bed and died less than a year after arriving in Tennessee. They say she had trouble adjusting."

Jackson certainly wasn't for everybody.

Mort cleared his throat. "Lord Thomas passed away several years later, on the night before he was to marry again." He shot us a pointed look. "Surely you heard."

"About the spiky fence, yes," Melody said quickly, "but that was a hundred years ago."

"Almost," Mort agreed. He moved to another portrait, this one of a younger man who bore a striking resemblance to Lord Thomas, only more wiry, making his strong features almost too pronounced. His eyes held a haunted quality that made me want to look away. "Finn Byrne." His voice went flat. "He died the same way as his grandfather Thomas. The house was locked up after that."

Wait. My hand darted to my chest. "Two men were...?" I couldn't finish the sentence.

"Impaled on the eve of their wedding." Mort said it for me, sparing a pointed glance at Alec. "Fifty years apart to the very day. Each of them fell from the honeymoon suite onto the iron fence below."

Melody gasped.

Alec stiffened.

And I? Well, I just had to ask. "Is the fence still there?"

"Verity—" Melody's eyes bugged.

"It's a fair question," Ellis said.

"Is it?" Alec asked.

He of all people should want to know.

Mort shifted uncomfortably. "It's a strong fence."

Ellis looked to his friend. "Maybe you should avoid the honeymoon suite."

"We can't." Melody's voice cracked. "I mean, that's where

Alec is staying tomorrow night. And where we'll celebrate our wedding night and..." She trailed off, her cheeks going pink.

Mort shot them a level look. "You should wait." He stood with his back to the portraits as if speaking for them from the grave. "Reschedule. I beg you." He shook his head, and for a moment, he looked older, tired. "Just leave and come back a different weekend."

"You can't be serious," Alec said.

"This is the weekend with the free offer," Melody piped up at the same time. At my look, she added, "What? It's perfect, and I want to get married."

Mort ran a hand through his graying hair. "Miss, it'll be fifty years tomorrow when Finn Byrne fell to his death. And one hundred years tomorrow when Lord Thomas took the same fall." He paused, letting that sink in. "I'm not one to tempt fate. Are you?"

The question hung in the air for a long moment.

"No. Of course not," Melody said, taking Alec's hand and squeezing it hard enough that her knuckles went white. She was telling the truth. Melody would never put the people she loved in danger. Not knowingly, anyway. "But you have to understand, my sister's a ghost hunter." When Mort gave her a long, skeptical look, she doubled down. "Verity will know if we have a problem. She always does."

Okay, well, I wasn't sure I was up to that kind of pressure.

"There's something in this foyer right now," I said, because it was true and because someone needed to acknowledge it. "I can feel it." Even if it hadn't shown itself to me. The air smelled faintly of tobacco and bay rum.

Melody startled and moved closer to Alec. Ellis stiffened as if he could somehow ready himself. And Mort didn't appear surprised at all.

"It's not *un*friendly," I added quickly, though I wasn't entirely sure that was true. It hadn't attacked us.

Yes, the bar was low in my kind of work.

"Well then," Melody said, pulling her shoulders back and channeling every steel-spined Southern belle who'd ever lived, "let's go see our honeymoon suite."

"If you're sure," Mort said, not moving.

Alec gave a stiff nod. "Let's check it out." He walked over to close the front door, which had somehow eased open while we'd been talking.

Mort didn't appear exactly surprised at that, either.

"I have my heart set on marrying the prettiest girl in the world this weekend," Alec said, wrapping an arm around my sister.

The caretaker let out a slow breath. "Then I'll show you to your rooms."

"There's a simple solution," Alec said as we ascended the grand staircase. "We just won't go out on the balcony."

"Won't matter," Mort said, leading the way, the wood creaking under his heavy work boots. "Something about that room draws folks outside. Both previous grooms were found pitched over the balcony, and neither had any business being out there in the middle of the night."

I didn't like it. "Have you seen anything unusual up there?" I asked, working to catch up to him.

He kept climbing.

"I'll believe you if you have," I promised. "I won't think you're crazy."

Mort halted on the landing, his back still to us. The silence stretched out long enough that I thought he wasn't going to answer. Then his shoulders sagged. "I saw something," he said stiffly, like each word cost him. "Once. Fifty years ago."

"The night—" Ellis began.

"What did it look like?" I pressed, stepping closer.

"A pale figure. Up in the window." He shot me a pointed look over his shoulder, and I felt my stomach drop.

"Last window on the right?"

He jerked out a nod. "There one minute, gone the next." The old man wiped a hand down his face. "I should have warned Mr.

Byrne. But I was a kid, and I was scared. My paps was the caretaker then. He told me to keep quiet, said nobody would believe a word out of my mouth and I'd just make trouble for the family." He shook his head, his eyes distant with the memory. "I did what I was told, and Finn Byrne died the next night." He shook his head. "I'll never forgive myself," he added, so quiet I almost didn't hear it.

The wind picked up outside, rattling the windows.

Mort cleared his throat. "Let's keep moving."

The second-floor hallway stretched in both directions, lit by electric sconces designed to look like gas lamps. The wallpaper was a rich burgundy with gold flocking. Elegant, yet it made the space feel narrower. "The Green and Blue suites are up on the third floor," Mort explained, turning right down the corridor. "This is the floor you'll be on."

We passed a pair of plain doors, then stopped at a fancy one at the very end of the hall. Carved roses and vines climbed the frame, and a gold heart inscribed with *Mr. & Mrs.* gleamed at the center.

"The honeymoon suite," he announced, revealing a room that looked like it had been plucked straight from a bridal magazine. White roses in crystal vases made it smell like a flower shop.

A massive four-poster bed dominated the center of the room, draped with a gauzy white canopy. The coverlet was ivory silk with delicate lace trim, and a dozen pillows in varying shades of cream were arranged just so. A small table with two burgundy velvet wingback chairs sat near the French doors, positioned to take advantage of the view.

"This is even better than the pictures," Melody gasped, stepping inside like she was entering a cathedral.

Then I caught a scent that wasn't flowers. Sharp and unmistakable, cutting through the sweetness like a knife. There, on the marble mantel next to an antique jewelry box, a ghostly cigar lay carelessly snubbed out in a crystal vase, the last wisps of smoke curling away into nothing.

Okay, we were in business.

My heart thudded in my chest as I scanned the room. "Hello?"

No response.

Tall windows looked out over the front of the house, their heavy brocade curtains pulled back to frame the view. Wait. We were in the last room on the north side of the house. That was the window where I'd spotted the ghost earlier, the pale hand pressed against the glass.

But I didn't see a soul. At least not any dead ones. Not yet.

"Verity, look!" Melody pressed both hands to her chest, her eyes going wide. In the corner by the door, a dressmaker's mannequin stood draped in the most gorgeous wedding gown I'd ever seen. Made of shimmering silk and trimmed in lace so delicate it almost didn't look real. It had a sweetheart neckline and pearl buttons trailing down the back. A cathedral-length veil cascaded from a delicate crown, the tulle so fine it looked like spun sugar. "My wedding dress!" Melody rushed to see.

"It's gorgeous." It was. It even had a train in the back that pooled on the floor. I took one last glance at the mantel, to the cigar fading away. "You're going to look so pretty."

Like a princess. Like the happiest girl in the world.

"I didn't know this was *the* dress until I saw it," she said, reaching out to brush her fingers over the silk. "Now I can't imagine wearing anything else. Help me try it on."

"Not with Alec in the room," I said, admiring the trim. "Bad luck and all that."

"We'll kick him out." She laughed.

"In a minute," I promised, scanning to see where the men had gone.

Melody couldn't resist. She lifted the delicate veil from the mannequin, holding it up to admire the pearls on the crown. "Out there," she said, nodding toward a pair of French doors opening onto a stone balcony.

My stomach dropped.

Ellis stood at the railing, leaning too far out over the edge.

Alec had joined him, both men peering down onto the garden below. At the fence, no doubt.

I braced myself and joined them, the evening air hitting me with a swift gust of wind to the face. "Let's go back inside," I urged, sneaking a peek despite every instinct screaming at me to get the heck out of Dodge.

The fence was classic Southern gothic wrought iron, its bars worked into elegant spirals and curves that were beautiful in that deadly sort of way. Lovely until you got to the tops. Each spike tapered to a wicked point sharp enough to run a man through, and there had to be two dozen of them running the length of the garden bed below, spaced close enough that you couldn't hope to fall between them.

You'd land right on top.

"Oh hey, Verity," Ellis said, not bothering to pull back up. "You'd think the new owners would have gotten rid of this."

"Maybe I'll stick some tennis balls on the points for tomorrow night," Alec joked, leaning farther to get a better look.

"Stop it," I said, fighting the urge to cover my eyes. "You two are going to give me a heart attack."

"Gallows humor," he said, straightening up and pulling me close. "We're just checking to see what we've got." At least he had the decency to step back from the edge.

"I'd like it noted that I'm the only sensible one," Melody called from the mirror over the fireplace, trying on the veil.

"How about we discuss this *inside* the room?" I suggested, ushering Ellis off the balcony.

"Listen to the lady," Mort said from the doorway to the hall. "It's a curse. I swear it. After Lord Byrne died, his bride-to-be tried to carry on. But they say she was never the same after losing him. Doctors said consumption took her three months later, but those who knew said it was really a broken heart." He paused, his expression going dark. "And fifty years later, Finn's bride-to-be took her own life not three months after his death."

Unfortunately, that was not the way to convince Alec.

Or Ellis, who doubled back and immediately began checking the bolts holding down the rail.

The wind picked up, rustling through the garden below.

"There has to be a logical explanation," Alec said. "Maybe the balcony was structurally unsound—"

"The balcony was rebuilt during Finn's lifetime," Mort cut in. "Stone foundation, reinforced joists, a much taller iron railing. Sturdy as she goes. It still didn't stop Finn from going over it fifty years ago." He crossed his arms over his chest. "And the fence is tied in with the history of the estate. The current owners refuse to touch it."

"Why don't we all just stay out of this room?" I suggested, heading for Mort and the hall.

Safe to say, if I owned a wedding venue, I'd get rid of the death spikes on day one. Though some couples would probably think it added character.

Melody chewed her lip, her hand going to the veil still draped over her head. For the first time, she looked uncertain.

Alec closed the balcony doors tight behind him and joined her, his hands gentle on her shoulders. "We're not part of this family, this legend, or this town," he reminded her, his voice steady and calm. "We're just two people who want to get married. That's all."

"We'll make sure it's safe," Ellis promised.

I stopped. "Can we have this discussion out in the hall?"

But Alec was in no hurry. He looked at me directly, his gray eyes solemn. "If there really are dangerous spirits around, you'll sense them, right? You'll warn us?"

I was good, but I wasn't sure I was that good. "I mean, I wouldn't bet your life on it." And certainly not my sister's.

Because that was what this was really about. Not some abstract ghost or century-old curse. It was about Melody sleeping in this house where sad, dead brides-to-be could be lurking. About Alec sleeping in a place that didn't have the best track record for keeping grooms alive.

And even as I pondered the problem, I noticed that the French doors stood slightly ajar.

"Are all the locks in this house broken?" Ellis asked, striding over to refasten them. He threw the bolt and tested it twice.

"It's not the locks or the doors," Mort said, watching Ellis work with the resigned expression of a man who'd tried the same thing too many times to count. "Don't matter how many different locks I install, how much I tighten the hinges, or what kind of weather stripping I use. It's something else." He shook his head. "I don't know what."

I exchanged a glance with Ellis.

"Let me show you where you should be staying," Mort said, herding us back into the hallway.

He led us down the hall to the next room. Smaller than the honeymoon suite, but lovely in its own right, with lily-patterned wallpaper and mullioned windows instead of a balcony.

I liked it better already.

"There's a room similar to this one a little farther down," Mort said, lingering in the doorway, "then two more suites on the third floor, complete with kitchenettes. The stairs are steep, so you'll have to head up yourselves. Doors are unlocked."

Of course they were.

"Honey Sue can show you the rest when she arrives," Mort said, leading us back downstairs, as if he couldn't wait to leave. "I should head back to my cottage. It's just beyond the carriage house if you need anything." He gave Ellis and Alec a sharp nod. "Stay away from that balcony."

"We'll do our best," Alec pledged.

And then some, if I had anything to say about it.

After Mort left, we stood in the grand foyer, looking at each other. Full darkness had fallen outside. The house felt different now. Bigger. Colder. Like it had been waiting for night to show its true face.

"Well," Ellis said finally, breaking the silence, "this is certainly atmospheric."

"It's romantic," Melody insisted, though she moved closer to Alec. "Let's go grab the luggage," she said, giving Alec a peck on the cheek that made him smile.

How she made him googly eyed every time, I did not know. But the man was a goner. I watched her dash out the door and him give chase.

I'd once nicknamed him Robocop on account of how stoic he was, how he never showed emotion, how he moved through the world like he was wearing iron underwear. But around her? He came to life.

Ellis headed for the door. "I'll grab our luggage, too."

"Not with those two kissing by the car." I grinned, glancing out the window as Melody wrapped her arms around Alec's neck.

"I don't think I'll stop them for long," Ellis said, heading out into the night.

Ellis joked with my sister and Alec as he grabbed my rolling suitcase and his duffel bag from the Jeep, but I hung back in the foyer.

I braced my back against the window frame, thinking. I needed to learn more about that honeymoon suite. The ghostly cigar. The doors that wouldn't stay closed. The pale figure in the window. All of it made me distinctly uncomfortable.

Happy voices filtered from the drive. Lucy had returned from her adventure in the garden and was now frolicking by the cars. Melody scooped her up, laughing, as my skunk tried to climb her like a tree.

At least someone was relaxed.

That was when Frankie's head popped up through the floor and nearly scared me out of my skin.

"This is it, Verity," he said, eyes wide. "You gotta see what I found!"

"Can it wait?" I asked, glancing toward the staircase. I didn't have time for the mobster or his treasure hunt or for him to be trying on the crown jewels. "I've got bigger fish to fry." Like keeping Alec alive. And Melody out of danger.

"That's just it," Frankie said, shoving himself up through the floorboards. "What I found downstairs? It might explain why those fellas took a dive."

## Chapter Four

"Follow me." Frankie dove back through the floor.

Sometimes he forgot I couldn't follow.

I eyed the spot where he'd vanished as Ellis and the rest paraded back through the door, the guys schlepping luggage and Lucy trying to escape from Melody's grip.

Why did it have to be a creepy basement? Why couldn't I learn more about why those poor grooms died by doing something fun like browsing an elegant old library or enjoying a sweet tea on the porch?

Lucy danced a circle around me before following Melody and Alec upstairs.

Ellis caught my look and drew close, lowering his backpack and abandoning my roller bag. "Let me guess. Frankie wants you to go somewhere you shouldn't and investigate something you'd rather not, while telling you less than you ought to know."

Bingo. "Is it that easy to read on my face?"

"I just know Frankie." He tucked a strand of hair behind my ear, his touch gentle. "What did he find?"

"I don't know yet." Something I probably didn't want to see. "It's in the basement. He thinks it might explain the deaths."

"Then let's head down," he said, already scanning the foyer for the entrance.

A grinding motor drew our attention to the front of the house. A work truck pulled up outside, headlights cutting through the night. "That's Mort."

What was he doing back? He'd said he was heading to his cottage.

The caretaker climbed out of the cab, carrying a toolbox that looked like it weighed more than I did. "He'd better not be checking the generator again."

Ellis's mouth formed a thin line. "You do what you need to do. I'll handle him." I could tell he wanted to come with me. "If Frankie found a lead, you need to follow it. The sooner we tackle this complication in the honeymoon suite, the better."

I gave my gloriously practical man a kiss on the cheek. "Wish me luck."

"I'm wishing you an easy time with your gangster."

He might as well have wished for the moon.

I hurried to find the entrance to the basement while Ellis headed for the front door, already putting on his friendly deputy smile.

"Hidden door under the staircase," Ellis called back, waving to Mort through the window.

No kidding? I should have guessed. Grand old houses loved their secret passages and hidden doors.

I caught the outline in the decorative wood paneling at the side of the staircase. A servants' entrance designed to be unobtrusive, to let the help move through the house without disturbing the family. Ellis never missed a detail. I ran my fingers along the edge until I found the catch. It slid open smoothly, revealing narrow wooden stairs that disappeared into darkness.

"You're the best," I called back to Ellis.

"I know."

It was one of the things I loved about him. No false modesty. Just facts.

"And be careful," he added, his voice going serious.

I always was. Or at least, I always tried to be.

I closed myself into the darkness and left the light off in case Mort could see the glow from the foyer. No sense taking chances or raising questions. I felt my way down the first step, then the second, keeping one hand on the rough stone wall for balance.

This was fine. Great, even. Frankie had a lead, and I was going to follow it.

My fingers brushed something cold and wet and—eww—sticky. I yanked them back, wiping them on my sundress.

No worries. I cleared my throat. Caught my breath.

I'd been in sketchy basements before. I could do this. After all, I'd survived a haunted asylum, been tossed off a ghost train, and even teamed up with a dead Belgian detective to solve a cold case.

A churning groan vibrated from somewhere below.

No problem. I was a professional.

The air grew colder with each step, thick with the smell of damp earth and something sickly sweet, like rotting fruit.

Goodness gracious.

Being maid of honor was supposed to mean picking out dresses and organizing the bachelorette party and maybe giving a slightly embarrassing speech at the reception. Never in a million years could I have imagined it would mean following a gangster ghost into a creepy haunted basement to keep the groom from dying before the ceremony.

Then again, this was my sister's wedding, and when had anything in our lives ever gone according to plan?

I dug the phone out of my pocket as I neared the bottom and turned on the flashlight. The basement sprawled larger than I'd expected, a maze of stone archways and low ceilings. Support beams cast skeletal shadows across uneven flagstone floors. Exposed pipes ran overhead, some wrapped in crumbling asbestos insulation that probably violated every code in the book.

Well, no venue was perfect.

Water dripped down onto a box spring in the corner. Renovation debris was piled against the left wall—broken plaster, splintered wood, coils of copper wire, and what appeared to be the remains of an old furnace.

The generator Mort had mentioned sat in an alcove to my right, its white casing and digital readout looking out of place in the old limestone basement. It was solar powered, according to the label on the side. A newer model, but apparently it still gave Mort trouble.

"Frankie?" I called softly, then more urgently when I heard voices overhead. Ellis's deep rumble and Mort's gravelly response, their footsteps echoing across the foyer. If the caretaker decided to come down those stairs behind me, well, I'd have to find someplace to hide. Probably behind that old furnace. In the dark. With the spiders.

Frankie poked his head out of the archway at the far end of the basement. "Over here. And make it snappy."

I hurried toward the archway slower than I'd have liked, cursing my decision to change out of my faithful Keds and into cute, clacky sandals for the trip to the estate. Every step echoed like a gunshot in the cavernous space.

A single bare bulb dangled above the entrance.

I pulled the string.

It illuminated a circle of light that somehow made the shadows deeper.

"Oh, for heaven's sake." Frankie stepped out of a darkened doorway to my left, scaring the bejesus out of me. "What? You haven't seen a ghost before?" He jerked his thumb. "In here."

"This had better be good." I stepped inside and found the light switch.

The wine cellar stretched out long and narrow, carved directly into the limestone foundation. The arched ceiling was fitted with a series of stained-glass sconces in geometric patterns and deep jewel tones. Built-in racks lined both walls. It was recent construction, smelling of pine and varnish.

Frankie stood at the back, near a nook in the rock that

appeared to hold a few dozen choice bottles. He'd cracked one open on the ghostly side, a bottle thick with dust and trailing a cobweb.

"Make yourself at home," I said as he took a swig.

He didn't even have the courtesy to appear offended. "I had to do something while I was waiting for you."

"I was upstairs for maybe five minutes," I said, inspecting the bottles.

He wiped his mouth on his sleeve. "Like I said. Forever."

The ghostly side of the space seemed to harken back to the time the mansion had been abandoned. Decrepit racks sagged, their wood blackened and rotting, their bottles thick with decades of grime. Several bottles had burst, their contents long since dried into black stains on the stone floor.

Haunted places appeared as the dominant ghost saw them. The ghost who controlled this space had been lurking here long before the renovation.

"What did you want to show me?" I asked, dodging a ghostly cobweb that hung from the ceiling like Spanish moss.

He took another swig and pointed the bottle toward the wall behind him. "It's back there."

"Where?" I didn't see anything. And then I noticed a spot different from the rest.

I drew closer. In the real world, the space looked recently restored, the mortar fresh and even. But on the ghostly side... I squinted to see. One section stood out like a scar—newer brick, cruder mortar, done in a hurry. Like someone had tried to match the color but hadn't quite succeeded.

"You gotta dig," Frankie said.

I glanced at him. "What about this is going to tell us why those grooms died?" Unlike my ghost buddy, I couldn't—and shouldn't—be going through walls.

"Hey." He pointed the bottle at me, sloshing ghostly wine. "While you were flitting around upstairs, playing dress-up with your sister, I was investigating. Doing the hard work."

"Sticking your head through walls and drinking stolen wine," I finished for him.

"Among other things," he said, corking the bottle. "I think I found an old friend of mine." He adjusted his hat. "Well, sometimes friend. Mostly enemy. It's complicated."

That was gangster code for "we shot at each other regularly."

I drew closer. "Who?"

"Lenny the Ghost. And yes, I get the irony. He's an ace thief. Better than me, even. Only, I have more class. Anyhow, he's dead in that wall, and from the look of him, he's been there a long time."

My breath caught. "Long enough to know what happened to those grooms?"

Ghosts liked to haunt their death spots, especially when they had unfinished business. Which I could see if one were buried in the wall of a wine cellar.

Frankie eyed me. "There's one surefire way to find out."

"Oh, no."

"You need to dig him up."

That was what I was afraid he was going to say.

"Here's the deal." Frankie deposited his half-drunk bottle back on the rack. "Lenny the Ghost went missing in 1924. We all figured Ice Pick Charlie snuck up on him or Bruce 'The Lout' fit him for a pair of concrete shoes." He hitched a shoulder. "Lenny was an ace thief, but quick on the trigger. He'd shoot you through the heart for looking at him funny."

"Whereas you shoot people for reasons," I mused.

"I stuff guys in car trunks for reasons," Frankie corrected. "The rest is a numbers game. You plug enough guys, some of their friends are gonna take revenge. That's how life works. Word is, Lenny found out the hard way. Twelve different guys claimed responsibility for his death. That's gotta be a record," he chuffed. "But if Lenny's still haunting this pile of bricks, my bet is he's been casing the place for the jewels. And if he hasn't found 'em yet, he'll still be here."

"Even if he found them, he couldn't take them." Not if he was dead. Ghosts could only keep what they'd died with.

Although, that didn't stop them from wanting to score. Case in point: Frankie.

"And you're sure it's him?"

"He's wearing the watch he lifted from Lucky Luciano."

As you do.

Frankie tipped the Panama hat low over his forehead. "He's right behind that wall. You dig him out. You steal his watch." The corner of his mouth tipped into a grin. "Old Lenny will come running."

"Oh, sure. Tick off a murdering gangster and then ask him to help me."

Frankie drew a silver cigarette case from his jacket pocket and flipped it open.

"Worked for you when you met me." He selected a smoke and tucked it onto his bottom lip.

"Doesn't mean I don't regret it."

Frankie smirked. "You're the only one who *can* do it, sweetheart." He lit the cigarette with a ghostly match that he tossed over his shoulder. "I can't touch that wall, not in your world. And if Lenny is after the jewels—which he is—he's going to avoid me. He won't want to share the loot. Or admit it's here. But if you steal his watch?" Frankie grinned. "He'll have to come after you."

"Remember, you're talking me into this."

"You'll sweet-talk him." He took a hearty drag. "You always do."

Yes, but I usually didn't rob the ghost first.

I brought a hand to my head, though I could already feel myself caving. The logic was sound, even if the execution was set to be a Frankie-style disaster.

"You got a better idea?"

The trouble was, I didn't.

If Lenny had been around for the death of the second groom fifty years ago. If he was a master thief and had been casing the property this entire time, it stood to reason he might very well know something about how Finn Byrne died. He might even have seen it happen.

It was our best lead so far. Our only lead, really.

"Okay." I grabbed the first bottle before I could change my mind. "But if this goes sideways, I'm haunting you first."

"Deal," Frankie smirked.

I began removing bottles from the nook, working quickly. The first few I stashed on the wine rack, hoping they'd blend. When that was filled up, well, the rest went on the floor next to me. It wasn't like I could exactly hide what I was doing. Not if I was going to make a big hole in the wall.

In a way, I considered it justice. Ellis and I had almost been walled in once under an old distillery. I remembered that moment of pure animal panic when I realized we might not get out. The clawing desperation, the way my lungs felt too small, the certainty that if we didn't escape right then, we'd die slowly over days, faced with dehydration, starvation, total darkness. We'd made it out, but this man hadn't.

He'd lived my nightmare.

He deserved to be found.

"There's only one catch," Frankie said, knocking the ash off his cigarette.

"Do I want to know?" I pulled the last bottle and got an unobstructed view of the wall. The bricks themselves appeared older, most likely repurposed from somewhere else on the property. The mortar appeared in my world exactly as it did in the ghostly realm. It was crude, crumbling, hasty work done by someone who either didn't know what they were doing or didn't care.

A cold draft leaked from the seams.

The gangster cleared his throat. "If you bring Lenny back, you might also get the attention of his killer."

I ran my fingers along the mortar. It flaked away like old chalk. "Why are you telling me this?"

"Because somebody had to wall Lenny in." Frankie took a drag. "It's very *Cask of Amontillado*."

I stared at him.

Smoke trailed from his nose. "What?" he said defensively. "I read."

"No, you don't."

"Fine." Frankie stubbed out his cigarette on the wall. "I'm just saying we do this smart." He scanned the cellar. "We draw out Lenny. We get him to talk. And then we skedaddle."

Not on my sister's wedding weekend.

This was getting better and better.

My phone buzzed with a text from Ellis. *Mort wants to check the generator. Running out of excuses.*

*Keep stalling*, I texted back.

I tested the edge of a brick with my thumbnail. The mortar crumbled away easily, releasing a puff of limestone dust that made me cough. The smell hit me then—damp earth and something mineral, like pennies left in water.

I kept working.

Dust coated my hands, turning them gray. My fingernails ached from digging at the mortar. Each brick I removed made a soft scraping sound that seemed too loud in the enclosed space, echoing off the vaulted ceiling. I wiped sweat from my forehead with the back of my hand, leaving a streak of grit across my skin.

This was my time to come up with a better plan.

Unfortunately, our best idea still involved me digging into the wall of a house I didn't own, while the caretaker was upstairs, to unearth a long-dead mob killer who might or might not be willing to help us but who would certainly have no qualms about killing us if the mood struck him.

Death would only knock Frankie out for a while. It would make me a permanent resident of the other side. Watching my sister get married without me, watching Ellis move on with his life, watching Lucy wonder why I never came home.

"This is it. I've lost my mind." I'd gone completely bonkers, I decided, grabbing another brick and wiggling it loose.

Then I thought about Alec in that honeymoon suite tomorrow night. About Melody's face when she talked about her dream wedding. About being the maid of honor, which apparently now included amateur grave robbing.

"I always knew you'd be good at this," Frankie said, rubbing his hands together.

"We are not making this a habit," I warned, pulling out another brick.

The cold intensified with each brick I removed. Goosebumps rose on my arms despite my exertion and the sweat trickling down my spine.

The hole was big enough now. I shone my phone light inside and immediately wished I hadn't.

The beam caught bone. I gasped as the light revealed the curve of a skull. A hollow eye socket stared back at me. The mouth hung open, frozen in mid-scream.

"Oh my God." I nearly dropped my light, the beam dancing across the wall like a spastic firefly.

The skeleton lay slumped against the corner, legs sprawled, arms crossed over its chest. Bricks littered the ground from a partially collapsed section of ceiling.

"Oh good," I said, eyeballing the hole in his head against the bricks on the floor. "His skull was smashed. Fatal cave-in."

"You don't have to sound so stoked about it," Frankie groused.

I drew back and straightened. "If he had to go, I'm sure he'd rather go quick."

Although I couldn't imagine who'd hole him up in a wall.

In a way, I was glad we'd found him. I turned to my housemate. "This was someone's son. Someone's friend. He deserves better than to be forgotten down here."

"Eyes on the prize, doll," Frankie drawled.

It was a jerk thing to say, but he was right. Alec deserved to live to see his wedding. Melody deserved to have her happy ever after.

"I'm sorry," I whispered to the skeleton as I reached inside the hole.

The clothes had mostly rotted away, black fabric gone gray and brittle. I detected the remains of a white shirt, diamond shirt studs glinting dully along what remained of the placket. A skeletal hand clutched a snub-nosed revolver.

And on that wrist, a gold watch.

"That's it." Frankie did a little dance. "That's Lenny's watch. Well, Lucky Luciano's, but Lenny's fair and square! And now ours if he don't show up. You hear me, Lenny?" He raised his voice. "We got your watch!"

Even tarnished and dusty, I could tell it had been expensive. Diamonds circled the watch face in a way that caught my phone light and threw tiny rainbows.

"Get the shirt studs, too," Frankie urged.

"We're not robbing him," I insisted.

"You are absolutely zero fun."

I leaned farther into the hole, trying not to think about touching the skeleton. My fingers brushed the knobby wrist bones, and I winced as they closed around the watch band.

Leather. Dried and cracking and probably about to fall apart in my hands.

I tugged gently.

The skeletal hand moved.

I winced and tugged harder. The skeleton cracked and shifted, and the whole arm dropped away from the chest with a sound like kindling snapping. Bones separated at the joints, clattering against the brick.

Heavens to Betsy! I jerked back, my heart hammering against my ribs. "I broke him. I broke Lenny the Ghost."

"Yeah, but you still need to finish the job."

My hands shook so badly I could barely hold my phone. The light beam stuttered across the walls.

I approached the skeleton again. Took in the arm lying at an unnatural angle. The gun on the ground next to what remained of Lenny.

The thought of touching those bones again made my stomach turn. But the gun...

"I'm taking the gun," I said, my voice steadier than I felt.

"Even better," Frankie said like a proud papa. "That'll tick him off more."

Lovely.

The gun was cold and heavy, more solid than I'd expected. Heavier than it looked. I pulled it free from the skeletal grip and stepped back from the wall, cradling it against my chest.

There. "I did it." I'd robbed the ghost. "Now what?"

Nothing happened.

Frankie and I stood there looking at each other, surrounded by scattered bricks and mortar dust, bottles on the floor, me holding the dead gangster's gun.

The bones of the skeleton shifted behind me, and I thought I might have a heart attack. I spun toward the wall, only to witness half the arm clattering to the floor. The watch tumbled free, and I snatched it up, just in case.

Wouldn't it be terrible if Ellis and Mort walked in on me now?

Five seconds passed. Ten.

Or worse—what if nothing happened at all? If we'd done this for nothing?

"Maybe he's not—" I began.

The temperature plummeted.

I sucked in a breath, and it came out as a cloud so thick I could barely see through it. Frost spread across the wine bottles on my side of the veil, crackling across the glass like spiderwebs. The lights overhead flickered.

"Here we go," Frankie muttered.

A voice spoke directly behind us. "Looking for something?"

I spun around.

A man materialized in the doorway behind us, blocking our only escape.

He wore a sharp tuxedo with glittering diamond studs down the front, the same ones I'd seen on the skeleton. He was shorter than Frankie, stockier, with a flat nose, a heavy brow, and a square jaw that looked like it had taken more than a few punches in its day.

His eyes flicked to the gun in my hands as he drew an identical revolver from inside his jacket. "Drop it," he said, his voice like gravel scraping concrete.

I tightened my grip on the revolver. "You first."

His lips curled into something that wasn't quite a smile. "I don't think so, doll."

## Chapter Five

Frankie slapped a hand on his thigh. "Hot diggety dog!"

I shot a hairy eyeball at my housemate. "You want to help with the mobster holding a gun on me?"

"Just keep holding your gun on him," Frankie said, as if that solved everything.

The cellar felt smaller with three of us in it—me, my impossibly delighted gangster ghost, and a very angry killer blocking the only exit.

Frost clung to the wine bottles. My breath came out in clouds. And I was standing in front of a hole in the wall with a crumbling dead guy inside.

Lenny the Ghost took a step closer, his diamond tuxedo studs glittering. He didn't look like the kind of guy who'd blink before pulling the trigger.

Frankie huffed. "You know what your problem is, Verity? You're always so worried about yourself, you haven't stopped to appreciate my brilliance." He tossed his hands out to the sides. "Lenny's here."

"Ready to shoot me."

"That means the rocks are still here, too."

Lenny's finger tightened on the trigger as I looked down the round, black barrel of the gun. "You trying to rob me again?"

"No." It was the truth. "I don't steal," I said quickly, holding up my free hand.

Danged if I wasn't still holding his watch. "I'll put it back," I promised, taking a careful step backward toward the wall. "This is all a huge misunderstanding."

One that would get me killed if I wasn't careful.

I kept my eyes on Lenny's revolver and my gun—well, technically, his gun—which I pointed in his general direction. I reached behind me, fumbling for the skeletal wrist. "Look." I connected with bone. "See?" I set the watch down on what I hoped was his wrist lying approximately where I'd found it. "All better."

The entire arm collapsed into a pile of bones.

"Whoops." I winced. "Sorry about that."

"Now you're desecrating me?" Lenny's voice hit a high pitch, echoing off the vaulted ceiling.

"I—" It wasn't what it looked like.

Although it kind of was.

He rushed me. Chilling the air, ice cold on my skin. I retreated to the wall with the hole and the bones and—

His eyes bugged out. "You dig me up, you rob me, you point my own gun at me, and then you mash my very bones?"

"They're fine." My heart hammered against my ribs. "Just a little rearranged." I wasn't making it better. "I mean, these things happen, right?"

Although they only seemed to happen to me.

"Let's fix this." I swallowed hard. We were getting nowhere by threatening each other. "I'll go first. I'll put down my gun."

Frankie shrieked. "Have I taught you *nothing*?"

Well, he certainly wasn't helping now.

"Here." I laid the revolver next to the skeleton.

Now it was his turn.

Lenny didn't move.

"You know what? I don't even care." Frankie waved a hand

and plucked a fresh cigarette from behind his ear. "He's a ghost, and your revolver is in the mortal realm. You can't use that gun on him anyway."

Yes, but Lenny didn't need to know that.

"Frankie!" I hissed, ready to pick it back up and toss it at him. I didn't care that it would pass straight through.

"Too bad his ghostly gun can kill you."

"Are you trying to get me shot?" I demanded.

It was true. When I was tuned in to the other side, the bullet in that barrel could end me.

"He won't shoot you," Frankie said, lighting his smoke.

"You're the one who told me he likes to kill people!"

Lenny grinned and cocked the hammer. "Only people who tick me off."

Like me.

The click echoed in the small space. The acrid smell of gun oil struck me. Icy metal pressed against my forehead, and I felt the awful, invasive, cold wet sting of the other side.

I sucked in a breath and felt the hollowed-out wall at my back. This was bad, real bad.

My mortal touch would make his ghostly gun disappear, but not fast enough.

My legs trembled. "Frankie," I demanded.

Now was not the time for him to be screwing around.

"He'll let you live," Frankie said with the kind of blissful confidence that had probably earned him the bullet hole in his forehead.

"That so?" Lenny dug the barrel in. Deathly cold seared into my skull. My vision tunneled.

"Lenny'll even help you with your little ghost problem," Frankie announced.

"And why's that?" Lenny's lips tugged into a predatory snarl.

I had the sinking feeling this was the last thing his victims saw.

Frankie snorted. "Because I know where the Irish Crown Jewels are hidden."

From the look on Lenny's face, it was clear he hadn't found them yet.

His gun dipped a fraction, and I used that moment to pull back from the ghostly sting.

"Picture it," Frankie crooned. "A large eight-pointed star made up of Brazilian diamonds. A shamrock of emeralds in the middle. Crusted with a ruby cross."

Lenny cast a glance at Frankie. "You seen it?"

Frankie smirked. "Come on, Lenny. Do I look like the kind of guy who'd waste your time with a story about a picture?"

Spoiler alert: Frankie was exactly that kind of guy.

And Lenny was no fool. His eyes narrowed.

"Think about it." Frankie took a drag. "You're talking to the guy who lifted Greta Garbo's sapphire necklace right off her neck while we danced the foxtrot." He blew a smoke ring. "The guy who robbed the Peabody Hotel while being chased by the Memphis police force and about a half a dozen ducks."

I'd heard that story. The ducks were the least of his problems that night.

He grinned, sucking down his cigarette. "The guy who personally stole Babe Ruth's lucky socks right out of his locker at Yankee Stadium."

He hadn't told me about that last one.

Unless he was making it up.

Lenny's gun wavered slightly. "Yeah, I remember you." A hint of respect crept into his voice. "Boss told us to bet on the Cardinals."

"You're welcome." Frankie tossed the cigarette, and it disappeared into thin air. "I'm telling you I know where to find that brooch, and I've got a live girl here who can dig it up."

Oh, hold on. "Say what now?" I straightened against the wall.

Frankie held his hands out. "All we want is your cooperation on another matter," he said as if he hadn't just volunteered me for jewel theft.

Lenny's eyes narrowed, and he leveled the gun at my forehead again. "I don't think either of you are in a position to negotiate."

"Whoops," Frankie said.

My head snapped toward him. "What do you mean 'whoops'?"

"He's kind of got us there."

Of all the—"Then why did you tell him everything while he has the gun?"

Frankie needed to *think* for once. To reason. To stop for a nanosecond and consider the consequences of his actions and to realize that I had a gun to my head that could kill me.

But he wasn't even listening. He'd gone all distant, calculating. Probably a half second from disappearing and leaving me here all alone.

Typical Frankie.

Was I going to lecture him during what could be my last minutes on Earth?

Yes. Yes, I was. "Are you seriously—"

Frankie launched himself at Lenny.

My housemate moved faster than I'd ever seen him before. In a blur of pinstripes, he slammed Lenny into a wine rack, stuck his fingers in the guy's eye sockets, and broke the bottles with his head. Glass shattered on the ghostly plane. Wine bubbled up like blood. And Lenny's gun clattered across the flagstones.

In the next blink, Frankie had Lenny on the ground with a knee planted on his back and a black, snub-nosed revolver pointed at his head.

"Nice work," I managed. Times like these, I could see how ruthless Frankie had been in life. And still was in death.

"It was the only way to stop your yammering," Frankie said. "And save your life."

I decided not to debate it.

Lenny went rigid, and his shoulders bunched as he tested my housemate's grip. Frankie responded by banging his head on the floor. "I'd thank you for distracting him so I could take him down, but you didn't realize you were doing it."

I crossed my arms and scooted away from the bones in the wall. "Anytime." And by that, I meant never again.

Lenny glared at me, cheek mashed onto the floor. Frankie planted a knee harder on his back and kept the gun trained on his head.

I stepped closer, careful to stay out of arm's reach. "Tell us what you know about the death of the groom. The man who fell from the honeymoon suite."

It was Frankie's turn to cock the trigger.

"Nothing to tell," Lenny said. "The guy bit it on a fence."

Exactly. My heart leapt. "Was he pushed?"

Lenny winced. "Yeah. I was there. I saw the whole thing."

Now we were getting somewhere. "Who did it?"

"That's the million-dollar question, ain't it?" His eyes shifted between us. "And it's gonna cost you."

"You want a bullet?" Frankie asked.

Lenny shrugged a shoulder. "I could use a nap."

The gangster was baiting us. He knew more, and he wasn't going to give it by force.

"What do you want?" I asked. We didn't have time to play games. My mom was arriving tomorrow. Alec's parents, too. We had the bridal photo shoot, the wedding rehearsal. And Alec was going to want to stay in that haunted honeymoon suite.

Lenny shifted under Frankie's weight. "I want the ruby earrings from the Irish haul. I dug 'em out right here. I had 'em in my hand before Dapper Dan bashed me over the head."

A hundred years ago. "Then they're long gone," I told him.

"I know where he stashed 'em. After I died, I found his hidey-hole. I keep stealing 'em on my side of the veil, but then they go back."

"That's because you didn't die with them," I said.

His expression clouded. "Don't rub it in." He looked to

Frankie. "I want your live girl to dig 'em out for me. I want to keep them in both realms."

More digging?

"He hid 'em in the chapel," Lenny continued. "You bring 'em back here and bury 'em with me. Then they're mine. Forever."

Or at least until someone renovated the wine cellar and claimed finders keepers, but that was the least of our problems.

"I'm not desecrating a church," I said automatically.

"Think of it as giving the earrings a new life," Frankie corrected as if they'd been unjustly imprisoned in holy solitude.

Well, too bad for him and Lenny, I had rules. Limits. Up until now, I didn't realize this was one of them, but in my gut, I knew it was.

Frankie eased up slightly, and Lenny lifted his chin off the floor. "Do it and I'll introduce you to my mother."

My housemate barked out a laugh.

"Your mother?" That was unexpected. "She's here?"

"She stops in from time to time." Lenny aimed an elbow at Frankie and missed. "My mama worked as a lady's maid to Lord Byrne's new bride and his wife before that." The corner of his mouth curled. "She knows all about the family. She's the one who told me about the rubies down here in the safe box."

That had certainly panned out.

I studied the gangster. "Okay. It's a deal."

He gave me a sharp nod. "We just gotta avoid Dapper Dan." He shot me a cold look. "Dan was after the earrings. Still is. He thinks they're all that's here."

"We won't tell him different," Frankie vowed.

Lenny's mouth pressed into a thin line. "Live people talk too much, and there are too many of them around lately. If he figures out the truth, he'll try to beat us to them." He turned his gaze to me. "I know exactly where he hid the earrings. You'll need a hammer and a crowbar from the workbench near the basement stairs."

"A crowbar? You can't be serious."

He looked me dead in the eye. "We go tonight, or we don't go at all."

Like *he* was the one on a time schedule.

I glanced at my phone. Nearly nine o'clock. Melody would be off with Alec. The estate would be quiet.

Was I actually considering this?

"I'm up for it." Frankie grinned.

Probably because he planned on stealing the earrings himself.

I ran a hand down the side of my face. "You're asking me to dig up part of my sister's wedding chapel."

"Or we can hope to run into Dapper Dan on our own," Frankie mused, examining his fingernails. "You can go into tomorrow night blind. Take your chances with your sister's fiancé. The church might be perfect, but the groom could get a few holes in him. From what I hear, Alec Duranja can be a pain in the neck anyway."

He could, and he still was at times, but Alec and I had resolved our issues, and my sister loved him more than life itself.

My chest tightened, picturing Alec out on that balcony this evening. Melody's face when she talked about her wedding. The ghostly cigar left behind on the mantel.

I winced at the bones in the wall. At Lenny pinned to the floor. At Frankie, who knew he had me.

Fine. I let out a slow breath. "I don't see any harm in relocating the earrings." Back to the wine cellar where the original family had kept them. "We're not stealing."

"Speak for yourself." Lenny's smirk widened.

"I'm serious." We'd find them, I'd talk to Lenny's mom, and we'd hide the jewels as the family had intended. It wasn't up to me to advertise to the world that Lord Byrne had stolen part of the Irish Crown Jewels. Or admit to illicit digging in a chapel.

"She's cute, isn't she?" Frankie asked Lenny.

"A little batty, but we can work with that." Lenny shrugged.

I glared at them both. "So, are we doing this or not?"

Frankie hauled Lenny to his feet, keeping the gun trained on him. "We understand you're gonna help us dig up those rubies tonight, and we're gonna help you keep that groom alive tomorrow." He grinned. "Everything else is just details."

Lenny eyed me as he brushed the dust off his tuxedo. "Trust us."

Not as far as I could throw them. But I was used to that. "Let's do this."

Lenny grinned, and I had a sinking feeling I'd just made a deal with the devil.

Two devils, technically.

And the night was only getting started.

## Chapter Six

Naturally, the two gangsters zipped straight up through the ceiling.

I had to take the long way.

I bolted out into the darkened basement. Something skittered behind the old mattress. I didn't stop to look. I grabbed a hammer from the workbench and slipped it into my bag. Then I hefted a crowbar and tried to forget what I was about to do with it.

I headed for the stairs.

The first trick would be getting through the servants' door in the foyer without Mort spotting me. Now that I wasn't grave robbing, being pimped out for a jewel heist, or staring down the barrel of a gun, I could hear their footsteps echoing on the hardwood upstairs. Ellis had done a stellar job of keeping Mort out of the basement. Now I just had to make his effort worthwhile and nail the final leg.

The stairs felt twice as steep going up, every creak of wood, every clack of my sandals making me wince. I pressed my ear against the servants' door, listening for any sound from the foyer beyond.

Nothing.

I eased the door open, hitching my breath at the faint scrape of wood on wood as I slipped into the foyer. The carved panel slid shut behind me with a soft click.

So far so good.

The foyer lay empty.

I fought the urge to do a mini jig.

The front door swung open, and I jumped.

Alec eased inside, cradling Lucy in his arms. For a moment, I feared the worst. Then I saw my skunk had all four legs splayed out and her belly up.

Lucy knew how to be carried in style.

"Verity." Alec halted. He seemed as surprised to see me as I was to see him. "Um, working?" he asked, his attention landing on my crowbar.

It was hard to miss. "This looks crazier than it is," I assured him.

If only that were true.

For once in his life, Alec didn't push it. Maybe because Lucy picked that very moment to press a paw to his cheek.

He glanced down at my little girl, who yawned wider than a barn door. "I was just taking her out. Figured she'd want to frolic a bit before bed."

She lazed her head my way and blinked. "She looks like she had a little too much fun." She had pink rose petals stuck to her fur, and her tail swished against his arm as she tried to keep her eyes open. I scratched her in her favorite spot behind her ear and was rewarded with the happy kick of her left back leg. It was as if it were attached by a string.

A smile played on Alec's lips. "She went straight for a big rose-bush by the fountain and refused to come out of it when I called. But that's okay." He gave her a scritch under the chin, and she raised her head for more. "I bribed her with a grape, and she was all mine."

"You're a natural." He really was. Practical. Patient. Good with animals and kids.

"She's easy to love," he said, ruffling her fur. His hand stilled.

"I appreciate what you're doing, easing Melody's mind about the dead grooms."

And his. But Alec wasn't the type to say it.

"You're going to have a beautiful wedding day," I promised him.

I'd make sure of it.

Voices drifted from the ballroom. I made out Ellis's steady tone and Mort's gruffer responses, punctuated by what sounded like hammering.

"Avoid those two," Alec advised. "Ellis has way too many handyman questions for the poor guy. Last I heard, they were debating toggle bolts versus molly bolts. Mort can't shake him."

I couldn't help but smile. Hopefully, Ellis was learning a few things while he had my back. And with any luck, Mort wouldn't hammer him to the wall.

Lucy let out a loud snore, and I realized she'd fallen asleep in Alec's arms.

"Off to bed with this one," he said, adjusting his hold. "She's heavier than she looks."

"I'll grab her later," I promised, glancing toward the door. "I've got a bit of investigating to do first."

He nodded once. "You know what you're doing." He paused a beat. "Just be smart about it."

"That's always the goal," I said, though I had serious doubts about the smart part given what I was about to do.

I watched him carry Lucy toward the stairs, her tail draped over his arm like a furry scarf.

I had this.

I hoped.

All I knew was I wouldn't let him or my sister down.

I stepped out into the night and shivered. A cool breeze carried the scent of fresh-cut wood and damp earth.

All I had to do was help two gangsters with questionable morals go digging in my sister's dream wedding chapel.

Piece of cake.

I promised myself we wouldn't disturb a thing.

Well, except for whatever I was going to attack with a crowbar.

*I can still back out.*

Although, that would mean putting Alec's life at risk and possibly even my sister's.

I pulled the phone from my bag and clicked on the flashlight, hurrying down the stairs, following the stone path that skirted the darkened garden. The fountain tinkled gently, and I slowed to notice the laughing cupid holding court over a bed of roses gone wild.

Light spilled from the ballroom windows at the back of the house. I caught a glimpse of Ellis standing on a chair, dismantling a ceiling light fixture while Mort steadied the chair below him. Bless that man.

The estate stretched out before me. I could barely make out the grove of oaks ahead, their branches creating a tunnel of shadows.

It was better than the basement.

I pressed forward through the darkness. I could do this. I had to.

Within a few minutes, the chapel rose in the distance, a two-story structure with a peaked roof and narrow stained-glass windows dimly lit from within.

Strange.

I hoped there wasn't someone in there.

But there couldn't be. Ellis had Mort distracted. Alec had his hands full with Lucy, and Melody wouldn't be wandering the property alone at night.

That was my job.

A pair of ghostly figures glowed silver in the small cemetery beside the chapel.

I slowed my pace. With any luck, they were my ghosts.

Although, I'd had plenty of surprises over the years.

As I drew closer, I made out Frankie's pinstripes and Panama hat. Lenny guffawed at something my housemate said, then lost the smirk when he saw me.

"She sure took her time." Lenny gave me the once-over as I stepped past the old cemetery gate.

"You see what I put up with?" Frankie asked, doing a quick double-check of the bullets in his gun before shoving it back into his coat.

They stood next to a tall Celtic cross, its surface carved with intricate knotwork that had weathered to soft curves. Behind it rose a mausoleum no taller than I was, made of limestone. The name *BYRNE* was cut deep into the lintel in bold letters, and Celtic knotwork wound around the frame. Moss crept up the sides, and the arched door was sealed with an iron gate, rusted and padlocked.

I stopped at the edge of the cemetery, the crowbar heavy in my hand. "I'm not breaking into a tomb."

Lenny shot me a pointed look. "You already did."

"Well..." He had me there. "Once per night is my limit." I rested a hand on my hip. "If Thomas Byrne was buried wearing King John's Crown, he can keep it."

Frankie snorted.

Lenny's eyes went wide. "She's the worst thief ever."

"We're working on it," Frankie assured him.

"No, we aren't," I said.

They might have conned me into jewel theft—jewel *borrowing*—but I wasn't going to grave rob the lord of the manor, and I was absolutely, positively, done with skeletons.

Frankie waved me off. "Relax. We're only liberating the earrings from the chapel. You might even learn something."

Like what not to do.

"Never in my life have I had to convince somebody to steal." Lenny tsked, floating ahead of us toward the chapel.

"Yeah, but I can't give up on the kid," Frankie said, joining him. "There's too much potential."

His urn clanked in my bag as I followed. I'd never been so tempted to drive him back to Sugarland and leave him there.

The chapel loomed ahead, its limestone walls dark with age and crusted with moss along the foundation. Overgrown camellia bushes flanked the entrance, their dark leaves glossy, their fat white blooms with ruffled petals glowing like pale ghosts against the shadows. Narrow lancet windows rose toward the peaked roof, their stained glass too dark to make out.

Graves rose up on my left and right, tilted headstones, lichen-crusted crosses, and weeping angels.

"Lord Byrne had this shipped over from County Wicklow," Lenny was saying to Frankie. "Stone by stone. It overlooked the sea for centuries. It was their family chapel, built in the 1600s." He gestured to the building with something like pride. "Cost him a fortune to move it, but he wanted his estate just like it was in the old country."

Minus the view.

The path ended at double doors of heavy oak reinforced with iron bands, carved with Celtic knots winding around a central cross. White tulle and ivy garlands hung from ancient hooks, ready for the ceremony Saturday. This place, these touches, were exactly Melody's style. No wonder she'd jumped at the chance to get married here.

I froze as the heavy door creaked open on its own. "I do not like how all the doors on this estate like to open themselves."

"I think it comes in handy," Frankie said, ducking inside.

I had no choice but to follow.

The chapel was bigger than it looked from the outside. Wall sconces with bulbs that flickered like gas lamps cast an old-world glow that barely reached the vaulted ceiling two stories above. The antique chandelier gracing the nave stood dark. Arrangements of autumn leaves, white roses, and trailing ivy waited on every window ledge. Cream-colored ribbons tied in elaborate bows marked the ends of each dark wood pew.

My footsteps echoed as we walked down the center aisle. I glanced up at the wood choir loft hanging over the entrance behind us, the narrow gallery running along both sides of the nave. Too many dark corners. Too many places to hide.

The altar stood at the far end on a platform, carved from a single piece of dark marble veined with silver. A triptych graced the space behind it—three panels of painted wood showing scenes of death and resurrection.

Candlesticks as tall as I was flanked each side. Arrangements of white lilies and greenery stood on either end of the platform. Their perfume hung heavy in the air, rich and sweet.

My hands felt clammy. I took turns wiping them on my dress.

"There." Lenny pointed toward the altar. "That's where Dapper Dan hid them."

Heck to the no. "I am *not* digging into the altar of a church." No way. Nohow. These ghosts had pushed me too far.

Lenny materialized between me and the marble altar. "Good. Because you're gonna dig here." He pointed to a stone slab set into the floor directly in front of the altar steps, right at my feet.

"Well, that presents another problem because that's right where the minister will stand when my sister gets married in about thirty-six hours."

Lenny's forehead crinkled. "I'm not talking about thirty-six hours. I'm talking now."

No wonder he and Frankie were getting along.

"Assuming I have the strength to move the stone slab after I dig it out," I drawled, "how, pray tell, do I explain a hole the size of Cleveland in the floor of the wedding chapel?"

Lenny blinked. "I don't see how this is relevant."

"She's just being dramatic," Frankie huffed. My gangster crouched low, studying the edges of the slab. "It's a hidey-hole. How hard can it be?"

In case he hadn't noticed, I said, "Someone grouted it in."

Frankie sighed like he was dealing with a six-year-old. "You dig out the mortar. You take out the stone. You put it back."

"I can't seal it back up the way it is now." Maybe Ellis could, but he'd have to sneak in with a bucket of grout, and even then, it wouldn't match. Plus, it might not dry in time for the wedding. "At the very least, it's going to wobble." I could barely hang a picture without it going cock-eyed.

"Details." He waved a dismissive hand. "Nobody's gonna notice if the preacher rocks a little."

"Or falls into a hole?" I prompted.

"They'll think he's just really feeling it," Frankie finished.

"I don't know what kind of weddings you've been to," I said, kneeling to get a closer look.

"Shotgun, mostly," he said.

I set my crowbar on the floor and ran my fingers over the mortar securing the slab, hoping against hope there was some way this could work. The stone was about three feet square, and now that I'd gotten closer, I could see it was made of slate, worn smooth by the years.

Elaborate scrollwork framed an inscription carved deep into the surface:

*Tógtha ag Tiarna Uilliam Ó Broin*
*1683*
*Go Raibh Grásta Dé Ar a Chlann*

My stomach squinched. "Do you think Lord Byrne's great-great-whomever is still down there?"

"Five bucks says they left him in Ireland," Frankie said, digging in his jacket for a cigarette.

I didn't want to find out.

I snapped a picture of the marker with my phone.

"These kids and their gadgets," Lenny said, bumming a smoke from Frankie. "I'd have lifted the earrings and been halfway to Oz by now."

Frankie set a match to the tip of his cigarette. "You and me both, buddy."

I ignored them and fed the image into Google translate.

*Built by Lord William Ó Broin*
*1683*
*May the Grace of God Be Upon His Family*

I heaved out a sigh. "Thank you, sweet baby Jesus." I read the translation aloud. "It's not a grave marker. It's a tribute to the builder."

"Somehow, that's not as fun." Lenny took a drag.

"Stealing is stealing," Frankie reminded him.

"Technically *re-stealing*." Lenny blew smoke out his nose. "I stole it first."

*Borrowing*. But I was done correcting them because they wouldn't listen anyway. Too bad for them, I controlled the jewels in the real world. I'd keep my end of the bargain. I'd bury them with Lenny.

Then maybe I'd tell the owners where to dig them up if they seemed decent and willing to treat the Byrne legacy well.

"She's daydreaming now," Lenny said, staring at me. "I mean, I've got eternity, but..."

"I'm on it," I said, dreading what I had to do next.

It was the only way.

I'd be careful. Give the gangsters what they wanted. Meet Lenny's mom. All in a night's work, right? Then I'd learn what really happened to those grooms. And make sure it never happened to Alec.

I knelt once more. I could do this. The cold stone bit into my knees through the light cotton fabric of my dress. Sure, this wasn't technically part of the duties of the maid of honor, but I was more than that. I was Melody's sister.

Strong. Determined. I pulled the hammer from my bag.

At least it was only mortar I was digging into. "I've got this," I murmured as I stood and set the straight edge of the crowbar against the seam.

"Give it a good whack." Frankie leaned too close, chilling my shoulder. "Pretend it owes you money."

I wasn't going to break it. "Will you let me handle this?"

"I have no choice."

"All right." The metal rang softly against stone as I bent awkwardly and tapped with the hammer. Once. Twice. The mortar crumbled away.

I worked my way around the edges, dust settling over my sandals. My lower back ached from bending.

"It's like she's never done this before," Lenny said to Frankie.

"She dug you out," Frankie answered, working on his smoke.

This was wrong. It was technically stealing. And this was not the place to do it.

*It's just a hole in the wedding chapel.*

Melody would understand.

I hoped she hadn't put down a deposit.

I winced as I pried the slab up and gripped it by the edges.

It took all my strength to slide it toward me, the slate scraping against the floor with a *screeeeeee* that echoed through the chapel.

"Yes, yes, yes." Lenny rubbed his hands together.

"Jackpot," Frankie said over him as they peered into the round, dark hole beneath.

I scrambled to see.

Lenny was right! It was a hidey-hole.

A pair of ghostly gray earrings glowed in the darkness below.

I fumbled for my phone flashlight and clicked it on, catching the rough stone walls of the cavity.

There. Real ruby earrings sat exactly where their ghostly counterparts glowed. Teardrop stones the size of my thumbnail glittered, set in gold.

They rested on top of a very real, very flattened skull.

The hollow eye sockets stared up at me.

I jerked back, my phone clattering to the floor. "Oh my God." I scrambled to my feet. "There's a dead guy down there."

A real, live dead guy. Well, not alive, alive. "You said this wasn't a grave."

Lenny held up the ghostly earrings, admiring them. "You're the one who said that."

I retrieved my phone and shone it down again. The bones were smashed but in decent condition. They didn't look crazy old.

Frankie leaned over the hole and ventured a look down. "Is that who I think it is?" He pointed with his cigarette. "Check it out. Six fingers on the right hand. And is that a rhinestone belt buckle?"

It was. The stones lay dull and pitted in the real world. The ghostly version glittered on top of what appeared to be a pelvic bone. The rest of the legs crumpled underneath.

"That's Dan, all right." Lenny drifted closer, studying the bones. "He always said those were diamonds."

"He's a liar," Frankie said.

"And a bad friend." Lenny pocketed the ghostly earrings.

A chill crept up my spine, and the hair on my neck stood up. Lenny dropped his cigarette.

Frankie tucked his smoke under his bottom lip and drew a gun. "He's also right behind us."

# Chapter Seven

A gun cocked directly behind me. Cold. Sharp. "Give me the stones back."

I couldn't move. Couldn't breathe. Didn't dare turn around.

Why did this keep happening to me?

I forced myself to look over my shoulder.

A steely-eyed ghost loomed in my wake. He sported a thin mustache and an argyle sweater under a jacket and tie. His fedora sat at a rakish angle, his rhinestone belt glittered, and he held a silver revolver pointed directly at Lenny's chest. "Now."

"Over my dead body," Lenny snarled, reaching into his tuxedo coat for his own gun.

Oh, great. A shoot-out. Just what we needed.

Then again, if Lenny plugged this guy, he'd get to keep the earrings. Our deal would be done, and I'd be one step closer to learning what killed those grooms.

I ducked, giving him a clear shot. Only Lenny's hand came up empty. He stared at it, then reached back in again like maybe he'd somehow missed his gun the first time.

Oh no! I'd made his revolver disappear back in the wine cellar. Well, my living touch had. To be fair, it was his fault for jamming it against my forehead.

Lenny went rigid. His hand dropped to his side, fingers curling into a fist. For a long moment, he just stood there, his eyes locked on the silver gun. And I didn't think he was admiring the ivory handle or the intricate scrollwork on the barrel.

Dapper Dan's finger twitched on the trigger. "Any time, Len."

Lenny let out a low growl as he slowly, reluctantly, pulled the ghostly ruby earrings from his pocket.

Dang it all.

The teardrop stones sparkled while the scowl on Lenny's face could have curdled milk. He held them out, his arm stiff, shoulders tight. "Here. I hope you choke on 'em."

"Thank you kindly." Dapper Dan plucked them from his hand with two fingers and pocketed them in a flash. The gun never wavered.

"I got you the stones," I insisted.

Lenny's lip curled. "I don't see them in my pocket." He glared at Dapper Dan. "You got a lot of nerve robbing me twice."

Dapper Dan had the audacity to appear offended. "I never robbed you once. Well, except for in Cleveland. But now I'm just taking back what you stole from my hidey-hole."

Lenny reared back. "I didn't steal from you. The ruby earrings were in a lockbox in the back wall of the wine cellar. I crashed Lord Thomas's engagement party in 1924. I broke 'em out. I had them in my hand for two seconds before I got bashed in the head and buried in that wall."

"You're nuts. I didn't go anywhere near the wine cellar." Dapper Dan backed toward the door. "Sure. I was a regular at all the parties. Who do you think got Lord Byrne the liquor? And sure, I was at that engagement party with a stunning debutante named Hazel." He let out a low whistle. "Ah, Hazel. Anyhow, I heard the earrings were in the master bedroom. Hazel wanted to make out in the garden and drop a penny in the well. That's where we found Knuckles McGee, facedown and floating. She screamed and ran. I snagged the ruby earrings lying next to a couple of pennies on the edge."

I straightened slowly. "So Knuckles stole the earrings from Lenny." At least it looked that way. Maybe if I solved Lenny's murder, he'd find his mom for me. Oh, who was I kidding? I needed to get those stones back like I'd promised.

"Knuckles worked the circuit," Dapper Dan said. "He didn't stash anything in a hidey-hole, so he'd get caught leaving. A lot. Got to the point there was so much stealing Lord Byrne stationed cops at the gates."

The type of police who overlooked an illegal party. He must have paid them well. "Lord Byrne kind of deserved it for inviting all the gangsters."

"My mom got me in," Lenny chuffed.

"That's not a flex," Frankie said.

Dan massaged the gems in his pocket. "All I know is I nicked these babies off Knuckles, was about to grab my girl and exit the party pronto, but the cops were already at the gates. I had to get rid of the rocks, so I ducked into the chapel and lifted the stone. I was all ready to tuck 'em in real nice when somebody clocked me in the head and stashed me under the floor."

"No kidding." I glanced back at the stone. "Must have been before they mortared it in."

Dapper Dan followed my gaze. "It was already chipped out when I found it."

That hidey-hole got a lot of work.

I rested my hands on my hips, attempting to piece it together. "So both of you died on the same night. Minutes, or in Lenny's case, seconds after you stole the earrings."

And yet, they refused to stop.

"I was hoping they'd lead me to the Irish Crown Jewels," Dapper Dan said, waving his gun slightly before aiming it firmly at Lenny again.

"You knew?" Lenny gaped.

Dan smirked. "Those rubies originally belonged to Queen Charlotte. They were on loan from the British Museum in 1907.

Queen Alexandra was slated to wear them on a state visit to see the crown jewels. Lord Byrne nicked the lot."

"I don't care," Lenny said, eyeing the door. In less than a minute, Dan would be gone with the loot.

Dan patted his pocket. "It's all I think about."

"You find the crown jewels?" Frankie asked, watching him go.

"I'm not saying," Dapper Dan mused.

But he hadn't, or he wouldn't still be here.

Dapper Dan's mouth ticked up at the corner. "When I found it, the hidey-hole already had a diamond necklace, two gold bracelets with little pearls, a full set of serving silver with a crest on it—"

"Whose crest?"

He shrugged. "I melted it down. Gave one of the bracelets to a lady friend," Dapper Dan added with a twinkle in his eye.

"You see what I'm missing out on?" Frankie glared at me. "I'm just here with her," he added to the guys, jabbing a thumb at me.

What a sweetheart.

Lenny shook his head. "I've been hanging around my body too much."

Dan's grin widened. "I think I can rustle us up a party—"

A gun barrel pressed against Dapper Dan's temple.

I hadn't even seen Frankie coming, and neither had the two gangsters. But there he was, behind Dapper Dan, with his own gun pressed to the guy's slicked-back hair. "Give me the stones. Now."

Dapper Dan went very still.

In one smooth motion, Frankie plucked the silver revolver from Dan's hand and slipped it into his coat pocket. A second later, he did the same with the ruby earrings.

"Rookie mistake," Lenny said, only his eyes moving as he watched Frankie score. "Taking your eye off Frankie the German."

I whistled under my breath.

*Way to go, Frankie.* We had the rubies. Now Lenny would have to help me.

Sure, ghosts could only keep what they'd died with, and the rubies would eventually vanish anyway. But try telling that to a bunch of dead gangsters with sticky fingers.

Dapper Dan's gun hand tightened in a fist. "You two in cahoots?"

Lenny cocked his head. "I'm not against it."

"I work alone," Frankie shot back.

Since when?

"The. Rocks. Ain't. Yours," Dapper Dan bit out.

"They are now," Frankie said, making for the door with our one and only bargaining chip.

"Hold up," I ordered.

"I stole 'em fair and square," Dan called after him.

"Not so fast." My voice rang out across the chapel, echoing off the vaulted ceiling.

All three gangsters whipped their heads to stare at me. I had a feeling they'd forgotten I was there.

Dapper Dan narrowed his eyes. "Who *is* this broad?"

I notched up my chin. "I'm Frankie's partner."

"Try liability," my gangster muttered.

Seriously? "Do you want me to drive your urn home and leave you in the driveway?"

"Don't say that in front of the guys," Frankie hissed.

I held my ground next to the gaping hole in the floor, the open grave where the rubies glinted in my world, where Dapper Dan's flattened skull stared up at us. I cast a single long shadow down the aisle under the flickering sconces. "Frankie will give you the ruby earrings"—I ignored it when he gasped like a girl—"*after* your mom tells me who killed those grooms."

Frankie looked at me like I'd sold his mama's pearls for bus fare. "Do you even understand how stealing works?"

"I'll tell you," Dapper Dan's voice rang out. "You don't need Lenny's mom."

"You're going to steal my deal?" Lenny shrieked.

I didn't care who told me what was going on. I just needed to find out fast. I turned to Dapper Dan. "Do you really know what happened to the grooms?" I didn't have time for games.

Dapper Dan shifted uneasily. "He'll give me my property back?"

"Until I steal it again," Frankie said with the kind of confidence that had gotten him killed.

"You get the rubies back," I said to Dan.

Frankie lowered his gun and used the other hand to straighten his tie. "No skin off my nose. I'm going for a bigger score anyway."

Dapper Dan studied me for a long moment before tucking a hand into the pocket of his stylish wool trousers. "It happened in 1975. The groom-to-be was having a whiskey and a cigar on the balcony. Celebrating." He gave a small shrug. "Skinny kid. Some guy came up behind him and gave him a shove. Didn't take much. Two hands, right between the shoulder blades. He went over the railing and splat."

I held still, memorizing every detail. "You saw it?"

Dapper Dan's mustache twitched. "I wasn't there. But Knuckles McGee was. He was hanging out on the balcony, trying to lift the guy's watch." He let out a small chuff. "Somebody needs to tell Knuckles you can't steal from the living." He shook his head. "Anyways, Knuckles said the guy didn't even scream. Just went over silent. Then this other fella walked back inside like he was happy with the job."

"What did the guy look like?" I pressed.

"You'd have to ask Knuckles," he said, eyeing Frankie, who was trying to slip out the door with the jewels.

"Frankie—" I warned. "We have a deal."

"You have a deal," he corrected. But he stayed where he was.

"He haunts the garden where he died," Dan said, eyeing Frankie's gun. "Says he can't leave. Maybe he's not smart enough."

"Or maybe he got hosed into the rosebushes," Frankie snapped.

"That's oddly specific," Lenny said, trying to ease out the back way.

Dapper Dan's expression darkened. "I don't think he'll go until he finds his lucky silver dollar, the one with the bullet dent in it. He dropped it when he died and hasn't seen it since."

"Let me fix the floor, and we'll go see him." I turned to the gaping hole in the center aisle and the heavy slate slab lying beside it.

This was going to be a problem.

I crouched down and gripped the edges. The stone was cold and rough under my fingers. I heaved, I strained, I sweated more than any Southern belle should, but I managed to slide it inch by painful inch.

It scraped across the floor with a sound that made even the gangsters wince.

Until at last, it dropped into place with a heavy *thunk*.

And a wobble.

I tested it with a foot. Yeah, that wasn't sturdy at all.

Dapper Dan's forehead pinched. "It's supposed to blend. You made it all crooked."

He was right. One end sat higher than the other.

"I didn't do anything," I said, not fooling anybody.

Ellis and I would figure out a way to fix it tomorrow. Somehow. Maybe he had quick-dry mortar in his Jeep. Or maybe I could convince the minister to stand very, very still during the ceremony. For now, there was nothing else we could do. I stood. "Let's go."

Lenny eyed me. "You might want to let me do the talking. Knuckles don't like the living."

"That's never stopped me before," I told him.

My housemate was already on his way out of the chapel, no doubt hoping everyone had forgotten about the rubies in his pocket.

"Frankie." I hurried after him, with the ghostly gangsters in hot pursuit. He just *had* to rob them. "Give the earrings to Dapper Dan."

"Fat chance," he said, skirting ahead of us. "You're the one who took your eye off 'em."

It didn't matter. "We had a deal."

"You had a deal." He disappeared through the wall.

The heavy oak doors swung open with a groan as I hurried out into the night with the gangsters hot on my heels. Frankie was already several paces ahead, moving fast.

The graveyard spread out before us. I broke into a jog. Beyond, the iron gate stood open, creaking softly.

Lenny materialized in front of me, blocking my path. "You are responsible for getting my stones back."

I didn't see how.

"Darn it, Frankie." I dodged around him.

Melody needed my help. Alec had better be staying out of the honeymoon suite. And Ellis was going to have to loosen, tighten, and inspect every nut, bolt, and fixture in the place at this rate.

Lenny reappeared at the gate, and I stopped in my tracks. He had the barrel of a gun jammed in his tuxedo pocket, pointing it at Frankie.

These things didn't disappear forever.

Frankie froze. Then his eyes narrowed. "You don't have a gun."

"Frankie," I warned. We couldn't afford for him to get shot. A ghostly bullet couldn't kill him like it could me—him being already dead and all—but it would knock him out for hours. He'd be no more help tonight, and I needed him.

Lenny shoved the muzzle harder against the fabric of his pocket. "What do you call this?"

Frankie studied him for a long moment; then his shoulders relaxed. "That's your finger."

He turned his back on Lenny and headed toward the cemetery gate and the path leading to the garden.

I sidestepped Lenny as he withdrew his bare hand from his pocket. Well, look at that. Good. I certainly didn't need these guys getting caught up in a shoot-out over stolen jewels in a graveyard.

Not on my time, at least.

"If it weren't my finger," Lenny called after Frankie as I jogged to catch up, "you'd have another bullet hole between your eyes!"

Frankie didn't break stride. "That hurts, Lenny."

"Not as much as a bullet," Dapper Dan said as I caught up to Frankie. Dan stood between us and the garden, his pleated wool pants pressed with a sharp crease down the front.

"Can I get my gun back?" he asked, falling into step beside Frankie.

Frankie reached into his pocket for a cigarette. "Not until we're done with you."

"Yeah, I'd probably just shoot you," Dan admitted.

Lenny brought up the rear, cursing under his breath. "I'm the one who told you where to find the rubies."

Frankie kept walking, refusing to look at him. "You didn't get us the intel on the grooms."

"There was also a dead gangster down there with those earrings," I added to Lenny. "I thought I wasn't supposed to rob the dead." He'd made a positive fuss about his watch.

Lenny waved a hand. "It hits different when *I* do it."

We made our way back toward the main house, following the stone path through the tunnel of oaks. The rose garden sprawled straight ahead.

"Knuckles?" I called, feeling ridiculous. "Knuckles McGee? I need to talk to you about the groom who was pushed."

Nothing. Just the fountain's gentle trickle and the gangsters trailing behind me. Frankie smoking. Lenny scowling. Dapper Dan watching for his chance to turn the tables on us.

I stopped at the edge of the garden. The honeymoon suite balcony jutted out from the second floor, its railing dark against the lit windows behind it. Below, the iron fence with its tall, deadly spikes.

My stomach turned. That was where they'd landed.

The ballroom windows on the first floor glowed softly, but I couldn't see Ellis anymore. I hoped he hadn't gotten Mort so excited about crown molding restoration that they'd decided to tear down a wall.

I turned back to the garden, my frustration building. "Come on," I murmured. "I know you're here somewhere."

The roses rustled. The fountain burbled.

I needed answers. Now.

Tomorrow night, Alec would be standing on that balcony at his rehearsal dinner. The pattern was clear. The night before the wedding, the groom dies.

I couldn't let that happen.

Dapper Dan stepped in front of me. "Okay, tell your pet gangster to hand over the rocks."

"Let me think," I said, trying to sidestep him.

He blocked my way. "I took you here. I told you what I saw. We had a deal."

I crossed my arms. "I knew where the garden was. I need you to locate Knuckles McGee for me."

"Well, now, that's going to cost you extra," Dapper Dan mused.

Of course it would. "Name it." I didn't have time to play around.

He smiled. His teeth were impossibly white. "I want the Irish Crown Jewels."

"And I want a pony." He had to be reasonable. "They might not even be here."

"That's my price," he said, as if it were my problem instead of his.

Frankie tucked the ruby earrings deeper into his pocket and kept a steady grip on his gun. "She can't deliver that, Dan. Nobody can. They've been missing for over a century."

"Then I guess you're on your own." Dapper Dan clapped

Frankie on the shoulder, then tipped his fedora and started to fade.

"Wait—"

He was already gone.

Lenny shot me a look and *tsked* like it was somehow my fault. "Told you Knuckles don't like the living. Good luck finding him without help." He disappeared in a shimmer of gray light.

I stood alone in the rose garden. Well, alone except for Frankie. I looked up at the balcony where my future brother-in-law might die tomorrow night.

"Son of a—" Frankie started and drew a hand from his coat. "Dan nicked them out of my pocket."

Dapper Dan was good.

But so were we.

And it looked like I was going to have to find Knuckles, and the answers, on my own.

Something rustled in the bushes behind me. I spun around but saw nothing but shadows.

"Did you see that?" I asked Frankie.

He'd already disappeared. Of course he had.

A light flicked on in the honeymoon suite.

Someone was up there.

Someone who shouldn't be.

## Chapter Eight

I broke into a run.

My sandals clacked across the gravel path and up to the front porch. I yanked open the heavy door and took the grand staircase two steps at a time. Someone was in that suite. Someone who could be in danger. Or worse—someone who *was* the danger.

My lungs burned as I reached the second-floor landing and rounded the corner toward the honeymoon suite. The hallway stretched before me.

Ahead on the left, a door stood ajar, light spilling into the hallway.

I slowed, trying to catch my breath, and a figure stepped out, blocking my path.

My throat caught.

Melody stood in the doorway, decked out in her wedding dress. If I hadn't known better, I'd have said she looked like a ghost. The silk gown hugged her curves, the sweetheart neckline plunging just far enough. The cathedral-length veil cascaded behind her. She looked ethereal. Magnificent. Like a dream.

"Verity!" Her face lit up when she saw me, then immediately fell. "Is something wrong?"

"Absolutely not," I said, recovering. Not in a million years. "You look amazing."

Her cheeks reddened. "I went to try it on, and I loved it so much I couldn't take it off."

My little sister was actually getting married.

I mean, I knew she was. I'd been there for the engagement. And I'd never forget this morning's surprise announcement in my backyard. But there was something special about seeing her in that dress for the first time.

Her eyes narrowed. "You're out of breath." She drew closer. "You've been investigating like you said you would. I mean, I figured that was where you went and why Ellis helped Mort change out every single light fixture in the ballroom. What did you find?"

"Ghosts," I said, not sure how specific I wanted to get.

She tilted her head, the rhinestones on her veil twinkling. "Verity...what have you been up to?"

"Err..." *Hammering a crowbar into your wedding chapel floor? Getting pickpocketed by a gangster ghost? Trying to figure out who murdered two grooms so your fiancé won't be next?* "I didn't meet the dead grooms, if that's what you're asking."

"Yet you ran up here at a full sprint." She stepped closer, the dress rustling. "Let me help."

"In that getup?" I grinned, trying to lighten the moment.

She didn't go for it. "I'd burn it in the fireplace if it meant helping you."

"Let's not give Honey Sue a heart attack," I said, glancing toward the carved roses and vines climbing the door of the honeymoon suite.

I wanted to tell her. About Lenny and Dapper Dan. About Knuckles witnessing the murder. About the fact that Finn Byrne might have been pushed.

But I didn't know enough yet. I was still gathering information. Still trying to find my witness. So I settled on what I *could* tell her.

"The truth is I'm dealing with a bunch of dead gangsters who would rather steal from each other than help me. And I still need to find my witness, a ghost named Knuckles McGee, who saw what happened in 1975. He haunts the rose garden, but he's not around tonight. Or if he is, he's not exactly cooperating."

"So business as usual," she quipped.

That made me smile. "Tell you what, if I need your help to figure something out, I promise I'll ask." Melody had investigated with me plenty of times. She was great in a crisis and even better as a researcher. But this weekend was different. "I need you to promise to focus on you. This is your big day."

"It is, isn't it?" she asked, caressing a pearl on her skirt.

"In the meantime, I want to see who's in the honeymoon suite. I saw the light from the garden. That's why I rushed up here."

She let out a breath. "Well, why didn't you say so?" She shot me a grin. "The guys are having an impromptu bachelor party in there."

"What?" My stomach dropped.

"I know, right?" she gushed. "They didn't exactly have time to plan one, seeing as we didn't know we were getting married until this morning." She shook her head, still seeming amazed by it herself. "Ellis showed up with a bottle of Southern Spirits about twenty minutes ago. Said Alec was here to marry the love of his life, and they needed to celebrate properly."

"Tonight?" I asked. "Not tomorrow night after the rehearsal dinner?"

"Who wants to risk a hangover on the wedding day? Plus, tomorrow Mom and Carl arrive, not to mention Alec's parents. This way, the boys get their moment before the chaos."

"In a cursed honeymoon suite."

Her face fell. "Did you learn that tonight?"

"No," I admitted. I'd learned nothing this evening that would put Alec or Ellis in immediate danger. "The verdict is still out."

"And they are two smart, observant guys who want to mark the occasion."

Ellis was quite brilliant. He deserved to cut loose after what I'd put him through tonight. And nothing got past Alec. Even if I'd wanted it to so very many times in the past.

"I suppose it couldn't hurt..."

A loud whoop echoed from behind the door, followed by the clink of glasses.

"See?" Melody said. "They're happy. Let them have their fun." She tugged on my hand. "Come on. If they get a party, we get a party."

She pulled me toward the room she was sharing with Alec. Along the way, we passed the smaller suite with the lily wallpaper, the one I was sharing with Ellis.

I popped the door open. "Where's Lucy?" Her pink pillow bed sat empty.

"I gave her a quick bath in the sink with a bit of Pantene. She's silky smooth and smells like coconuts." Melody's eyes sparkled. "Now she's in with Alec and Ellis, getting spoiled rotten. They have a whole charcuterie board in there. Mort brought it up. I thought it was to keep Ellis busy, but turns out it's all part of the package. Lucy's been helping herself to the blueberries and grapes."

I couldn't help but smile. Lucy did love a good blueberry.

"Tomorrow morning, Alec and I are having breakfast in bed while you and Ellis have a special outdoor brunch set up just for you." Her smile widened. "After that, I'm doing bridal photos all over the estate. Plus some posed shots in an actual carriage."

"That sounds amazing," I said, meaning it. This was the ultimate package.

"They want the whole wedding party in some of them, but I'd love it if you could be there from the start and sneak in a few extra pictures with me."

"Count me in." I'd do cartwheels for any chance to be a part of her day.

Plus, the rose garden was where Knuckles had been murdered. I'd love to run into him there.

Melody brightened. "It'll be fun. Very vintage. Very romantic."

She tucked a strand of blonde hair behind her ear. "Your bridesmaid dress is hanging in your closet. I peeked. It's gorgeous. There'll be a seamstress here tomorrow if it doesn't fit."

"If it's half as beautiful as your dress, I'm sure it will be great." And if it wasn't, it didn't matter.

This was her day.

We reached the room Melody shared with Alec. It was larger than ours, with a four-poster bed and antique furniture. A vase of fresh white roses and baby's breath sat on the bedside table, and someone had laid a fire in the small marble fireplace. "Oh, now this is cozy."

Melody grabbed a canvas tote bag from beside the bed. "I brought supplies." She pulled out two plastic wineglasses and a bottle of rosé with a label I didn't recognize.

Oh, shoot. "That was my job," I said, feeling like the world's worst maid of honor.

"Does it really matter where we get the wine?" Her smile was playful, teasing. "Besides, you've been a little busy keeping my fiancé safe."

"You know I'll always be here for you," I said, joining her on the bed.

She handed me a glass, then pulled out a small wooden board with cheese, crackers, and chocolate-covered strawberries. "I swiped this from the kitchen while Mort wasn't looking."

"You're a criminal mastermind," I said, settling onto the bed as she arranged everything.

She poured the wine and handed me a glass. "They wanted to give us a veggie plate. I guess because we're women? I call that discrimination." She grabbed a strawberry and bit into it, a bit of chocolate catching on her lower lip.

"How about we change you out of that white wedding dress?" I suggested, depositing my wine on the dresser.

Melody licked the chocolate away and grinned. "I'm never taking it off. Besides, I can control myself."

"You sure?"

She laughed as she settled onto the bed across from me, the silk dress pooling around her. She looked ridiculously beautiful and completely at ease.

"To sisterhood," she said, raising her plastic glass.

"To the happiest day of your life," I countered, clinking my glass against hers.

"So far, today is the happiest day of my life. Then tomorrow will be. And then the day after that." She took a sip, then set down her glass and reached for a piece of cheese. "I know this weekend is different. I know I'm asking a lot—"

"You're asking me to share in the most important day of your life, and I couldn't be more honored," I told her. "I want to be here." In whatever way she needed me. "I want to help." I wanted to see her shining and in love and perfectly happy.

"Thanks, Verity." Her voice softened. "This is all I've ever wanted."

To be with the people she loved. The man she loved.

She grasped her wineglass by the stem. "I also know you're worried." She cut me off before I could try to deny it or soothe her. "You're worried about me. About Alec. About the balcony. About whatever you're not telling me about tonight." She met my eyes. "You're not as good a liar as you think."

"You always could read me." It was why I never bothered keeping secrets from her.

"I just want you to know I trust you. Completely. If you say we need to call this off, I will. No wedding is more important than the people I love."

The weight of her faith settled on my shoulders.

"I'll learn what's happening. I'll make sure everyone is safe and happy, that this goes off without a hitch," I promised. "I won't let anything bad happen."

She smiled, and for a moment, sitting on that bed with wine and strawberries and my sister in her wedding dress, everything felt normal. Good. Right.

Like this weekend might work out after all.

We'd made a healthy dent in the strawberries when a knock rattled the door.

"Those boys just can't live without us," Melody teased with a tilt of her wineglass. "Come in," she called like the Queen of Sheba.

But the door was already opening, and Ellis shoved his way through, smelling like whiskey and cigars, supporting Alec with an arm around his waist. Lucy trotted in behind them, looking quite pleased with herself. My future brother-in-law swayed on his feet, a dopey grin plastered across his face.

"Special delivery," Ellis said, his voice strained as Alec tried to step sideways and nearly brained himself on the doorjamb.

My mouth dropped open. I'd never seen Alec like this.

In all the years I'd known the man—and they hadn't all been pleasant—he'd always been infuriatingly stoic. Even when we'd tumbled down a cliff, been left to die in a cave, and been attacked by pirate ghosts, Alec Duranja had maintained his Robocop charm.

He shot us a saucy grin.

This was not that Alec.

"Is he okay?" Melody scrambled off the bed to grab him as he stumbled two steps sideways, gave a salute, and plopped down on the floor.

"I want to say he's fine," Ellis hedged, though his expression said otherwise. "He didn't eat much, and we were toasting lots of things."

"We toasted the wedding. We toasted your smile," Alec warbled to Melody.

"Alec's first day on the force," Ellis added. "The town of Sugarland. Peaches. Verity not killing me when I surprised her with a bubble bath using Dawn dish soap."

"It makes bubbles!" Alec giggled like a teenage girl. "We toasted Dolly Parton. And...and the invention of the wheel. We even toasted the skunk!"

Yes, well, Lucy deserved it after hanging out with these two.

I moved the cheese board off the bed to make room for Alec. Melody and Ellis helped him up, and he landed like a wet sack of rice, grinning like a fool.

Melody fussed with his hair. "He doesn't really drink."

He was making up for it now.

"That's the thing," Ellis said, lifting his friend's feet back onto the bed after he'd sprawled them over the sides. "He only had the one glass, not the entire bottle."

Alec began singing "Livin' La Vida Loca."

"Looks like it hit him fast," I said as he added arm motions.

Lucy hopped up onto the bed and gave Alec a sniff.

Alec's head lolled toward Melody. "There's my beautiful bride." His words slurred together. "Most gorgeous woman in the entire world. In the entire *universe*." He looked to the skunk. "Now if she's so smart, why's she marrying me?"

Melody's hand flew to her mouth, but I could see she was trying not to laugh. "Alec, honey—"

Lucy swished her tail and abandoned the fool.

Meanwhile I opened a window. Neither one of us liked the stale smell of cigar smoke.

"I love you. Soooo much." Alec rolled toward Melody, nearly falling off the bed. She reached out to steady him, and he caught a hand and kissed it. "So, so much. You know that, right? I tell you that?"

"You do," Melody said gently, sitting next to him and wrapping an arm around him. "Every day."

"Oh, good." Alec flopped back onto the bed with a sigh.

His eyes were already drifting closed. I exchanged a look with Ellis while Melody grabbed the pillow Alec had knocked off the bed.

I planted my back against the window frame. "What exactly happened at your little party?"

This didn't seem normal. Even for someone who'd had too much.

Ellis stood next to his friend. "One minute we were toasting, the next he could barely hold himself upright. It came on really fast."

Alec's eyes fluttered open. He focused on Melody with an intensity that would have been romantic if he weren't three sheets to the wind. "Promise me you'll always smell like strawberries."

"I promise." She laughed, softly brushing hair back from his forehead.

Ellis ran both hands through his hair. "I mean, I had more than he did."

"What are you saying?" Melody asked as she retrieved an extra blanket from the closet.

"There was a decanter on the table next to the balcony." Ellis paced to the window then back. "It was crystal. It looked expensive. We figured it was part of the setup. You know, like the charcuterie board. Oh, and the pair of cigars on the mantel. Alec was already drinking when I joined him with my bottle of Southern Spirits."

Alec let out a low groan. I didn't want to alarm Melody. But I also couldn't ignore the timing. The honeymoon suite. The cigars. The fact that both previous grooms had been drinking before they died.

"Let's make sure we keep an eye on him," I said carefully. "Keep him in bed tonight. No wandering. No balconies."

Ellis tensed. He understood what I wasn't saying.

"None of this makes sense," Melody said, fussing with her

fiancé. "This just isn't like Alec." She sighed. "Maybe I pushed this too fast. I'm stressing him out."

"Sure, I'll go out with you," Alec tried to pat her hand and ended up patting the bed. "But I don't think we should date until after the wedding."

She shouldn't jump to conclusions. "Look, he's fine." At her incredulous look, I added, "At least he'll be good in the morning."

Melody fluffed the pillow and gently tucked it behind her fiancé's head. "It's not like Alec to start early or drink alone."

"We both ate the charcuterie and smoked the cigars," Ellis said, beginning to pace again.

I crossed my arms as well. "I wonder where the cigars came from." The 1975 groom had been smoking a cigar on the balcony when he was pushed.

Ellis frowned. "The pair of them were just sitting there on the mantel. Hand-rolled by the look of them."

"You drank your own whiskey," I added.

"Could the whiskey be bad?" Melody asked. "Or a stronger proof than normal?"

Ellis halted. "I don't know."

The caretaker was the only one here besides us. "Maybe he started toasting with Mort." After all, Mort was here to help make sure we had a good time.

Still, I found it hard to imagine.

Ellis shook his head. "Mort left when the bachelor party started, and the second glass was clean." He hooked a thumb under his belt. "He delivered the charcuterie and was out of there. I think he was afraid I'd start talking again."

"Thank you." I really owed him for earlier.

He gave a stiff nod.

Guilt twisted in my chest. I'd kept Ellis busy on purpose, dragging him into my ghost hunt. If something had happened to Alec while we were gone...

"I'm sorry—" I started.

"Stop." Ellis shook his head. "You were helping, same as I was. We're not even sure anything is wrong."

We shared a look.

"I know." Ellis crossed his arms. His gut was telling him the same thing mine was. He glanced at his friend.

Melody smoothed Alec's hair back from his forehead. "Should we get him to the hospital?" she asked. "Get his stomach pumped?" She looked to Ellis. "Have his blood tested for drugs?"

Ellis rubbed his jaw. "I hate to say it, but I don't think he'd want that, even if he was drugged. If he tests positive, he'll have proof of drug use on his record." He glanced at his friend. "Yes, we can bring in the Jackson police to investigate, but we have no guarantee they'll focus on the right things. Some of those good ol' boys would be thrilled to have a Sugarland officer in their drunk tank."

He was right. As much as it pained me. "Alec would have to claim he was assaulted, and we're not sure that's true. The wedding would be off."

Melody took Alec's hand. "It would be years before we could save enough to try again."

Ellis met my eyes.

Meanwhile Alec let out a soft snore.

Melody's hand stilled on Alec's shoulder. She hovered over him in her beautiful wedding dress, her veil cascading down her back. "I think he's asleep."

"Good." He needed to recover.

"I'm sorry." She stood, then sat back down. "All I wanted was to get married. Maybe this deal was too good to be true."

"Hey." Ellis held up a hand. "Everything's going to be fine." He stood, shoulders back, the police officer taking charge. "We'll stick together like we always do." He glanced at Alec, then back to us. "In the meantime, don't let Alec out of your sight."

"Never." Melody vowed, her chin notching up. "I'll make sure he stays right here tonight." She softened. "I'll take good care of him."

Ellis glanced to me. "I want to check out that honeymoon suite again."

"I'll go with you." I nodded.

We ducked out into the hall.

Ghosts couldn't have caused this mess. A live person might have wanted to hurt us tonight, and we had less than twenty-four hours to figure out who.

# Chapter Nine

Ellis closed the bedroom door with a soft click, sealing Melody and Alec inside.

He ushered me down the hall. "Melody is onto something. I don't think this was alcohol."

My stomach tightened. "That's what I was going to say." I fell into step beside him.

"I've seen drunk plenty of times. Hell, I've been drunk." He ran a hand through his hair. "That wasn't it. Alec had one glass, maybe two fingers' worth, from that decanter. I had twice that from my bottle, and I'm stone-cold sober."

We passed the door to our room. The honeymoon suite loomed at the end of the hall.

"Someone left laced whiskey in the room where two grooms died." The same room where Alec was supposed to sleep tomorrow night.

"Yes, but who would leave drugged alcohol for a pair of police officers?" Ellis pulled out his phone as he walked. "Whoever put it in that decanter didn't know I'd brought my own. I'd planned to share with Alec, but he'd already poured a drink."

We were halfway to the honeymoon suite now.

"Whatever was in there was meant for both of you. If you ended up as bad as Alec, either one of you could have fallen off that balcony, and the other wouldn't have been able to stop it."

He gave a sharp nod. "Sedative, hallucinogen, who knows. We have a limited amount of time to figure out what drug was used. Some of them have a short detection window." Ellis didn't slow down. "I'm texting Jeannie at the lab. I'm getting that whiskey over to her. Tonight."

"You think the Sugarland crime lab works weekends?" Jeannie had two kids and coached Little League soccer on Saturday mornings.

Ellis reached for the door handle. "For this? For us? She'll be there."

He opened the door, and I led the way into the suite. The air was frigid. The balcony doors flung wide.

Ellis stiffened beside me. "I don't remember leaving those open."

A cold breeze wafted in from the garden below, carrying the scent of fresh roses. White curtains billowed like ghosts.

I smelled the cigar before I saw it. There, resting on the balcony rail. It lay at an angle, ash drooping over the edge. A thin trail of smoke curled upward into the night sky.

I stepped outside for a closer look.

The cold of the stone seeped through my thin sandals. The iron railing was slick with evening dew. But this wasn't Alec's cigar. It belonged firmly on the ghostly plane. The cigar lay half smoked, as if I'd interrupted a gentleman taking in the air and surveying the garden below.

I ventured a glance down at the iron fence bathed in moonlight. Each spike tapered to a lethal point.

The wind picked up, whipping my hair across my face. The balcony suddenly felt too small, too exposed. Like standing on the edge of a cliff.

I backed away from the rail and hurried inside. Ellis stood

frozen in front of the small table between the balcony doors and the fireplace. Two wingback chairs flanked it, one tipped over, no doubt courtesy of Alec. The charcuterie board dominated the table, stripped of every blueberry. Lucy's handiwork, no doubt.

Ellis gripped his phone in one hand, his other hand forming a tight fist as if he couldn't quite believe what he was seeing.

Or rather, what he wasn't seeing.

"It's gone." His voice came out flat. "We left everything right here." He gestured to the table.

My throat tightened. Someone had been in this room. Recently. While we were just down the hall with Melody and Alec.

"Maybe Alec tried to take it with him?" Stranger things had happened.

Ellis shook his head. "He wasn't exactly in control of his hands or his feet."

"He would have made a mess of the decanter."

"And set the house on fire with his cigar."

We were joking. Mostly. Although the fact remained. Ellis had practically carried Alec through Melody's door. He hadn't been holding anything. He'd had enough trouble holding himself up.

"Then it has to be here," I said, even as dread wound through my stomach. "Here." I pointed. A single bottle of Southern Spirits whiskey sat alone on the mantel with the cap upturned next to it.

"That was mine," Ellis said, moving to inspect it. "I left it pretty much like that."

I scanned the room. The massive four-poster bed with its flowing white canopy. The marble fireplace with its dying embers. The crystal vases filled with white roses on the dresser and nightstand.

No more whiskey. No crystal holder.

"The glasses are gone," Ellis said. "Both of them."

"Someone took them." Along with everything else.

"While we were twenty feet away." He cursed.

Then it hit me. Someone had crept into the honeymoon suite and stolen every shred of evidence that a crime might have been committed.

I thought back. Had we heard anything? Footsteps in the hall? A door opening? But no. We'd been focused on Alec, on the shock of it all, on figuring out what had happened.

Someone had slipped in and out, quiet as a ghost.

"Wait." I held up a hand. "Who had access to this room?" I started ticking off fingers. "Mort has a key."

"He wouldn't be cleaning up during the bachelor party," Ellis said, "and the decanter was mostly full." He surveyed the room. "Besides, Mort went home an hour ago. I watched him drive away."

I made my way to the window overlooking the front of the house. Ellis's Jeep and Alec's pickup stood alone on the driveway.

Ellis walked out onto the balcony and scanned the yard.

I joined him at the rail, gripping the cold iron. "It could be Honey Sue." She'd have a house key. Except she wasn't arriving until tomorrow.

Ellis pulled out his phone, checking the time. "Honey Sue would announce herself. Probably with a bullhorn and a checklist."

This was the woman who'd wrangled the Henderson-Clarkson wedding with seventeen bridesmaids, a flower girl who'd released butterflies during the vows, and twin ring bearers with matching black eyes. She'd used a PA system rented from the high school just to keep everyone on schedule.

The garden below lay still, the fountain's gentle trickle the only sound. No movement in the shadows. No footsteps on gravel.

Ellis turned to me, his mouth set in a grim line. "This confirms it. We have a problem with the living."

A chill ran down my spine. The ghosts I could handle. The

dead gangsters, the cursed balcony, even Knuckles McGee lurking somewhere in the rosebushes.

But someone alive had drugged Alec. Someone alive had stolen the evidence.

They'd been in this room minutes ago. They'd been bold, calculated. And if they'd wanted Alec and Ellis out of commission tonight, what would they try tomorrow?

## Chapter Ten

My alarm jolted me awake at eight a.m. sharp. I slapped it off and thanked my lucky stars I'd set it last night after lying awake far too long. I couldn't stop thinking about Alec barely able to stand. The missing evidence. And the biggest question of all—who might want to wreck the wedding, and why?

This wasn't just about a haunted honeymoon suite and its legacy of dead grooms. Not anymore.

Ellis was already up, leaning against the wall by the window. He wore jeans and a cerulean button-down that made his eyes look impossibly blue, not that I could tell at the moment. He was too busy staring at his phone.

"Anything?" I asked, leaning up on my elbows.

He strolled over to give me a kiss on my messy bedhead. "Mort's still not answering."

It had made sense last night. We'd been up way too late. But now? "How's Alec?"

"I checked in on him this morning. He said we made the right call about not taking him to the hospital." Ellis glanced at me. "He's rough around the edges, but doing okay. He tried to reenact his proposal to her last night and almost gave himself a black eye on the bedpost."

At least the sentiment was there, even if the coordination wasn't. "Bet he has a wicked headache this morning."

"She's already asked the caterer to send up aspirin and a ginger ale with their bridal breakfast in bed this morning."

"Good thinking." Although knowing Alec, he'd probably insist he was fine and try to do jumping jacks to prove it.

"You'd better hop to it." Ellis checked his watch. "We're due downstairs in a few minutes for brunch on the lawn."

Right. Part of the picture-perfect wedding weekend package.

I'd almost forgotten.

I popped into the shower, letting the hot water chase away some of the tension in my shoulders. When I emerged, I slipped on a burnt orange sundress with tiny cream-colored leaves and my trusty white Keds. I tied a carefree ribbon in my hair.

I didn't feel carefree.

Today was the day we absolutely, positively must get answers. Because tonight was the rehearsal dinner. The same night both previous grooms had died.

I grabbed the bag with my lipstick and Frankie's urn and headed for the door with Ellis right behind me. Lucy scampered ahead of us down the stairs, her tail swishing as she took the steps two at a time.

A young woman in a crisp white shirt and black slacks waited at the foot of the grand staircase, clipboard in hand. She shot us a confident smile as we descended, her professional demeanor faltering slightly when she spotted Lucy.

"Oh!" Her eyes went wide. "Is that a—"

"Skunk," I said quickly. "Lucy's very well behaved."

Our host's smile snapped back into place. "Of course. How lovely to meet you...Lucy," she managed as my skunk parked herself on the woman's black flats and gazed up as if to say *pet me now*. She adjusted her clipboard, and I pretended not to notice the way her eye twitched.

Some people took a few minutes to get used to skunks.

She raised her chin. "I'm Claire, your server this morning. I'm here to dazzle and delight you with our signature garden brunch experience."

"Lead the way," I said, knowing she'd do great even as she attempted to navigate the skunk at her feet. Claire didn't have to work for long. Lucy recognized the word *brunch* and spun a few happy circles in anticipation.

She knew how to work up an appetite.

Ellis's attention, however, was focused on a pair of expensive leather suitcases near the front door. They were monogrammed with the initials KPL.

He walked over to them. "Who else is here?"

Claire followed his gaze. "The owners got in late last night. They have a small apartment on the third floor and are still settling in, but I'm sure they'll be down to greet you soon."

That was news. "What time was that?"

Ellis crouched to inspect the luggage tags, turning one over in his hand.

Claire's clipboard shifted to her chest. "I'm not sure exactly. Chef was the only one here when they arrived."

"Chef told you that?" I asked.

She seemed surprised at the question. "This morning, yes." Claire shot us a conspiratorial grin. "Evidently, they raided the kitchen for snacks. Drives Chef crazy, but there's nothing he can do, you know?"

I exchanged a look with Ellis. "Seems like we weren't the only ones who had a late night."

"It's all part of the job," she said. "Chef had to prepare for today's meals and for the wedding tomorrow." She gestured toward the back of the house. "Let me lead you to the garden."

I stepped between them as Claire headed down the hall, and Ellis snapped a quick photo of a luggage tag. I shot him a questioning glance as he tucked the phone into his pocket and stood.

Claire hadn't noticed we'd lagged behind. "The grounds were originally designed and planted by Lady Brigid Byrne herself in 1907, with cuttings brought over from her family estate in

Ireland." We caught up with her halfway to the ballroom, with Lucy prancing next to me. "Lady Brigid was Lord Byrne's first wife, married in 1889..."

Ellis brought up the rear. "Where's the kitchen? I'd like to speak with the chef."

"Oh, he's not here at the moment," Claire said over her shoulder. "There was an issue with the food delivery. Not that it will affect your breakfast," she hastily added. "He bought all fresh ingredients for your brunch and the bridal breakfast in bed. But he's having a word with his supplier." She leaned toward me with a conspiratorial whisper. "In person. I would not want to be them."

Ellis stopped short. "Who's the supplier?"

Claire's smile wavered. "I'd rather not—"

"Then who's the chef?" I asked.

She glanced at a dark wood door just before the entrance to the ballroom. "Remy Duchamp, from Duchamp Catering." Her voice held a note of reverence. "Best in Jackson."

I could name every chef in Sugarland. Well, both of them. Three if you counted my friend Lauralee. "I've never heard of Remy Duchamp."

Her shoulders squared, and she pressed the clipboard against her side like a shield. "He's award-winning. Featured in *Southern Living* twice."

Well, then clearly *Southern Living* needed to visit Sugarland. I'd pen them an invite as soon as I got home.

Ellis pulled out his phone, already typing. "Tell Remy Duchamp I want to see him the moment he gets back."

"Oh." Claire's steps faltered, her practiced smile slipping. She glanced back at Ellis, then at me, as if trying to decide whether answering his question fell under "dazzle and delight."

"He's with the police," I explained.

But that only appeared to confuse her more. She cleared her throat and gestured ahead with renewed determination. "I will make sure Chef finds you as soon as he returns. Now"—she smoothed her hair—"if you will follow me, our rose garden is truly spectacular this time of year."

We followed. Although, I'd admit I walked slowly enough to put some distance between us and our hostess. "What kind of chef prepares a signature brunch and then leaves before the guests taste it?" I asked Ellis. "Unless he had a very good reason to be somewhere else."

"Or he wanted to avoid questions," Ellis said. "Look, if Alec was drugged last night, we don't have a lot of time to find that decanter. The half-life on a lot of these drugs is short."

"Not only that," I said, "but if we don't find that decanter, there goes our evidence."

"I think you'll be pleased," Claire said way too cheerfully. "Chef Duchamp has prepared a feast that showcases the very best of Tennessee's autumn harvest."

She led us through the ballroom, past the elegantly set tables we'd admired last night. We went out through a set of French doors and down a set of lovely stone steps I hadn't noticed in the dark.

The garden sprawled before us, transformed by sunshine. What had looked wild and overgrown now revealed itself as deliberately romantic—creamy white climbing roses wound up wrought-iron arbors, their blooms heavy and fragrant. Stone pathways curved between beds of late-season dahlias and chrysanthemums in shades of burgundy and gold. The cupid fountain I'd seen last night gurgled cheerfully, surrounded by its moat of giant pink roses spilling over onto moss-covered stones.

I scanned for any sign of Knuckles McGee. But I saw nothing ghostly. Not yet at least.

He had to be here somewhere.

Lucy made a beeline for the bed of pink roses, burying her nose in a particularly fat bloom before rolling onto her back in a patch of clover, all four paws in the air.

My skunk knew how to appreciate the finer things.

A small bistro table sat beneath a rose-covered arbor on a

terraced level near the fountain, positioned to overlook the main garden. The cream linen tablecloth caught the breeze. Two delicate china place settings waited, each with a folded napkin tied with a sprig of rosemary. A pair of crystal glasses and a silver coffee service gleamed between them. A three-tiered stand held an array of pastries—croissants, scones, and tiny fruit tarts dusted with powdered sugar.

"These light bites are from the Cozy Crumb Bakery here in Jackson, delivered fresh this morning. I'll be out soon with the main course," Claire said, already backing away as if afraid we'd ask more questions. "Please, enjoy."

She hurried back into the house.

A lanky man in his thirties stood a short distance away, knees locked, taking pictures. He wore dark jeans, a fitted black polo, and had the kind of carefully tousled hair that probably took twenty minutes to achieve.

"Morning!" He lifted the camera. "Brett Garrett. Your photographer for the weekend. Are you the bride and groom?"

My face heated.

Ellis choked out a startled laugh. "Not yet."

I felt myself go more red. "We're just the best man—"

"And the maid of honor," Ellis finished for me.

A couple of fools was what we were.

"Gotcha," he said, framing us through the camera lens. "The owners want me to get some candid shots during the romantic garden brunch." He took a few steps closer as the camera lens gave a rapid *snap-snap-snap*. "Just pretend I'm not here."

Ellis pulled out my chair before settling in across from me. He reached for the coffee pot and poured for both of us, the rich aroma curling up. For a moment, we were the picture of a relaxed couple enjoying a romantic garden breakfast.

I reached for my coffee cup. "Nothing awkward about this at all."

"Not even a little bit," Ellis agreed, his tone so deadpan I nearly choked on my first sip.

"Treat me like I'm one of the rosebushes!" Brett called, circling around the fountain as he framed a wider shot, his attention fixed on his viewfinder.

Heavens. "I wouldn't last one second with the paparazzi."

"It's the price we pay for a free wedding," Ellis said, clearly not regretting it a bit. He leaned forward, his voice dropping. "So. Mort, the owners, and the chef."

I matched his posture. "All here last night." I reached across the table for his hand. "All with access to the house and the honeymoon suite."

"The caterer would have managed the bar." Ellis's fingers threaded through mine.

"But both the owners and Mort were also in the kitchen." I weighed the possibilities as his thumb traced slow circles on the back of my hand. I kept quiet, aware that voices carried. "Although what could Chef Duchamp's motive be? I doubt he knows our groom."

"I'll ask Alec about Chef, the owners, and Mort." Ellis glanced at the photographer, who appeared to be changing a lens. "Although that could have nothing to do with it. This could be a for-hire job. Keep the groom out of commission, ruin the wedding, make the venue look bad."

I considered it. "The owners would want the opposite, though. They need this weekend to go perfectly." They were giving Melody a free wedding to make it happen. "It's their big promotional launch."

"Unless they want history to repeat itself." Ellis's expression went dark. "Think about it. Two grooms died here, fifty years apart. Now we're at the hundred-year mark. One more death and the publicity alone would be massive."

A chill ran down my spine. "That's morbid. And risky. They'd be accessories to murder."

Ellis squeezed my hand before letting go. "Or they didn't think it would go that far." He lifted his coffee cup. "Maybe they just wanted Alec sick enough to postpone. Add to the legend, get some press."

"I still don't see how that would make couples want to book this place. Most brides start off liking the groom."

Ellis chuckled.

We both reached for the same croissant. He laughed and let me take it. I tore off a piece and popped it into his mouth.

He caught my wrist, holding it while he chewed, his eyes never leaving mine. When he swallowed, he pressed a kiss to my palm before releasing me. "Dangerous game you're playing."

Didn't I know it?

I tore off another piece, this time for myself.

He plucked it from my fingers and ate it.

"Thief, I ought to have you arrested."

"Worth it," he teased.

He planted an elbow on the table. "So I'm thinking...what about Mort?" His voice dropped back to business. "He's lived here more than fifty years. He saw Finn Byrne die. He warned us not to come."

"He did." I scanned for the photographer taking shots of us from the other side of the cupid fountain. Aware that we'd just given him a show.

Dang it.

*This is for Melody*, I reminded myself.

We just needed to rein it in.

I cocked my head. "What if Mort's trying to protect the estate's reputation? Or what if he blames himself for not stopping the second death and he's... I don't know, trying to prevent another one in the worst possible way?"

"By drugging the groom?" He sipped his coffee. "That doesn't track."

"By scaring him off." I said, lifting my cup. "If Alec got sick, maybe he'd leave. Cancel the wedding. Stay alive."

It was twisted logic, but not impossible.

Lucy trotted to our table, tail high, a rose petal stuck to her nose. She sat at my feet and gazed up expectantly.

She had cute down to a science. I selected a tiny fruit tart and fed her a blueberry off the top.

Ellis pulled out his phone and scrolled down. "Have you ever heard of Kip and Lonnie Pierce?"

I stopped to think. "Should I?"

I mean, I knew pretty much every soul in Sugarland, Tennessee. But here in Jackson? I was out of my element.

Ellis showed me the photo he took in the lobby. "According to the luggage tags, Kip and Lonnie Pierce live in Greenwich, Connecticut."

"So the owners aren't even from here?" That would be a very unpopular choice in Sugarland. Bordering on scandal. "It's obvious we've slipped into foreign territory."

"Old-money territory." Ellis placed the phone facedown on the table. He had that focused detective look that I found unreasonably attractive, all sharp intelligence and quiet competence. "I'm talking hedge fund managers, estate lawyers, that kind of crowd."

I must have been staring because Ellis's expression softened, just slightly, before that devastating dimple appeared.

I felt myself blush. "So why buy a haunted wedding venue in Jackson, Tennessee?"

"Good question." He tapped his screen. "On the walk out here, I ordered background checks on all of them—the Pierces, Chef Duchamp, Mort." He popped an entire mini pastry into his mouth. "And Honey Sue."

I snagged a blueberry scone. "Honey Sue?"

"We're running out of time," he said, swallowing. "We have... today."

My stomach sank at the mention of it. He was right. We needed to know everything about everyone who had access to that room. Even the people we thought we knew.

His phone chirped. He met my eyes briefly before standing to take the call. "Sorry," he added to me before shifting into professional cop mode. "Yes, this is hot. Get Sonny on it too. I'll owe you both a barbeque dinner from Big Mike's and a slice of Mabel's cherry pie." He listened for a moment. "Okay, the whole pie."

I watched him work, the only man I'd want with me on my sister's wedding weekend. The man who'd kept Mort distracted last night so I could dig up a gangster in the wine cellar, who was now calling in favors to keep his friend, my future brother-in-law, alive.

"I need employment history, any priors, financial records if you can get them..."

Meanwhile, Lucy stole the blueberry scone I hadn't realized I'd been holding way too close to my lap. She scuttled under one of the big rosebushes by the fountain to enjoy her own fancy brunch.

Ellis paced along the stone terrace, phone pressed to his ear. "Right. Any connections between them. I'm talking business deals, shared properties, anything that links the Pierces to Jackson or this estate specifically." He paused. "And if Duchamp has any complaints filed against him, health code violations, anything. I need this by noon if possible. We're running out of time."

I sipped my coffee, watching him work. I always loved how Ellis thought of everything—in his police work and in how he treated me and the people he loved.

"One more thing," Ellis said. "Check if Mort Shackleton owns any part of the property or if he has any claim to it. Inheritance, will, anything like that." Another pause. "Great. Call me the second you have something."

He ended the call just as Claire popped around the side of the house, pushing a silver serving cart.

"You are in for a treat this morning," she announced as she rolled it up the ramp to our table.

She set down plate after plate with practiced efficiency. Fluffy buttermilk biscuits split and filled with thin-sliced country ham and a drizzle of honey. A frittata studded with caramelized onions, sharp cheddar, and fresh herbs, the eggs puffed and golden. Roasted cherry tomatoes still on the vine, their skins blistered and glistening. A bowl of mixed berries featuring blackberries, raspberries, and fat blueberries that looked like they'd been picked that morning. And finally, a basket of what could only be described as heaven, warm cinnamon rolls with cream cheese frosting pooled in their centers.

Lucy materialized at my feet so fast I wondered if she'd teleported.

"This..." I trailed off, at a loss for words.

"Isn't breakfast," Ellis finished for me as Claire set down a flight of homemade preserves. "This is a buffet."

"Chef Duchamp's signature brunch," Claire said. "He prepared everything fresh this morning before he left. The frittata can be served warm or at room temperature. Bride's choice. And the biscuits are best within the first hour, so it can be served as a buffet as well." She gestured to the spread. "Please, enjoy."

We watched her roll the cart away, neither one of us making a move, despite Lucy's frantic pawing on my leg.

The drama was Oscar-worthy.

I should dig in. I wanted to devour my plate. Instead, I stared at the frittata. Ellis fiddled with his butter knife.

"So," I said carefully, "the chef made every bite of this."

Ellis twirled the knife between his fingers. "The same chef who may have drugged Alec's whiskey last night."

"To be fair, we don't know it was him." I reached for a biscuit but stopped halfway to grabbing it and slathering it in butter. "If he wanted to poison us, this seems like an elaborate way to do it."

And a sure way to get caught.

Lucy let out a small whine, her nose twitching and her back paws dancing.

My stomach growled. The frittata beckoned me, golden and perfect, steam still rising from where Ellis had cut into it. The cinnamon rolls glistened, their frosting just beginning to melt down the sides.

Ellis shot me a wry look. "Tell you what. I'll try the frittata first. If I keel over, don't eat the biscuits."

"How heroic of you." I plucked a berry from the bowl and popped it in my mouth. The raspberry burst with sweetness. "Oh my God."

"Good?"

"Incredible." I tried a blackberry next. "Okay, if Chef Duchamp is trying to kill us, at least he's giving us a memorable last meal."

Ellis cut into the frittata, steam rising from the center. He took a bite, chewed thoughtfully. His eyes widened. "This might be the best thing I've ever eaten."

"Better than my eggs and bacon?"

"Don't make me choose." He took another bite. "Okay, it's safe. Probably. Try the biscuit."

I pulled one apart, the layers flaking under my fingers. The ham was paper-thin and salty-sweet, the honey adding just the right amount of sticky richness. "Oh, Ellis."

"That good?"

I nodded and held out a piece. He leaned forward to take it from my fingers, and I felt his breath warm against my palm.

My heart did a little skip.

"We might need to invite Chef Duchamp to Sugarland." I took another bite, closing my eyes. "Assuming he's not a would-be murderer."

"There's always a catch." Ellis served me a slice of frittata. "Although, if this is his signature brunch, I understand why he's award-winning."

I tried the frittata. The eggs were silky, the cheese sharp and nutty, the caramelized onions sweet and complex. "This is stupid good."

"We're definitely not dying." Ellis reached for a cinnamon roll. "If only all our suspects were this talented."

Lucy's patience finally ran out. She placed both paws on my knee and fixed me with her most pitiful expression.

I tore off a piece of biscuit—no ham, no honey—and handed it down. She took it delicately, then scurried back to her rosebush.

"She's got the right idea," I said, watching her. "Stuff your face and smell the roses." It was hard to argue with skunk philosophy.

Ellis reached across the table and took my hand. "Despite everything going on, I'm still glad we're here. Together."

"Even though someone might be trying to kill the groom?"

"Especially then." He kissed each of my knuckles one at a time. "Who else would I want to investigate a cursed wedding venue with?"

I smiled despite myself. "You really know how to sweet-talk a girl."

"I try." He squeezed my hand before releasing it to steal a berry from my plate. "Besides, the food's incredible, the garden's beautiful, and you look stunning in that dress."

A ribbon of pleasure wound through me. "Ellis Wydell, are you flirting with me during an active investigation?"

"Is it working?"

"It always does."

He grinned and leaned in for a kiss.

*Click-click-click.*

We both froze, then turned to see Brett by the cupid fountain, camera raised, grinning behind his lens.

"Don't stop on my account," he called cheerfully. "That was perfect."

Ellis sat back, his ears slightly pink. I bit back a laugh and wished I could melt into the ground.

Brett never let up on the grin. "I think I've got more than I need from you two," he said, lowering his camera. "I'll be back around ten for the bridal photos. Should be gorgeous." He trotted back toward the house with a wave.

Ellis and I stared at each other for a beat.

"So that happened," I said.

His mouth quirked. "We're never going to live that down." He rubbed the back of his neck.

I pressed my palms to my cheeks. "My mom's going to see those photos."

"Along with everyone who books this venue for the next five years." He reached across the table for my hand, threading his fingers through mine.

A laugh bubbled up before I could stop it. Ellis joined in, his shoulders shaking.

"We're professionals now," I managed, trying to catch my breath.

"Clearly." His eyes danced. "Very focused on the investigation."

I squeezed his hand. "So focused we forgot about the photographer with the camera."

"In my defense, you're very distracting." He lifted our joined hands, turned mine over, and pressed a kiss to my palm.

I fought the urge to fan my face. Then I noticed Lucy under the rosebush with her biscuit.

And she had company.

A white skunk with cream-colored markings gobbled up the last morsel Lucy had shared.

My smile faded. "Oh no." I drew back.

The white skunk went still and stared up at us with shockingly blue eyes.

"Shoo!" I ordered.

"He's a handsome fellow." Ellis held out a slice of bacon.

"Oh no. Don't. He could have diseases. Rabies. Parasites." This was a wild animal. Next to my Lucy. I would have scooped her up right then if I hadn't been worried it would startle the beast into biting.

The skunk's nose twitched.

"I'll get him away," Ellis said as the white skunk crept forward, hesitant but curious. He stretched his neck, grabbed the bacon from Ellis's fingers with surprising delicacy, and retreated into the roses.

"Well, shoot," Ellis said, watching him share it with Lucy.

She chomped the other half of the slice, and I gaped in horror as they devoured it *Lady and the Tramp* style.

"Lap, Lucy. Now," I called.

With a flick of her tail, she dashed to me, and I scooped her up.

"Good girl," I gushed, treating her to a slice of my bacon.

Ellis observed the interloper with the kind of focus he usually reserved for crime scenes. "You know, it's interesting. Lucy's chased off every wild skunk who so much as sniffed at the edge of your property. Remember that one who tried to hang out under your porch? He didn't stand a chance. But this one gets to share her breakfast."

"I think she's trying to give me a heart attack." As if to prove my point, Lucy squirmed out of my arms, snatched a piece of frittata off my plate, and leaped back down. She scampered straight under the big, pink rosebush and dropped it in front of the other skunk. "Lucy!"

She completely ignored me, settling down next to him like they did it every day. I stared at her. "Is this what the teenage years look like? Is she starting to rebel?"

Ellis quirked a brow. "I'll only worry if she comes home with a motorcycle."

A voice called out from behind us, "Oh, that's just Lucky."

Mort stood at the base of the terrace steps, toolbox in hand. He must have come from around the side of the house.

"He has a name?" I craned to get a better look. "He's not wearing a collar."

Mort climbed the steps and set his tools down near the table. "He hangs around because I feed him too much. All of 'em, really." He shoved a hand into his pocket, looking sheepish. "We had a tough winter a few years ago, and I started putting out food. Then I never stopped."

"You're sure he's safe?" I asked.

"Healthy as all get-out." Mort pulled a small bottle from his pocket. "I have a wildlife vet come check on my regulars. And I slip 'em vitamins. This one especially needs it. Can't hunt as easy when everyone sees you coming." He nodded toward Lucky, who blinked up at us. "He's got leucism. Born without most of his pigment, but not a full albino. Still has some color in there if you look close."

He did have the faintest cream-colored stripe, barely visible against his white fur.

Mort pocketed the vitamins and picked up his toolbox. "I'd appreciate it if you didn't mention this to the owners. They're..." He searched for the word. "Particular. About wild animals on the property."

Ellis stood and shook hands with Mort. "We haven't met the owners, but I understand they arrived last night." He hooked a thumb under his belt. "Do you have any idea when?"

The caretaker shifted his toolbox from one hand to the other. "Couldn't say for certain. I went home right after I set you boys up for your bachelor party."

"What about Chef Duchamp?" I asked.

Mort scratched his jaw. "He was here earlier in the evening, setting up. Why?"

Ellis fetched a strawberry from his plate. "We wanted to thank whoever left the whiskey and cigars for our groom's party last night. Nice touch."

"Ah." Mort's shoulders relaxed slightly. "The whiskey was from Chef. He left it by the fridge earlier. I brought it up to the suite before the party started, set it on the table for you. The cigars though, those were from the owners. A special tobacco blend from Charleston. They have them custom-made at some fancy shop down there."

"I'll have to ask them where," Ellis said, popping the strawberry into his mouth. "We were disappointed when someone collected everything from the room before we finished our party."

Mort rubbed the back of his neck. "Who would do that?"

"We have no idea." Ellis's voice stayed light. "They made off with the decanter, the cigars, even our glasses. We left the room for a few minutes, and it was all gone when we got back."

"That doesn't make sense." Mort set down his toolbox. "There's no reason for anyone to be going into the honeymoon suite while the groom's having his bachelor party. I'm sorry. I don't know what happened."

I stood to join them. "Could it have been housekeeping?"

Mort shook his head. "Claire does light tidying between events, but she was off last night so she could be back early this morning."

"I'd like that decanter back for the weekend," Ellis said. "Unwashed. Even if it's empty. Can you figure out what happened to it?"

Mort studied Ellis for a long moment. "I'll see what I can do."

"I'd also like to know who was upstairs with us last night," I added.

Mort gave a stiff nod. "I need to get the horses tacked up for the carriage pictures this morning." He picked up his toolbox. "But I've got a few minutes. I'll ask around and tell you what I know when I bring the carriage around. Should be about an hour."

"One more question," I said quickly. "Was Chef Duchamp the only one working in the kitchen yesterday, or did he have help?"

"Only him." Mort headed down the terrace steps. "He prefers to work alone. Says too many cooks spoil the broth."

We watched him disappear around the side of the house, his boots crunching along the path.

Ellis made a note on his phone. "Charleston custom cigars. That's specific."

"And expensive," I added. "Would they be easy to tamper with?"

"No. But I had one, and I was fine. I'd say they were clean."

"Then why take them?"

"I don't know."

Lucky wandered out from under the roses and gave a playful leap. Lucy trotted beside him, looking enormously pleased with herself.

I watched them for a moment, an idea forming. "I have one more way to learn who else was in the honeymoon suite last night."

Ellis tucked the phone into his back pocket. "Frankie? What's he been up to?"

"I don't think we want to know." And it didn't matter. "It's time to put our favorite gangster to work."

## Chapter Eleven

I dug through my bag and pulled out Frankie's urn where it had been clanking around next to my lipstick and compact. It was brass and heavier than it looked, wider at the top and tapered down to a flared base. Green stones circled the rim in an uneven arrangement, and a crude hand-painted scene marred one side. I plunked it onto the table between the frittata and the basket of cinnamon rolls, nearly knocking over a pot of peach jam. "Hiya, Frankie," I called, waiting for the ghost to appear.

Nothing. Not even a chill.

Lucy poked her head out from under the rosebush. She knew that name.

And the trouble it could bring.

Wisely, my little skunk retreated into her leafy hideout.

Oh, to be a skunk. I tried again, louder. *"Rise and shine, Frankie."*

A sparrow hopped along the stone terrace rail. The cupid fountain gurgled. A breeze rustled through the rose arbor above us, sending a shower of ivory petals across the white tablecloth.

Ellis's mouth quirked. "Let me guess. He's being difficult."

"This is the guy who wanted me to rob a dead gangster in the wine cellar last night." Never mind that I did. "Difficult doesn't begin to cover it."

Only this was worse. "He's ignoring me." Just like Lucy did whenever I called her away from a particularly fun compost pile.

"Too bad we can't lure him with a treat," Ellis said, tempting Lucy out with another bit of bacon.

"I'm fresh out of dice, cards, and laundered cash." My thumb came to rest on the healthy dent gouged into the lower half of the urn. "Come on, Frank."

His voice sounded in my ear. "Don't call me Frank."

My gangster housemate shimmered into existence between me and the rosebush. Lucy took one look at him and dove back in with Lucky.

He'd clearly been exploring the estate. A spider web dangled from the brim of his Panama hat. At my pointed look, he yanked the hat off and shook it away like it had cooties.

He tamped the hat back onto his head. "Satisfied?"

Maybe. "Where have you been?"

His mouth tipped into a grin. "You don't want to know."

Good point. I wasn't his mother. "At least you came when I called."

"You do realize I'm not the genie in the lamp."

"I need your help." I explained the events of the previous evening, ending with the missing whiskey and cigars.

Frankie's scowl melted like butter on a hot biscuit. "Sounds like a nice, clean job. Like the time I broke into that Chicago speakeasy through the coal chute and walked out with three cases of Canadian whiskey and the owner's pet parrot. Bird knew more secrets than the FBI."

I folded my hands in front of me. "Ellis and I need you to search Mort's apartment, Honey Sue's room, the carriage house, the chef's kitchen, and the owners' apartment." I tried to think if I'd left anything out.

Ellis ran a hand along his jaw. "Anywhere else you find locked or suspicious. Storage rooms, the attic."

Good catch.

Frankie yanked at his tie like it was choking him. "The entire estate. You want me to search the entire estate."

Oh, good. "That would be wonderful. Thanks."

Frankie's eyes bugged out. "Have you stopped to consider I have a life?"

Well, technically he was dead.

But I didn't think he'd want me bringing it up.

"I've got hobbies!" He threw his hands up. "I've got interests!"

"Let me guess. You've been digging in the chapel, seeing if you can find more of Lord Byrne's loot."

He had the nerve to appear offended. "A gangster never tells his secrets."

Yes, well, I knew him.

Meanwhile, Lucy's striped tail stuck straight up as she dug furiously at the base of her rosebush. Dirt flew out behind her like a Bugs Bunny cartoon, scattering over the pavers and onto Ellis's shoe. Lucky worked next to her like he was about to strike gold.

Ellis kicked the dirt off his loafer. "I can't tell if Lucy's the bad influence or if he is."

I'd deal with them in a second.

"I'm asking you to help keep my sister's fiancé alive," I said to Frankie.

The gangster's mouth pressed into a thin line. "You've always got an angle."

I met him straight on. "I'm asking you for a favor. As a friend."

Frankie whipped off his hat. "I'm already busy with a problem *you* created."

He couldn't be serious. Me? "What did I do?"

His eyes bugged out. "You dug up two guys who keep trying to kill each other and put a few holes in me." He twisted the brim to show me a brand-new bullet hole. "Things haven't exactly been easy since you decided to go picnicking." He jammed his hat back on his head. "This is worse than a speakeasy with three rival gangs and one bathroom."

It hadn't been my idea. "You asked me to dig them up."

"As a favor to you," he said as if he were the gallant one. "Now I got no peace." He brushed a cobweb off his shoulder. "Lenny's stealing what I'm trying to steal. Dapper Dan's just waiting to steal it back, and both of 'em want to kill me for the ruby earrings I found."

"Found?"

"In Dapper Dan's pocket."

Naturally.

Frankie stiffened. "The guy is relentless."

A relentless gangster? "I wonder how you manage."

Lucy's head popped up from the rapidly expanding hole under the rosebush, dirt smudged across her nose. Darn it. She was going to need another bath.

"Oh, baby. Stop," I said, starting for her.

"I've got her," Ellis said, moving fast.

Lucy was faster. She dove back down, sending up a fresh wave of dirt that smacked Ellis square in the chest as he reached for her. Lucky's white tail waved like a flag as he helped her excavate.

We had to get back on track. I focused on the gangster. "I'm asking for your help. As a friend." Surely that had to mean something after all we'd been through.

Frankie let out a snort. "I'll find your whiskey and cigars. I'll search the entire property, and if they're here, I'll find 'em. But first, you gotta do a favor for me."

I fought the urge to run a hand down my face. "That would be lovely, but I don't have time—"

"Dig up Knuckles," he finished.

I dropped my hand. He couldn't be serious. "Are you saying you want a *third* gangster trying to kill you?"

Frankie straightened his tie. "Knuckles is different. I met him a couple of times. He's the only one who can keep Dapper Dan and Lenny in line. Trust me. I know what I'm doing," he said at my dubious look. "Knuckles is a peacemaker."

"I can tell by the name."

"Think of him like a bouncer. Only terrifying." Frankie yanked down his cuffs. "Plus, he's the only witness to that second groom going bye-bye off the balcony."

A door slammed. Voices carried from the house. Melody's laugh rang out, bright and happy.

Frankie quirked a brow. "You want to save your brother-in-law or not?"

He had a point. A frustrating, inconvenient point.

Still. "I'm not digging up another body." Two was enough.

"According to Dapper Dan, all you need is his lucky silver dollar, and Knuckles will show up. It's got a bullet dent in it. You can't miss it."

It was never that easy.

This was all too much. I just wanted to help my sister. "Why do you have to make everything so complicated?"

Frankie threw up his hands. "I was about to ask the same thing about you."

A burst of activity shook the rosebush. Ellis stood covered in dirt. Lucky danced circles around him as Lucy backed out of the hole. She clutched something in her teeth that I sincerely hoped wasn't dangerous, poisonous, or alive.

Ellis was on her in a flash. "Drop it."

She did. My boyfriend scooped it up and let out a low whistle.

"What?" I pressed.

He tossed it to me. It was muddy and tarnished, but there was no mistaking it. A silver dollar. A sharp dent marred the center.

"I don't believe it." I looked to the white skunk now dancing circles around Lucy. "Maybe you really are Lucky."

"Bingo!" Frankie slapped his knee as a ghost shimmered into existence directly behind him. He was shorter than Frankie but twice as wide, his blunt fingers curling into fists and murder in his eyes.

Maybe our luck had just run out.

## Chapter Twelve

The ghost's gaze locked on the coin in my palm.

"That's mine." He lunged for me.

I dodged toward the fountain with the gangster on my tail.

"You stole my lucky dollar." Knuckles took a swipe at my head. Missed.

Barely.

This wasn't good. "Frankie!" He didn't seem bothered in the least. "A little help here."

"No, thanks. I want him to like me," he hollered from ten feet away and counting.

I dodged another swipe and focused on Knuckles. On the problem at hand. "I didn't steal anything," I insisted. "Here. Take it." I tossed the coin at the bruiser and watched it sail straight through his forehead.

"Argh!" He clutched his head like I'd scalded him. "You!" He pointed a fat finger at me. "You toss my property like it's nothing?"

"I was giving it back." Badly, yes. Awkwardly, maybe. But he had me over a barrel. Frankie was no help, and Ellis couldn't see either one of them. "You just said you didn't want me having it."

"Stealing it." He glowered.

"Tomato, tom-ah-to," Frankie said.

Oh, sure. Now he had an opinion.

Ellis scooped it up. "Verity, are you all right?" He pressed the coin into my palm.

Not again.

Knuckles jerked back. "You're both in on it." His beefy hands clamored for my neck. "You the leader?"

I wished. "More like a fixer." The one trying to herd cats and catch butterflies without a net. The one bailing out the *Titanic* with a teacup.

Not that he'd want to hear it.

I retreated lickety-split, the back of my knees hitting something solid and cold. The fountain. Water sprayed against my shoulders, soaking the back of my sundress. "Ellis, please run and tell Melody I might be late for pictures."

"I'm not going anywhere," my boyfriend said, trying to place himself between me and Knuckles.

Only he was about three feet off, and there was nothing he could do against a ghost.

"Mr. Knuckles." I raised my hands. "This is all a misunderstanding," I insisted, water filling my Keds. We'd started off wrong and made it worse. I offered him a hand. "Hi. My name is Verity Long, and I'm from Sugarland." He glared at me. I pasted on my brightest smile. "I hoped that by finding your lucky dollar, we could become acquainted, and you might be persuaded to tell me what you saw in 1925, or even in 1975 when—"

Knuckles drew so close I could smell the garlic on his breath. "I can't decide whether to drown you or pound you." His lip curled. "Either way, when your gang sees what I do to you, I guarantee they'll never touch my coin again."

Oh boy. Okay. "I dug up your coin so I could meet you," I insisted.

"So you could toss it through my head?" he demanded.

"To be fair, I hadn't planned that," I said, searching frantically for a way around, under, or—I cringed—through the gangster. "He's your friend, Frankie. Do something!"

My housemate straightened his tie. "I wouldn't exactly call him a friend."

"Frankie!" He was the one who'd told us to dig up the coin. He was the one who started the whole thing with Dapper Dan, who said we should talk to Knuckles. I was the one getting threatened, soaked, and very nearly pounded. And wouldn't you know Melody's bridal photos started in, oh, about fifteen minutes. I still had to change my dress and fix my hair.

The fountain spray hit the back of my neck.

"Frankie," Ellis hollered.

The gangster had cracked open his silver cigarette case and was busy selecting a smoke.

The jerk.

I didn't get it. I didn't get his nonchalant attitude or his complete lack of concern for me or my hide. But I did know one thing. I was tired of doing Frankie's dirty work. I was tired of gangsters popping up at every turn. I was tired of water leaking out of my shoes. I should be able to enjoy a lovely breakfast with my sweetie, without the threat of violence or drowning. "Franklin Rudolph Winkelmann, if I so much as muss my hair..."

Frankie was from the South. He understood the threat.

He materialized next to me in a flash. "Let's not get hysterical."

I turned to Ellis. "I'm fine. He's here. Can you please track down my sister before she leaves for pictures and tell her I'll join her as soon as I can? Also, double-check that my bridesmaid dress is hanging in the closet." In the chaos last night, I'd forgotten to venture a peek.

Ellis looked from me to the spot where Frankie stood.

He was getting better.

"Verity—" he began. He knew how unreliable my ghost could be.

"I've got this," I promised. "You can't help me with the

ghosts, but you can sure be my hero when it comes to making sure Melody's grand bridal photo shoot happens with as little drama as possible."

A muscle in his jaw jumped, but he nodded and looked toward the house. "Call me if you need me, and I'll come running," he vowed.

I had no doubt he would.

Ellis kept eyes on me as he bounded up the stairs to the ballroom.

My housemate locked in on the gangster, who dug a pair of brass knuckles out of his pocket and slipped them on.

"Frankie the German." The brute made a fist, and I could have sworn I heard his knuckles crack under the brass. "I shoulda known you were in on this."

"Whoops," Frankie said.

"What do you mean, 'whoops'?" My housemate was supposed to make this better. I couldn't be the only one trying to smooth things out.

Instead, I watched Knuckles's eyes narrow and his lips thin.

Frankie held out his hands, the unsmoked cigarette dangling between two fingers. "Knuckles. Buddy. I thought you were over the whole vehicular misunderstanding."

Knuckles clenched his fists. "You sold me a stolen police cruiser."

"With the guns still in the back," Frankie said. As if that made it better.

"They hunted me down." Knuckles's face darkened in a way that preceded either a stroke or a murder.

Frankie held out his hands. "To be fair, that sounds like fun."

"At my niece's christening!"

"Gotta start the kids off early," Frankie said, ignoring the vein now throbbing in Knuckles's temple.

"How is this helping?" I demanded.

"You're the one who wanted to meet him," he said. Then he turned to Knuckles. "Don't mind my protégée here." He tucked the smoke onto his bottom lip. "She's the type to run a protection racket and actually protect people. But don't worry"—he struck a match on his hat—"I'm in charge now."

Knuckles eyed me like a bug under glass.

Frankie lit the smoke and tossed the match over his shoulder. "In this case, the kid dug up your doodad fair and square. She's alive."

Knuckles glared at me like that was my fault. "I been looking for that coin for a hundred years."

"And now you can keep it safe," Frankie said, taking a drag. "Safer than it was buried in the dirt."

Knuckles unclenched his fists.

I pinched the silver dollar between two fingers and held it out for him. "I can relocate this anywhere you'd like."

He swiped at it, his hand passing straight through. He let out a curse.

Dang it. I didn't mean to tease.

I studied the tarnished dollar, which wasn't enough to buy a cup of coffee anymore. "Why is this coin so important?" So far, it hadn't been at all lucky for me.

Knuckles didn't take his eyes off it. "I used that dollar to stop a bloodbath between the Eastman Gang and the Five Points crew." He reached for it again. Failed. "Borrowed it from Diamond Hal. Then we flipped it to decide who got to rob Al Capone's vault. Diamond Hal's boys got the speakeasy upstairs. Mugsy's Seven got the vault." He passed a single finger through the tarnished silver dollar. "I walked off with the change as my negotiating fee. A rare 1921 Peace dollar."

Because he was such a peace-loving guy.

Frankie reared back. "You..." He jabbed two fingers and a cigarette at Knuckles. "You also stiffed the South Town Boys that night. We'd been hiding in Al Capone's boiler room since Tuesday. All twelve of us!"

Knuckles shifted his weight, blocking any escape route for me while he glared at Frankie. "So...it was you who called the cops."

"No." Frankie tossed up his hands. "We were dressed as the cops."

Knuckles smirked. "Then I appreciate you running off the crews. Gave me time to clear the vault."

Frankie's jaw went slack. "*That's* why it was empty!"

Knuckles's mouth twitched. "Should've seen the look on Al Capone's face. Almost as good as the one on Geraldo's face sixty years later. Made the whole thing worthwhile."

At least he'd backed off a little. I stepped away from the fountain, ignoring the slosh of water in my shoes. "Let's start over," I suggested, ignoring Frankie angry-smoking way too close to me. "I'll put this back where we found it." I scanned for the skunk hole.

Knuckles's beady eyes bored into me. "It needs to go under the fountain."

"Why?" There had to be a better place.

"I'm under the fountain!" Knuckles boomed.

Of course he was.

"Didn't even see it coming," he added under his breath.

"What happened to you?" I pressed. "What's the last thing you remember?"

He shook his head. "One minute, I'm scoring a sweet pair of ruby earrings. The next minute, I'm clocked on the head and tossed down a well."

Frankie and I exchanged a look. Those earrings got around.

"The fountain was installed afterward?" I guessed.

"They said it tied the garden together," he said gloomily.

It kind of did. But I didn't think he'd want to hear it.

Instead, I focused on the problem at hand. I wanted to help. Still... "I don't see how we can pull this off," I mused, considering the fountain was large and stone and not going anywhere.

"Stop talking." Frankie took a hard drag, eyeing Knuckles. "Don't say another word until we make a deal."

Where we couldn't uphold our end of the bargain.

*Focus on what you can control.* I smoothed my dress. Checked my hair. It was soaked in the back, mostly dry in the front. Mussed, certainly. But I could work with that. I had about five minutes before I was due at the bridal photo shoot.

Knuckles crossed his arms. "You bury my coin with me. I'll tell you about the murder in 1975."

I gasped. "You knew exactly what I was talking about earlier."

He gave no reaction. "The difference between us is I have game."

Sure. That was the only difference.

Frankie exhaled smoke out his nose. "Tell us about the murder, and she'll bury your coin with you."

Wait. "Isn't that what he just said?"

"No," they both said in unison.

Okay, then. "What did you see?"

Knuckles's expression darkened. "October 14, 1975." He crossed his arms, his brass knuckles glinting. "I was up on the balcony, casing the place for something to steal, seeing as I lost the earrings."

His gaze drifted up to the honeymoon suite.

"Finn Byrne was celebrating with a whiskey and a cigar. He'd found a real pretty bracelet in the stuck drawer of an old jewelry box on the mantel." His mouth twisted. "Said how it would make a fine wedding gift for his bride." His lip curled. "It was better than the earrings, I'll give him that."

I tilted my head. "You wanted to take it."

He spread his hands. "How could I resist? I was onto a great score. Until I couldn't touch it." His hands clenched into fists. "You know how nuts that drives me? Anyhow, that's when a lady called his name from down by the pointy fence."

I held my breath, waiting.

Knuckles shifted his weight, and for the first time, he looked... unsettled.

"Did you see who it was?" I pressed. "Dapper Dan said it was a man."

"He wasn't there." Knuckles scrubbed a hand over his face.

"It was a ghost in a white wedding dress. Long hair all wild." His voice dropped. "Crazy eyes. Like she wasn't all there."

My stomach twisted. That wasn't good.

"She shot up to the balcony, quick as a flash." He took a reflexive step back. "Finn couldn't see her. And when he bent to look down, she shoved him straight over."

I went cold. A ghost.

A ghost had pushed Finn Byrne off that balcony. "She murdered him." She made him look over, and then she pushed him.

Frankie let out a low whistle. "I wonder if that was Lord Byrne's bride from 1925."

Could be. I looked to Knuckles. "Did you recognize her?"

The gangster shook his head. "I wasn't around in 1925."

Right. He'd died in 1924, and it could take months, even years, for a spirit to be able to manifest.

Okay. "Suppose it was Lord Byrne's bride," I ventured. "Maybe she wasn't so sad he died. Maybe she killed Thomas and then killed Finn fifty years later."

"That's cold," Knuckles huffed.

"But possible," Frankie countered. "She could've mistaken Finn for his granddad."

Maybe. "They didn't look that much alike to me. At least not from the portraits downstairs."

"Close enough," Frankie concluded. "We're talking about a murderous poltergeist here. They operate on rage, not close photographic comparisons."

He had a point.

"She might be on a loop," Knuckles said. "One big murdering loop."

Which would be awful for us. Poor Melody.

"We need to know more." I turned to Knuckles. "Have you ever seen this ghost again?"

"Once or twice." He gave a slight shiver. "She hates weddings. She goes poltergeist and rants about men." He shook his head. "I keep trying to get her to tear up the fountain. You know, let me breathe a little."

Maybe I could track her down. Ghosts tended to haunt specific places. Often where they'd died. "Where does she hang out?"

He glanced at the balcony. "Up there and in the basement. I follow her sometimes. I say, hey, dig me up. Dig my coin up. I'll bet you find your rocks. But noooo... She's too busy banging away at the generator. She's nuts."

Wow. I was glad I hadn't run into her in the basement. "Do you know her name?" She was a person. Or she had been...

He snorted like I was the crazy one. "I'm not trying to make friends."

I was. At least I wasn't opposed to it. "I have to find her," I murmured to myself.

"Bad idea," Knuckles drawled. "She's half-poltergeist on a good day."

I'd take my chances.

Knuckles pounded a fist into his palm. "Now, a bargain's a bargain. I want you to put my coin under my fountain. Real nice."

Right.

"Verity," Ellis called.

I turned to find him standing on the deadly balcony.

Oh no.

"Go back inside," I urged. "Please."

"Are you all right?" he asked, walking to the edge.

"I'm fine. The ghost is gone," I fibbed. "I'll be there in a second."

He leaned his elbows on the rail. "I found Melody. She's putting your dress on our bed. But Alec and I need to go to the tux place before pictures. Our pants don't fit."

"Go," I urged. I wished I could drag him off the precipice and into the room.

"Love you!" He waved.

I blew him a kiss and was so, so glad to see him go.

Whoever said weddings were stressful was right.

First things first. I scanned the base of the fountain. The stone basin sat on a pedestal surrounded by giant pink rosebushes. Lucy emerged with Lucky, both of them covered in mud and looking enormously pleased with themselves.

"Lucy!" Oh, that was it. She was going to need a bath and a blow-dry fluff.

I looked down at myself. Wet dress. Muddy arms. My heart sank. I was going to need a bath too.

There was no fixing it now. I pushed aside the roses and saw where they'd excavated a small drainage grate half-buried in dirt and old leaves.

"That'll do," Knuckles said, drawing up behind me.

"Give me space." I knelt beside the grate, the damp ground soaking through my already-wet dress. The silver dollar felt heavy in my palm. I owed this to him to get it right.

He'd given me what I needed to save Alec or at least confront the ghost who might want him dead tonight.

My stomach clenched. We were running out of time.

I positioned the coin at the edge and flicked it as hard as I could down the pipe.

It hit deep with a clear *ping*, bounced once, then rattled down into darkness, landing with a faint splash.

Knuckles let out a breath. "Now I can keep an eye on it."

"You're welcome—" I began.

But he'd already vanished. It seemed Knuckles wasn't one for long goodbyes.

"Aww." Frankie tossed his cigarette. "I was gonna see if he wanted to partner up."

I stood, brushed myself off, and wedged a bit of mud off my knee. "You are not going to commit any crimes on Melody's wedding weekend."

"As far as you know," he said.

"Verity!" Melody's voice rang out from the balcony of the

honeymoon suite. Her eyes widened when she saw me. "There you are! We need you for photos! Like, right now!"

I looked up to see my sister in that deadly spot, radiant in her wedding dress.

"I'm almost ready," I called, running my fingers through my out-of-control hair, wringing water from the hem of my dress. "I'll be right up!"

Her hair was styled in perfect waves, her face clear and bright. "Your bridesmaid dress is in your room. Hurry."

"No problem." I waved a muddy hand, starting for the house with Lucy and Lucky trotting behind me like a mismatched honor guard.

"You actually got three problems," Frankie said, gliding next to me. "One, you got a ghost strong enough to physically push people off balconies. Knuckles is right. That's poltergeist territory." He held up a second finger. "Two, it seems to me you got someone alive helping that ghost. Or at least making things worse. Someone with keys and access and a real good reason to want your sister's groom dead."

"Do you have any good news?" I asked, racing up the back steps.

"Well, that's where number three comes in." The ghost passed through the window wall as I pried open the ballroom door. "You got this afternoon to figure out who both of them are."

I stood holding the door. He was right. About all of it.

And in the second it took me to think, both dirty skunks dashed into the ballroom ahead of me.

Oh no. "Lucy!" She knew better. "Lucky!" He most certainly didn't.

After a quick search, it was clear they'd escaped. Shoot. They'd probably find the kitchen. Or the owners' suite. Or—please no—the bridal preparations room. But I didn't have time to track them down. I'd just have to trust Lucy to keep Lucky out of trouble and hope the damage was minimal.

In the meantime, I needed to find out who the ghost in the

wedding dress was. I needed to figure out who was helping her from the living world. And I needed to do it fast. I also needed to be beautiful for my sister's dream wedding photo shoot. And somehow keep her from seeing the panic clawing at my chest.

I turned to Frankie. "I need you to work your magic. Find that missing whiskey and those cigars."

Frankie gave a curt nod and tamped out his ghostly cigarette on the ballroom floor. "I'll search the main house. Lenny will do the carriage house and the caretaker's cottage. Dapper Dan will take the chapel."

"Can you trust them?" I asked, heading for the stairs.

"No, but they'll do a good job. We have a deal."

Those three were going to be worse than skunks in a ballroom.

I raced up the stairs, my wet shoes squelching with every movement. I needed to warn Alec about tonight. But what would I say? *A ghost in a white dress has a thing against weddings and a habit of pushing grooms off the balcony.* He'd think I was crazy. Or worse, he'd cancel the wedding and break Melody's heart.

No. I needed proof. I needed to find out who the ghost was and why she was killing grooms. Then I could stop her.

Melody appeared at the top, her face lighting up when she saw me, then immediately falling.

"Verity, what happened?" She met me halfway down. "You're soaked!"

"I tripped into the fountain." I'd explain the rest later. "Give me five minutes to change and brush my hair."

She pulled a twig out of my cleavage. "Make it thirty and wash your hair."

She studied my face. "You're sure you're okay?"

I forced a smile. "Don't worry about me."

She didn't look convinced, but she also didn't pressure me. Instead, she took my hand. "Don't worry, sweetie. The photographer wants lots of shots of me on the carriage, and I'm going to enjoy every second of it. It'll be fine."

She deserved that. She deserved her dream wedding and more. "I promise this will be the only thing that goes wrong."

Somewhere on this estate was the answer. The reason why a ghost had become a killer. The connection between past and present that would explain why Alec had been targeted.

And I had until sunset to find it.

## Chapter Thirteen

I headed straight for the honeymoon suite. Yes, I needed to get ready for pictures, and yes, my hair was currently dripping a small river of water down my back. But I had to tend to one thing first.

The heavy French doors stood open to the balcony. Again.

Somehow, I doubted that had been Melody's doing.

I crossed the room and yanked the doors closed, then latched them good and tight. I gave them a rattle to make sure they held fast.

Normally I would have been satisfied, but I'd had just about enough of this room. And its ghost.

I grabbed the closest burgundy wingback chair and dragged it toward the balcony doors, ignoring the screech against the hardwood. Then I wedged it under the handles.

There. I admired my handiwork. *Let's see the ghost get past that.*

I shook out my aching wrists and had a mind to pile the dresser on top, but I wasn't Hercules. Or the Hulk. This would have to do.

I strode to the center of the room, catching my breath, eyeing the corners, half expecting to see the ghost. I was messing with her balcony, after all.

The massive four-poster bed dominated the suite, its white canopy serene, the crystal lamps on the dressers elegant. Above the bed hung an old-fashioned oil painting of a woman in a garden. I recognized her from downstairs. Lady Brigid.

She was in her thirties and quite regal, dressed in burgundy silk and positively dripping with jewels from her tiara to her diamond-flecked fan.

I did like her style.

"What do you think of all this?" I asked, not really expecting an answer.

Every inch the aristocrat, her chin tilted just so, dark hair swept up in an elaborate style popular in the late 1800s. Emeralds at her throat. Emeralds on her fingers. Rubies in her ears.

Her teardrop ruby earrings had triggered the mess with the ghost, although she didn't seem anything like the desperate phantom bride. Lady Brigid had been properly married, after all. No doubt with lots of pomp back in the Old World.

It had to have been hard, coming from a lifetime of wealth and privilege, of nobility, to start over in Jackson, Tennessee, when it was nothing but dirt roads and cow farms. It would be unimaginable.

The colors in the painting were exquisite. She posed in front of a magnolia tree in full bloom.

Gracious.

This portrait wasn't painted in the old country. It was painted here. In Jackson, Tennessee.

That meant...

"Lord Almighty. Your husband stole the crown jewels, and you knew it." Worse, she'd posed with royal rubies for a fricking portrait here in Tennessee!

Hadn't she been worried about being caught?

Or had she been too bold, too proud of her prize to care?

A cool breeze wafted from the window where I'd seen the ghost. Quite the trick, seeing as I'd closed it myself.

Knuckles said the angry bride haunted this place.

"Were you jealous?" I asked, hoping to draw her out.

It had to be hard to be the girl who came after a woman like that.

If Brigid had died shortly after arriving, then Thomas had taken a long time to remarry. I wondered if he'd kept her portrait here in the room he was about to share with his new bride. Had she stared up at it, comparing herself to a dead woman she could never replace?

Perhaps the first big, Southern wedding planned for this estate had simply been a marriage of convenience, planned by older men to tie a rich new-world family to European minor royalty. I wonder if she'd had a choice at all.

Had our ghost been trapped, even when she was alive?

"Hello?" I asked, wishing I knew her name. "I can see you if you want to be seen. Or we can simply talk."

I waited, straining for any response—a whisper, a chill, the faintest sign that I'd been heard.

"I'd be glad to visit."

Nothing.

It was strange to think that a woman haunted this place. Yet the only ghostly images I'd seen had been half-smoked stogies.

And the figure in the window.

I saw none of that now.

No cigar on the balcony or in the vase on the mantel.

Then...wait. My gaze settled on the antique jewelry box on the mantel next to the crystal vase full of roses. It was no wider than my hand and very old, the rich wood burnished from decades of use, the brass hinges aged to bronze. A swan in flight was inlaid on the lid in mother-of-pearl, its wings spread in an elegant arc.

Had Finn found the bracelet here?

No. Not after all this time.

Even if it was the same jewelry box, it would no doubt be empty by now.

But what if it wasn't...

My heart kicked up. There was only one way to find out.

I crossed to the mantel and ran my fingers along the edge of the box. The wood felt smooth and slightly cold. I lifted the lid.

Faded pink velvet lined the once elegant, now empty interior.

Well, what had I expected? That Lady Brigid's bracelet would just be sitting here, waiting? I closed the lid, feeling a bit foolish.

Until I spotted a drawer at the bottom. A gnarled hole resided where the pull handle had been. I caught the edges with my fingernails and eased it open.

The shallow drawer lay empty, lined with faded pink silk.

Of course it was.

I left the box on the mantel and turned to think. Finn had found a ruby bracelet in this room almost fifty years ago. I crossed to the window where I'd first seen the ghost. He'd planned to gift a bracelet to his wife-to-be. But before he could, a ghost in white pushed him off the balcony.

My breath fogged the window.

Lenny, Knuckles, and Dapper Dan had all died on the same night, each one after stealing the matching ruby earrings.

I folded my arms over my chest.

Lenny hadn't made it out of the wine cellar before he was struck down. Knuckles made it as far as the garden before he was hit from behind and pitched into the well. Dapper Dan made it as far as the hidey-hole in the chapel before he was shoved into a shallow grave. I pressed my palms against the cool glass, staring out at the garden below.

Each of the gangsters had tried to escape with the earrings. Each had been struck from behind and killed.

That only left Lord Thomas. Was it possible Lord Thomas had planned to give his late wife's rubies to his bride-to-be?

He stole them. He would have seen them as his property to give away as he pleased. But he wasn't the one who *owned* them.

I turned back to the portrait of Lady Brigid, her chin lifted, her jewels gleaming. "Is it you?"

I kept an eye on the portrait as I returned to the jewelry box. Sparing a glance over my shoulder, I eased open the drawer once more. It was shallow, no more than a pinkie's length deep. But the box went much farther back.

It reminded me of my mom's jewelry box when I was a kid. Hers was from Sears, but I'd always loved the hidden drawer where she'd kept nothing, and where I'd kept my treasures—an extra pretty acorn, the dried marigold that had been a gift from Lauralee, and my walnut in the shell.

I pulled the shallow drawer all the way out and peeked inside.

My heart leapt. A false drawer lay at the back.

I glanced behind me, expecting to see who? Lady Brigid?

No sense taking chances.

When I was sure the coast was clear, I coaxed the hidden drawer out. I almost had it when a rush of cold hit me like a wave. It came so suddenly, so fiercely, I gasped. The temperature in the room plummeted.

The doors to the balcony rattled.

Oh boy.

My breath came out in visible puffs.

Did I dare?

I really wished I'd had the strength to drag the dresser over to block the balcony. But it was too late now. I eased the drawer all the way out.

A figure materialized in front of me, a woman with dark hair trailing behind her. She wore a billowing white dressing gown with lace at the throat. The same woman from the portrait.

Her face twisted with rage, her eyes wild.

Brigid.

She flew straight at me. I tried to dodge, but she was faster. She slammed through me, bone cold. Invasive. Wrong.

I stumbled back, gasping, clutching my chest. It felt like she'd scraped ice along the inside of my ribs. My hands shook as I watched her soar straight into the painting above the bed and vanish.

I grasped the drawer. Looked down.

Inside, nestled on faded velvet, lay a ruby bracelet set in gold, the stones cut into shimmering teardrops. They matched the earrings exactly.

I swallowed the lump in my throat and faced the painting of Brigid. I had to make one thing clear. "I'm not touching your jewels." I set the entire drawer on the mantel behind me. "I'm not taking them." I didn't even want to look at them.

The room began to warm. The balcony doors settled.

I held my breath. "Are you still here?"

A sweet scent tickled my nose, like the dusting on marshmallows, with a hint of vanilla.

I took a step closer to the painting. Halted. One step was good enough. I folded my hands in front of me. "I think I understand."

The scent grew stronger.

Knuckles hadn't seen a bride. He'd seen Brigid in her dressing gown. Proud, regal Brigid had died sick in bed, which meant she didn't get to wear her jewels in the afterlife.

Then to make it worse, Thomas tried to give them away to his new bride.

Lenny, Dan, and Knuckles each tried to take her earrings, and then poor Finn thought he'd stumbled on a lucky gift for his beloved. He didn't know those rubies were being watched. Or that they were worth killing for.

"People keep taking your jewelry. You had to move because of those jewels. You had to come here to the middle of nowhere Tennessee, and it killed you." She hadn't survived a year. "Now people keep trying to take those jewels and give them away."

The scent went harsh, burning at the edges.

I held up my hands. "It's okay. You want to keep your rubies."

A voice echoed from the painting, stark and commanding. "Don't touch my jewels."

"I am not," I vowed.

Goosebumps shot up my arms.

"I am—" I really wanted to leave. Run out of there and never come back. Instead, I pasted on a smile and moved slowly toward the drawer on the mantel. "I am putting these back in the hidden drawer." Fingers shaking, I slid it in deep and placed the false one over it. "They are safe."

Alec would be safe.

"None of us will ever touch, look at, or even think about what's yours," I promised.

I closed the lid on the jewelry box and slid it to the back of the mantel. Then I shoved the vase of flowers in front of it for good measure.

"There." My voice came out steadier than I felt. "It's done."

We were done.

The sweet scent lingered for another moment, then faded away.

The room felt ordinary again. Just a luxury suite with fancy furniture and a garden view.

I backed toward the door, keeping my eyes on the painting until the last possible second. Lady Brigid stared down from her frame, serene and regal as if she hadn't just touched off a nightmare.

I closed the door behind me, wishing I could lock it for good measure. I leaned against it, my heart still racing.

Alec would be safe. That was what mattered.

Lady Brigid wasn't haunting this place because she'd hated weddings. She was haunting it because people kept trying to take her jewelry.

I'd seen ghosts turn poltergeist before. Any spirit could, given enough anger. When a soul let rage overtake them, they became something else entirely—violent, powerful, operating on pure instinct and fury. Poltergeists were terrifying precisely because they were out of control. But Brigid's trigger was crystal clear. Don't touch her jewels.

We could work with that.

But Brigid wasn't the only threat.

∼

I raced back to my room, still catching my breath from the honeymoon suite.

Fifteen minutes until pictures. I could do this.

Lucy sat on my bed, curled up with Lucky, both of them a muddy mess.

I gasped. "You're not allowed to have boys over." Especially rough-living, bad-influence, fast boys like him.

I scooped her up. She had leaves stuck to her tail and crumbs in her fur.

"Lucky, you are not welcome in this house," I snapped as he leapt off the bed with what I swore was a swagger and a tail flick. I chased him into the hall, down the stairs, and out the door.

She churned her little legs as if she were ready to go with him. "Lucy, I'm surprised at you," I said, escorting her back to our room.

This wasn't like her.

I hopped into the shower with her and broke the land-speed record for getting us both sweet smelling and clean. Then I wrapped her snug in a towel and yanked a comb through my damp hair, wincing as it caught on tangles. Five minutes for a dry and curl. Another five for makeup and a quick spritz of perfume.

This morning might have been messy, but I'd never complain. Not when I'd learned the ghost problem wasn't our problem if we behaved ourselves.

I fluffed my hair and ignored the fact that it was still damp underneath.

Lady Brigid had a right to her jewels or thought she did anyway. Stolen or not, they were hers now. And so long as we stayed away from her jewelry—her jewelry box, her rubies, anything that belonged to her—we'd be fine.

Thank God I hadn't touched those earrings in the chapel.

Once we fixed the wobbly floor tile, they'd be sealed in good.

It was fine. I was fine. Melody and Alec were going to have a lovely wedding.

We would not touch any ruby jewelry. We would not trigger the ghost. How hard could that be?

I unzipped the garment bag and saw my bridesmaid dress for the first time.

"Oh." I pressed a hand to my chest. Shocked all over again.

My phone alarm sounded. I was due downstairs.

*Hurry, hurry.* The bridesmaid dress slid over my head like silk because it *was* silk. Lilac purple with a fitted bodice that hugged in all the right places before flowing into a graceful A-line skirt. Delicate beading caught the light at the neckline, subtle but stunning. It was the kind of dress that made me stand a little straighter, that made me feel elegant without even trying.

I smoothed the fabric over my hips and caught my reflection in the full-length mirror.

Wow.

This was it. We were living Melody's dream wedding, and it was showtime.

I slipped on my heels and grabbed a pair of pearl earrings before I caught myself and put them back. Just in case. I hurried downstairs. Sunlight streamed through the windows. It was fixing to be a beautiful afternoon.

## Chapter Fourteen

My lilac silk bridesmaid dress swished as I stepped out onto the front porch. I felt like a princess.

Then I saw Melody.

Her wedding gown fit like a dream as she posed by an open carriage. Brett bent into an impossible angle and rattled off a steady series of *click-click-click*.

Last night, I'd seen the dress. Today, I saw the bride.

The sweetheart neckline revealed her delicate collarbones, her blonde hair swept up in a loose updo that showed off her graceful neck. She saw me and abandoned the shoot, rushing to meet me for a big, warm hug.

"Is everything okay?" she asked, pulling back to study my face.

"It is now," I said as she stepped back and did a little twirl, the skirt billowing out around her. "Alec's going to short-circuit when he sees you."

Her smile could have lit up the entire state of Tennessee. "That's the plan." She glanced past me to the carriage, dreamy-eyed. "Oh my God. It's perfect. It's absolutely perfect."

It was. Pure white lacquer gleamed with gold leaf scrollwork curling up the sides. Yellow roses and trailing vines tumbled from brass lanterns mounted at each corner, and the crimson velvet cushions looked plush enough to nap on.

Brett materialized at her elbow. "Okay, bride-to-be, let's get you in that carriage. I'm thinking we'll start with you stepping up, all smiles and romance."

"That won't be hard." Melody laughed.

"Not for you." Honey Sue Caldwell bustled up with energy to spare. "The Pierces are going to be so pleased." The wedding planner couldn't have been more than five feet tall, but her snow-blonde hair added another half foot, teased and sprayed into submission. Her pink blazer was ironed as sharp as a mint dollar bill, sequins sparkling at the cuffs as she brandished her clipboard.

"Verity!" She pulled me into a hug that smelled like orange blossoms. "It's so wonderful to see you. You look...stunning." She stepped back, hands on my shoulders, plucking a tiny piece of lint and tossing it. "I've been so excited for pictures today. Melody is just perfect isn't she?"

"Well, we have you to thank for making it happen." She could have picked any bride, but she'd asked my sister.

"I always say good things happen to good people." Honey Sue clapped her hands together. "Stars. I am in heaven." She turned to Brett and bellowed, "I want that sunshine streaming through her hair, like the angel she is." She beamed at me. "It'll be your turn next."

"I'm ready whenever you need me," I promised, resisting the urge to salute like one of her troops.

She gave my arm a playful swat. "I meant I can do your wedding too." She perked up. "Picture a lovely event in that gorgeous house your grandma left you. The whole town there as you take vows under the apple tree out back by your pond. I've even got a girl who can train your little skunk to carry the rings." She tapped a pink nail against her chin. "Don't tell me Lucy wouldn't look darling with a white silk ring pillow on her back and a matching bow for her tail."

For a split second, I forgot to breathe. "Lucy would—" Well, she'd probably love it. "But—" I caught myself before I could think on it too hard. "I'm not engaged."

She shot me a knowing smile. "I may love sparkles, but I'm not blind. I've seen the way Ellis looks at you." She leaned in close. "I was there at the diner last month when he told Kimmy Anne you were his dream girl through and through." She patted me on the arm. "It won't be long."

I opened my mouth. Closed it. What was I supposed to say to that?

I hadn't the foggiest. So I decided to do what every good Southern girl would do. I changed the subject. "What about you?" I asked. She was single. "Your business is love and happy endings. You ever been tempted to tie the knot?"

She blinked hard. It was a simple question, but it was clear I'd thrown her. "It's not in the cards for me." Her voice went flat, and for a split second, the sparkle dimmed from her eyes. Then she snapped back, waving a hand at Brett. "Adjust her dress. Remember, she's floating on the breeze!"

"Your job is intense," I said in attempt to smooth things over while Brett readjusted the shot. At the same time, I had to ask, "Did you make it by at all last night?" I kept my voice casual. "Maybe to leave cigars in the honeymoon suite? Or a nice decanter of whiskey?"

Her brow furrowed. "Cigars? Heavens, no." She made a face. "I wouldn't dream of it." She shook her head firmly. "This is a historic home. They might have stunk it up in the past with those awful things, but the current owners would have my head if I allowed smoking inside."

"The waitress at brunch said the owners stock custom cigars," I insisted, keeping my tone light.

She shot me a long look. "Tell the boys not to even think about lighting up."

Too late.

She tapped her clipboard with a manicured nail. "Now, Chef Duchamp does like to provide a bachelor's toasting bottle. A nice whiskey to go with the charcuterie plate. Alec wanted his a night early, which Chef assured me was no trouble at all." She smiled. "Did he like it?"

"He did at first." That was all I could safely say. I didn't want to venture more. At least not until we'd heard from Mort.

Frankie had gotten on me in the past for including everyone in our business. Which tended to tip off the bad guys. Well, I wasn't going to do it this time.

Too bad he wasn't around to appreciate it.

Honey Sue cocked her head. "Did you enjoy the cheese plate? And those chocolate-covered strawberries?"

"Oh my." Heat flooded my cheeks. "That was for us? Melody thought she'd commandeered it from the kitchen."

She laughed. "It was yours, along with a bottle of prosecco."

"We didn't see the bubbly, but no worries," I added when her face fell. "Melody smuggled in a bottle of rosé."

Honey Sue's smile faltered slightly. "I'm so sorry. That should have been all laid out for you in your room. If I'd been here, it would even have had a bow on it."

"It's fine. Honestly," I said quickly.

She glanced toward the carriage where Brett was adjusting Melody's veil. "Everything went a little sideways last night. I stopped to help someone who needed it, then when I got home, I discovered an entire shipment of flowers had arrived on my porch by mistake. I carted them over to the Freeman sweet sixteen, and when I got back out to my car, I had a flat tire." She raised a hand to her head. "By the time I got it sorted, I was an absolute wreck. Then when I came home to freshen up, my water heater pilot light was out, and I had no way to shower."

It seemed like too much to be a coincidence. "Do you think someone was trying to keep you distracted last night?"

She blinked at me, surprised. "Now why would they do that?"

So she wouldn't be around to see who could have drugged the whiskey or stolen the evidence. An alert and organized Honey Sue would have noticed someone sneaking upstairs. Not to mention she could have told us exactly when the owners arrived and what Chef was doing in the meantime.

She patted her hair. "At least it all worked out."

"It did," I agreed. It had worked out perfectly for whoever was targeting Alec.

Ellis and Alec pulled up in Ellis's black Jeep, the engine rumbling as they parked just beyond the carriage setup, careful not to block Brett's shot.

I glanced over as both men climbed out and ooh la la.

The tuxedos fit perfectly now. Ellis wore his with the same easy confidence he wore his police uniform or a snug pair of jeans on a Sunday. The black jacket emphasized his broad shoulders, the white shirt crisp against the strong column of his throat. His dark hair was cut in neat layers, not a strand out of place…which made me want to mess it up.

Alec looked sharp too, his tux fitting him like it had been custom-made, his posture military-straight as he grinned at something Ellis said.

His retort died in his throat when Melody posed with one foot in the carriage, one trailing behind. She dropped her shoulders back and held her bouquet out to the breeze.

"That boy has it bad," I said as Ellis strolled over to me.

He planted a sweet kiss on my cheek. "This boy too."

His smile turned crooked, and I couldn't help but smile. "You could make a girl forget her good sense, looking the way you do."

"The tux helps," he said, straightening his bow tie. "We figured we'd wear them out of the shop and save time changing." He dipped his head. "Had to stop for gas. The attendant asked if we were strippers heading to a bachelorette party."

"And here I am, fresh out of singles." I slipped a finger through his belt loop and gave a playful tug.

He let me draw him in. "We also stopped by the Sugarland Police Department on the way back."

Oh my. "And?"

"The background reports should be in soon." He kept his

voice low. "Katie has them on rush. She's working from home today, but she promised she'd get them to me by tonight."

"Before rehearsal?"

"God willing."

"Good." Because we were running out of time.

"Melody, darling!" Brett called, camera raised. "Step down from the carriage for me. Alec, you help her."

Alec moved into position at the carriage step, reaching up. Melody placed her hands on his shoulders and jumped down, her dress billowing around her.

Before her feet fully touched the ground, Alec caught her, lifting her slightly as she laughed. Then he kissed her—not the polite peck of a photo shoot, but a real kiss. The kind that made a girl swoon.

Brett dropped to his knees to get the angle, his camera firing off rapid shots. "Yes! *Yes.* That's it. That's the one." He sat back on his butt. "Perfect. Absolute magic!" He rose to his knees. "Now do it again."

Ellis slipped an arm around my waist, guiding us slightly away from the photo shoot. "What's going on with the ghosts?"

"Well, I met a poltergeist this afternoon." I leaned into him, watching Melody stroke Alec's cheek as the camera snapped.

"A poltergeist?" His hand stiffened against my hip. "Those are the most dangerous kind. I wish I'd been there with you."

"I'm fine. In fact, I think we're all okay. Lady Brigid just wants to keep her jewelry. As long as nobody touches her rubies, she'll leave us alone."

"Noted," he said, his gaze traveling to the window where I'd seen the ghost.

There was no sign of her now.

I turned to face him, resting my palm against his chest. "Also, you need to fix a stone slab on the chapel floor. It wobbles."

"I'm sure Mort can—"

"You'll also be sealing some ruby earrings underneath, which should solve one of our problems. Oh, and a skeleton. If we let Mort do it, he'll call the police."

"I'm the police," he reminded me.

Yes, but he was fine. "The dead guy was killed by the poltergeist a hundred years ago, and it's not as if you can arrest her. Besides, this is Melody's wedding weekend."

"Sure. Just your normal wedding weekend." He brushed a strand of hair away from my face. "Anything else? Maybe a dragon that needs slaying?"

"Not yet." I grinned up at him. "But give it time."

"Hey, lovebirds!" Brett called out. It took Ellis and me a second to realize he was talking about us. "I need everyone over by the garden. We're going to do a fun series with Melody tossing the bouquet."

"Lovebirds?" I nudged Ellis.

"We're not as sly as we think," he quipped, letting Brett position us in front of the rosebushes with the cupid fountain in the background. He stood Melody front and center with the rest of us clustered behind her.

"How are you feeling?" I asked Alec as Brett straightened his tie.

"Like a truck ran over me, then backed up to make sure it finished the job." He dodged away from the photographer and straightened his bow tie himself. "I'll live. Probably."

"Looking gorgeous, Verity," Brett said, walking backward. "Now when Melody tosses the bouquet, I want you all to jump in the air and try to catch it."

"Are men allowed to do that?" Ellis asked.

"Enjoy the fact that you can jump." Alec ran a hand over his face. "Right now my world is a tilt-a-whirl."

At least they were both athletic. My idea of exercise was chasing Lucy around the house when she stole my socks.

Alec swayed a little, and I fought the urge to hold him upright. "We asked Mort to find out who took the whiskey and cigars from your suite and to track them down so we can send them to the police lab." Maybe that would make him feel better.

Melody took her fiancé's hand, her eyes on me. "Do you trust Mort?"

"No. To be honest, I barely know him. But he was the only person I could ask. Mort has access to places and people we don't." It had been a calculated risk.

One I sincerely hoped I wouldn't regret.

"Stand a little closer together." Brett circled us, camera raised.

Two blurs of fur streaked behind him. Lucy and Lucky bounded from the rose garden toward the stand of oak trees, their tails high. Lucy paused mid-dash to grab a napkin Lucky had dropped in the grass, shaking it like a prize before Lucky tackled her, and they tumbled together in a rolling ball of black and white and more white.

"Should we—" I started. I mean, he'd tackled my baby girl.

Ellis shook his head, grinning. "Let them play. They're happy."

In the time it took him to say it, they were off again, disappearing into the trees.

"Everybody look at me," Brett said from behind the camera. "Now, Melody, when I count to three, toss the flowers high. Everyone else, look excited—like you'd trample your grandma to get the bouquet."

"Weddings should not be violent," Honey Sue said, tucking a loose curl back into Melody's updo.

"Says the woman who set us up in a haunted honeymoon suite," Alec murmured once she'd turned her back.

"Don't you be listening to rumors," Honey Sue said, plucking a rose petal off Ellis's shoulder.

"We're safe from the dead as long as we don't anger Lady Brigid," I said.

As for the live person after Alec...

Melody glanced over her shoulder. "I saw Mort talking to the chef earlier." She stole a glance at Brett, who was fiddling with his lens. "Whatever Mort said made Chef Duchamp really angry."

"Par for the course for that man," Honey Sue said, fluffing Melody's train with practiced efficiency. "Chef's a handful, but I assure you he's a genius."

Brett eyed us through his lens. "Honey Sue, you're in the shot."

"I'm just trying to make sure things run smoothly," she said, stepping back, eyeing Alec. "If there's a problem, I want to know."

Brett lowered his camera. "Yeah, I heard you might have been slipped some drugged whiskey last night."

Dang it.

Honey Sue gasped.

"What makes you say that?" She pressed a hand to her chest, her sequined cuffs glittering. "This is exactly the kind of thing I need to know."

I'd been hoping to be a little slyer than that. I'd rather catch Alec's assailant with the evidence before they knew we were onto them.

Honey Sue brought a shaking hand to her head. "No wonder you were asking me where I was last night. I should have been there. I will look into this right away."

Brett rested his camera hand on his shoulder. "Mort wanted to search my room this afternoon. With no warning. Because he said so. It was a little extreme."

So was drugging the groom.

Honey Sue went pink in the cheeks. "Did you let him?"

"I told him I'm busy." He wiggled his camera. "Wouldn't put it past him to do it anyway."

Alec loosened his tie. "Where are you staying?"

"Above the carriage house, down the hall from the business office." He glanced to the building beyond the gardens. "We all stay there. Makes it easier for the weekend."

"The rooms are small but lovely," Honey Sue managed. "I'll

talk to Mort," she said to Brett. "There's no need to be rude to staff. He's completely out of line."

Or the man was onto something.

I exchanged a look with Ellis. He seemed to be thinking the same thing.

What did we really know about Brett, anyway? He'd been friendly enough, enthusiastic about his work. But he had easy access to the grounds, to the carriage house, to the manor itself. And he'd been awfully quick to mention the drugged whiskey, almost like he wanted to gauge our reactions.

I couldn't wait to get my hands on those background reports. Something about this whole setup felt off.

Brett switched out his lens. "Okay, Melody and Alec, I need you to kiss like the ship is going down."

"For real?" She giggled.

"No." He grinned. "Be super sweet about it. Then, Verity, you're not in the shot, but I want you to hold up the bouquet in the background. Just duck down and hold your arm up. It'll look great."

"Got it," I said, making like an incognito flower stand as Alec laid a soft kiss on my sister.

Ellis dodged to the side, and Honey Sue escaped toward the carriage as Brett started another barrage of photos.

When Honey Sue was far enough away, Brett lowered his camera. "Let's take a quick break." He passed Melody a tissue. "See if you can dab the sweat from your groom's forehead." Brett stepped in closer to me, stealing a glance at the wedding planner, who was deep into her clipboard. "You know, I was up pretty late last night, working out the shot list for today." He wiped his lens with a cloth. "My bedroom window faces the back woods, near the parking area." He glanced toward the tree line. "I saw someone coming in on foot from that direction. Late. It had to be past midnight."

My pulse quickened. "Who was it?"

Brett glanced to Ellis, who'd joined us. "It was too dark to tell. Could've been a guest."

"We were the only guests," I said.

"I don't know, then." Brett shook his head. "We won't have much staff until tonight and tomorrow. They were moving fast though. Like they didn't want to be seen." He raised his camera again, glancing at Honey Sue. "Could have been someone sneaking a smoke or something."

Ellis leaned in. "Which direction were they heading?"

"Toward the manor." Brett backed up and motioned to Melody for another shot. "Like I said, it probably means nothing."

My gut said otherwise.

This place was surrounded by a fence. I wondered who had keys.

The wedding planner was walking toward the front gates, her clipboard under her arm, her thumbs flying over her phone.

I hurried to catch up. "Honey Sue?"

She hit *Send* and turned to me. Her smile was back in place, but her shoulders tensed. "Yes, sweetie?"

I slowed. "Are the gates locked after hours?"

"Why would they be?" She looked at me like I'd just put sugar in the cornbread. "Around here, I doubt they even lock the front doors."

"Oh." I supposed I couldn't argue with that. I'd proudly left my doors unlocked until I'd gotten into mystery solving.

"This is Jackson, after all," Honey Sue reasoned.

Goodness. Maybe Jackson did have one thing in common with Sugarland.

Though I wouldn't go so far as to admit it out loud.

A sleek black Mercedes pulled up the gravel drive, tires crunching to a stop near the garden entrance. Brett's head snapped toward it.

"The owners are here," he said under his breath, straightening. "Look busy." He grinned at us like it was a joke, but there was an edge to it.

Honey Sue immediately sprang into action, checking her clipboard and smoothing her blazer.

"Okay, everybody. Stand in front of the carriage." Brett ushered us over and backed up to get the shot. "We'll do a bouquet toss. Everybody jump as high as you can on three, two, one!"

Melody launched the bouquet into the air. Poor Alec barely made it off the ground. I leapt high, grinning like a maniac, completely forgetting to go for the flowers. Ellis raised a hand in the air like an offensive receiver catching a Hail Mary pass, one hand closing around the stems in midair.

"Ha!" Brett pumped his fist. "That was great!"

Ellis handed me the flowers. I passed them straight to Melody.

Honey Sue clasped her hands together. "Roses would be perfect for your wedding."

Ellis took my hand, and the look in his eyes, both soft and serious, made my heart do a little flip.

"Isn't this the most beautiful wedding party you've ever seen?" Honey Sue asked as the couple from the car joined her.

"You do know how to put on a show," the first man said. He was tall and lean, maybe in his early fifties, with silver-streaked hair swept back from a tanned face. He wore navy slacks and a crisp white linen shirt, expensive loafers with no socks. Everything about him said old money, effortless.

The second man was shorter and rounder, with a neatly trimmed beard going gray at the edges. He wore khakis and a burgundy polo with wire-rimmed glasses perched on his nose. He had the look of someone who spent more time in spreadsheets than sunlight, but his smile was genuine as he took in the scene.

"Kip Pierce," the tanned man said, extending a hand to Melody. "And this is my husband, Lonnie." He gestured to the bearded man beside him.

"Not to mention partner in crime," Lonnie added, chuckling at his own joke.

"Beautiful work, Brett," Kip said, his voice as smooth as aged bourbon. "Looks like you're settling into your job nicely."

The photographer tilted his head. "I think you'll be pleased with what we put together this weekend."

"Both of us," Honey Sue added as her phone buzzed. She glanced at the screen and frowned. "Excuse me one moment."

She stepped away, pressing the phone to her ear.

"Let's get as much footage as we can," Brett said as the first man nodded his approval. "We'll feature as much of the estate as possible."

"To showcase the bride and groom," Honey Sue added, scooting past him. She slipped her phone into the pocket of her skirt. "Now I need to check the lighting in the chapel. The videographer is having a fit about the sconces casting shadows."

"She's good," Kip said to Lonnie as the wedding planner hurried toward the stone building, making a wide arc through the oaks to stay out of the photographer's shot.

Brett repositioned Melody and Alec, backing them up until the weathered cemetery and the winding path to the chapel filled the frame behind them. "Alec, take Melody's hand. Look at her ring like you're just noticing how beautiful it is."

Alec lifted Melody's hand gently, his thumb brushing over the diamond. Melody smiled up at him, soft and genuine.

"No, no, no." Kip strode forward, waving his hands like he could erase the whole thing. "Don't show the cemetery. It's ugly."

Brett lowered his camera. "It's romantic."

Lonnie peered at the scene over his glasses. "Our brand is Southern elegance. Southern history. Not...that. We're taking care of that."

Kip planted his hands on his hips. "How soon before we get the permits to demolish the site?"

My knees went weak. "Excuse me?"

"Just the cemetery," Kip said breezily as if that made it better.

"The wedding chapel stays, of course. Have you seen it? Makes you feel like you're in the South."

Heat prickled up my neck. "You *are* in the South."

Lonnie patted his partner's shoulder. "I'm going to camp out in the office and make some calls." He turned toward the carriage house, already pulling his phone from his pocket.

Kip barely acknowledged him, his attention snapping back to Brett. "Did you get all of the carriage shots we talked about?"

"Sure did." Brett moved closer, angling his camera to show the small digital display. "I can show them to you if you'd like."

Kip checked out the display, but his eyes kept drifting to the grounds, scanning the property like he was mentally rearranging it. "I thought we were going to have horses out here for the shoot. Where are the horses?"

Brett scratched the back of his neck. "Mort went to get them a while ago."

Kip scrubbed a hand across his forehead. "Where is Mort?"

"I'll go check," I offered. I wasn't in any shots at the moment, and I needed to talk to Mort before anyone else did. Especially if he'd taken it upon himself to search the rooms above the carriage house.

"I'll go with you," Ellis said.

"Good." I was already moving toward the stables.

"No. Stop," Brett ordered. "I'm going to need you to admire the ring too."

"Alec's got it," Melody assured him, waving us away.

Alec looked glad to be standing upright.

We hurried across the field, leaving the wedding party and the owner and the chapel behind us. "You thinking what I'm thinking?" Ellis asked.

I lifted my silk dress, trying to keep my heels from digging into the grass as we jogged toward the carriage house. There was no way it had taken the caretaker an hour to fetch the horses. "Mort's been gone too long."

The building rose before us, two stories of weathered stone

with white-trimmed windows and a red slate roof. Ivy climbed the eastern wall, reaching toward the second-floor dormers. The wide double doors to the stable lay open.

We slowed. I stepped inside first. Dust motes danced in the shafts of sunlight that cut through the gaps in the wooden slats. The air was thick with the smell of hay and horses, earthy and sweet, mixed with the sharper tang of leather and old wood. Six stalls lined each side of the central corridor, but only two at the front appeared occupied, the horses shifting restlessly in their boxes.

"It's strange Mort hasn't hitched the horses," I said, peering into the first stall. A black mare stamped her hoof.

Ellis moved on down the aisle. "You'd think he'd do his job, even if he is helping us investigate."

"Unless he's the guilty one," I said under my breath.

Frankie would have a field day with that. I could hear him now: *You sent the bad guy to go catch...the bad guy?*

"Mort?" I called.

I didn't see him anywhere.

The stable wasn't that big.

Ellis peered into the second stall, running a hand along the wood. "If he's guilty, why would he be questioning the chef?"

"As an excuse to be in the kitchen, poisoning Alec's soup," I murmured.

Ellis stopped cold. "Are we even having soup?"

I wasn't sure. "I haven't seen the menu," I admitted.

That was the problem. We didn't know enough, and we were running out of time.

A slightly larger black horse nickered at Ellis. "What do you think about Brett?"

"He was here last night." I reached the third stall. There wasn't so much as a stray piece of hay in this one. "He could have planted the drugged whiskey."

Ellis's hand tightened on the stall door. "Mort did ask to see Brett's room."

I froze. "You think he's up there now?"

Ellis stared me down. "He's got to be somewhere nearby."

"Unless he fled the property."

We moved faster now, checking each stall. The fourth, the fifth.

I reached the last stall and froze.

Mort sprawled in a pile of hay. Blood matted the back of his head, pooling beneath him.

I grabbed Ellis's arm to steady myself. My head went light, and my stomach fluttered. The stable tilted. This couldn't be happening. Not here, not at Melody's wedding. Not to Mort, who'd been trying to help us.

Flickering streaks of white and yellow light rose up from the body. I'd experienced soul traces before. They marked the place of a recent death.

Next to his body lay the whiskey decanter from the honeymoon suite. Shattered, with the crystal stopper lying next to it.

Smeared dark red.

# Chapter Fifteen

Ellis crouched beside the body, two fingers pressed to Mort's neck. After a long moment, he pulled back and stood. He knew. We both knew.

Mort was dead.

"What can you tell me?" Ellis asked.

Red streaks pierced the white and yellow soul traces. "There was anger."

Although that much was clear from the body. He lay crumpled in the horse stall, his weathered cheek pressed against the dirt floor. One arm twisted beneath him at an impossible angle.

Someone had killed him in cold blood. With the whiskey decanter.

The one I'd asked him to find.

Ellis was already reaching for his phone. "I've got to call this in." His voice was steady, controlled. It was his police officer voice, the one that meant he was locking down his emotions and hell-bent on doing his job.

"Ellis—"

He met my eyes, and for just a second, I saw the worry there. Not for the case. For me. "Do you see more in the soul traces?"

"No, but Ellis—" I managed, unable to look away from

Mort's body. The blood. The shattered decanter. The absolute stillness of him. "His toolbox is missing."

I hadn't known Mort well, but I'd never seen him without it. And he'd definitely had it with him when he set out this morning.

Ellis nodded. "Stay here. Don't touch anything." He rested a hand on my shoulder. "We'll figure it out."

We certainly would.

Ellis strode toward the stable entrance, phone to his ear, speaking in low, urgent tones to the Jackson Police Department.

I wrapped my arms around myself, the silk of my bridesmaid dress suddenly feeling too thin as I searched each horse stall again. The toolbox was nowhere to be found.

I stopped short of the stall that contained Mort's body. How had this happened? Mort had been helping us, and now—

Now he was dead.

Heavy footsteps echoed on the floor above. Ellis glanced up, and I ducked out to see Lonnie hurrying down the exterior stairs, slightly out of breath, his wire-rimmed glasses askew. "Is it true? It just went over the police scanner."

"You were up in your office," I said, earning a quick nod from him.

"Working," he finished.

Or hiding out after he killed Mort. He'd certainly had the opportunity.

Ellis pressed the phone to his chest. "Don't move," he ordered Lonnie, who reached for his cell phone. "Don't call anybody."

"I called Kip," he said to both me and Ellis. "Where is he?" Lonnie ducked past me into the stables.

"You can't go near the crime scene," I called, hot on his heels as he jogged straight for the last stall, the one with Mort.

He stopped. Stared. The color draining from his face.

"It's really him." His voice went high and thin. He lurched backward, nearly running me over. "Is he—oh God. Oh God, we need to call someone. OSHA. We need to call OSHA." He fumbled for his phone. "Workers' comp. Insurance."

We had bigger problems. "This wasn't a work accident," I said, my voice sharper than I intended. "He was hit in the head with a whiskey decanter."

Lonnie's eyes went wide. "A decanter? But how—" He shook his head rapidly like he could shake the reality away. "I need to call our lawyer. Right now."

No. "Ellis told you to hold the phone and stay put."

He looked from me to Kip, who was striding into the stable with the confidence of a man who owned everything he surveyed. Which, technically, he did.

"I got your text," he said to Lonnie. "What's the situation?"

"Disaster." Lonnie scrubbed a hand over the back of his neck. "Mort's dead in stall six."

Kip scanned the stable, the blocked-off stall, Ellis on the phone. "Can we at least get the horses out before the police get involved? We've got a wedding to photograph."

"Ellis is still on the phone with the Jackson police," I said, my patience wearing dangerously thin. "And no. This is a crime scene."

Kip stiffened. "You don't know that."

I knew more than I'd ever wanted to know. "I'm pretty sure I've seen a crime scene before."

Lonnie adjusted his glasses. "It's tragic, but horses are dangerous. Clearly Mort got kicked."

He knew nothing of the sort. "We found him in an empty stall. There was no horse."

"It was no one's fault or liability," Lonnie concluded.

Kip snapped his fingers. "So we can still do a shoot with the horses," he said as if that were the best idea ever.

Footsteps crunched on the gravel outside.

Brett ducked in the door, the camera hanging forgotten around his neck. "Is it true? I heard Mort—" He stopped short when he saw us.

"Don't come any closer." We didn't need any more people in here. This was a disaster.

As if on cue, Melody appeared in the doorway with Alec right behind her. Her face was flushed, her eyes bright with what should have been joy.

"Verity?" Her smile faltered as she took in the scene. Ellis on the phone, Lonnie pale and sweating, Kip's grim expression. "What's going on?"

I moved toward her, blocking her view of the last stall. "There's been an incident."

"What kind of incident?" Alec braced a hand on the wall for support.

"Mort's dead," Kip said bluntly.

Melody's hand flew to her mouth. Alec pushed off the wall.

"Dead?" she whispered. "How?"

"Someone killed him," I said, wishing we could have been a little less callous about it.

"Oh my God," Melody squeaked.

Kip clapped his hands together, the sharp sound making us all jump. "There's nothing we can do except try to salvage the afternoon. Brett, go grab Starlight from her stall. I'll get Roxie. We can still do the outdoor carriage shots while we wait for the police."

I stared at him. "This whole place is a crime scene. In fact, what are we doing standing around? We should leave right now."

"Yep. Let's get back to the shoot," Kip decided, nudging Brett, who stood shocked.

"Are you out of your mind?" Melody's voice cracked. "A man is *dead*."

"Which is why we called the police," Kip said as if he were explaining it to a four-year-old.

"Ellis called the police," I corrected.

The owner tipped his chin down like he was addressing an illogical bride. "We've got perfect light right now, and you promised us a photo session."

Melody's nostrils flared. "I'm going to give you grace and assume the shock has you completely out of your mind."

"I'm with her," Brett said, escaping the stable.

Kip opened his mouth to argue, but Ellis ended his call and fixed Kip with a look that could have turned Medusa herself to stone. "Everybody out. I want you out on the lawn where I can see you until Jackson PD arrives."

Alec wrapped an arm around Melody and escorted her to an iron bench outside. Brett went and slumped down under a tree in the yard. Ellis stood between Kip and the body, while I struggled to make sense of it all.

Someone had killed Mort. Someone at this wedding. Someone who'd wanted that whiskey decanter badly enough to commit murder.

I still couldn't imagine who would do such a thing.

Lonnie had been upstairs in the office. He claimed he'd been working, but he had no witnesses. He'd had opportunity. The office overlooked the stables. He could have seen Mort heading down here, could have followed him. And he'd been awfully quick to declare it an accident, to worry about liability instead of a human life.

And where had Kip been? Sure, he'd been out in the yard, watching the shoot. But Lord knew where he'd been before that. Mort could have been dead by the time he'd driven his Mercedes through the front gate. He could have driven straight from the back lot by the stables.

The horse at the end whinnied in its stall. I looked to Brett under the tree.

He'd been taking photos, but he'd been in and out of the stable earlier at the same time Mort had. Mort had wanted to search his room.

And then there was Honey Sue, oblivious in the chapel. Or was she? She had a reputation for coordinating her weddings with military precision. She had access to every part of the property. She knew everyone's schedules, everyone's movements. She had a room in the stable house, same as Brett. Had Mort asked to search her room as well?

I brought a hand to my head. Everyone was a suspect. Each

one had the opportunity.

My throat tightened. I'd sent Mort down here. I'd asked him to search for evidence, to help us figure out who'd drugged Alec. He'd been doing me a favor, and now he was dead because of it.

If I hadn't involved him, he'd still be alive. He'd be up at the main house right now, fixing a loose hinge or replacing a light bulb. Not lying dead in a horse stall with the back of his skull caved in.

But one thing was clear. Mort had died because he'd been searching for that decanter. Someone had drugged Alec last night. And now it seemed they'd killed to keep that secret.

I caught Ellis's eye. "I'll be outside."

He gave me a slight nod. I needed a second to myself.

No one else noticed when I slipped around the side of the carriage house. I pressed my back against the stone wall and tried to breathe. Tried to think.

Frankie materialized next to me, arms crossed. "Hey, what are you doing lurking around the gangster clubhouse?"

"The what now?" I didn't see anything of the sort.

"Over there," he said, tilting his head toward the caretaker's cottage just beyond the back parking lot. "We call ourselves the Irish Dancers, on account of how sly we are."

I didn't even want to unpack that one. "In case you forgot, you are here to accompany me to a wedding."

"I don't see your sister getting married right now," he huffed.

Of course he had to make this difficult. "You were also supposed to help me locate the whiskey and cigars that went missing from the honeymoon suite."

"About those..." He adjusted his hat. "I don't think they're on the estate anymore."

"I found the whiskey decanter," I said. "It's next to Mort inside the carriage house."

"Then what are you complaining about?" He held out his hands. "You don't need me anymore."

"Someone bashed him over the head with it. He's dead."

"Tough break." Frankie winced.

Seriously? "Is that all you have to say?"

"What do you expect?" He threw up his hands. "Somebody shot me in the forehead, and you don't hear me complaining."

"Yes, I do. All the time." He kept his hat on twenty-four seven to cover the bullet hole.

He scoffed. But he didn't deny it. "So, when were you going to tell me you didn't need me no more?"

"For real?"

"I didn't see you rubbing my urn with that breaking news."

"I've been kind of busy," I said in the understatement of the year.

The gangster cocked his head. "Have you ever stopped to consider what I need?"

"Let's see—a fancy bootlegging still in my backyard, a party with a ghost tiger on a leash, a family of ghostly goats on my porch, a getaway car chase with gangsters shooting at me while I cart you around in my 1978 avocado green Cadillac—"

"All good choices," he allowed.

"I could go on." But we didn't have the time. I stepped back from the carriage house wall, putting a little more distance between myself and the stable where Mort lay dead. "I need your help."

Frankie looked me up and down. "You've got to be kidding me."

"I've hardly ever seen Mort without his toolbox," I said, keeping my voice low. "He had it on him this morning when he set out for the carriage house. But now it's nowhere to be found."

"Ahh." Frankie's expression shifted. "I've got a thing happening right now."

So did I. "I'm betting Mort had that toolbox on him when he was attacked. If his killer took it, there must be something in it they couldn't risk leaving behind. I need you to find it." When Frankie's gaze flattened, I added, "This is important."

His eyes bugged out. "So is stealing the Irish Crown Jewels."

Heat flashed through me. "Don't you dare."

"I always dare." He puffed out his chest. "It's what separates the men from the saps."

"Look." I took a breath. If I couldn't appeal to his good nature—and I knew better than that—I'd speak to his practical side. "I learned who killed your gangster buddies."

He stiffened. "I view them as my associates."

Whatever. "Will you listen to me?"

"I'm just saying Dapper Dan would shove his *mother* down a well for fifty bucks."

Cars pulled up. Doors slammed. I should have been done with Frankie by now.

It was like talking to a toddler. "Dapper Dan didn't kill anybody."

Frankie gave me a look. "What part of gangster don't you understand?"

"Don't get technical. What I'm trying to say is Dapper Dan didn't kill Knuckles." I took a breath and explained about Lady Brigid. How she'd turned poltergeist protecting her ruby earrings. How she'd hunted down each gangster after they'd stolen from her. Lenny in the wine cellar, Knuckles at the well, Dapper Dan in the chapel. How she'd pushed both grooms off the balcony for trying to give her jewelry to their new brides.

When I finished, Frankie was staring at me, his head cocked. "You gotta admire her dedication."

"No, you don't." That was not the lesson we were taking from this.

Before Frankie could respond, a trio of ghosts materialized behind him. Dapper Dan in his argyle sweater, Knuckles with his perpetual scowl, and Lenny still wearing dirt from the wine cellar.

Frankie whirled on them. "I told you guys to wait in the getaway Ford!"

"There's a horse standing in it," Knuckles grumbled.

"There's also a pair of cop cars parked out front." Dapper Dan ventured a fleeting glance over his shoulder. "You know what that means. Pat-downs, handcuffs, guys who've seen the wanted posters."

"The Jackson police? They're here?" That was fast. I needed to get back there.

"HQ is just up the road." Lenny hunched his shoulders, turning his back to the front yard. "Good thing they didn't see us."

He'd be waiting a long time for that.

"But see?" Dapper Dan added to Knuckles. "I may have robbed you after you were dead, but I didn't toss you down that well."

Knuckles turned to Lenny. "And I didn't bash your head in. I was nice and buried you in the wall after you died."

"Yeah, you don't want ladies screaming and police swarming," Dan said.

"He was my friend," Knuckles said simply.

Lenny punched Knuckles's shoulder.

Knuckles rubbed the spot and fought a grin.

They were all one big, happy criminal family.

Not that I wanted to lecture, but... "You guys might get a lot farther if you worked together. Stopped undermining each other." Stealing from each other.

Knuckles looked at me like I'd suggested he join the ballet.

"I have to go," I said, starting for the front yard. Ellis might need me.

"Go." Frankie waved me off, grinning like he'd won the lottery. He turned to the guys. "She's got a point. Now that we know you all didn't kill each other, we can be a team and steal the jewels."

"Absolutely not." I halted before they got any more terrible ideas. I turned to look each one of them in their beady little eyes. "Lady Brigid goes full poltergeist when anyone tries to take her ruby earrings. You saw it." Well, maybe none of them saw it coming, but they were all there. "She killed every last one of you."

Dapper Dan cocked his head. "It's not like Brigid can kill us again."

"I'm good as part of a gang." Knuckles rubbed his fist on his palm.

"We'll go after the Irish Crown Jewels instead of the earrings," Lenny said like he'd solved everything.

"I do like diamonds." Knuckles slapped him on the back.

They were crazy people. Every stinking one of them. "This is like Frankie times four."

"Heyyy..." My housemate snapped his fingers. "I like the sound of that. Frankie's Four!"

"No." I'd take his urn and drive to Canada before I let that happen. "You are not a gang."

"I prefer *a criminal enterprise*," Dapper Dan said.

"We can make that the subtitle," Frankie offered.

"What? Are you ordering T-shirts?" Lenny snarked.

"Nobody's stealing anything," I insisted.

Knuckles narrowed his eyes at me. "We didn't invite you."

"If the jewels are on the property—" I began.

"They are," Lenny interrupted.

"And even if you could locate them—" I hedged.

"Like you said. We'll work together." Dapper Dan grinned.

I sucked in a breath. "I ask—no, I *demand*—that you wait until my sister's wedding is over, her groom is safe, and we are off the property."

"Oh, so you're going to leave me out," Frankie balked.

I pulled him aside, lowering my voice. Never mind the others could obviously still hear us. "We don't even know that the jewels are here."

"Lady Brigid took the ruby earrings during the Irish crown jewel heist," Lenny said.

"Maybe so, but you have no way of knowing if she had the rest."

"She talked in her sleep," Lenny finished.

Dapper Dan elbowed him and grinned.

Lenny shrugged. "I'd like to claim credit for espionage, but remember, my mom was her lady's maid."

I looked at the four dead gangsters. "Here's the deal. You help me find Mort's toolbox, do your best to figure out who's targeting Alec, and keep this wedding from turning into a complete disaster, and I won't tell my police officer boyfriend exactly what you're up to."

Lenny shrieked. "She's a snitch!"

"She's alive," Frankie said practically.

Knuckles pounded a fist in his hand.

I got so close to Frankie I could feel the chill radiating off him. "*I* know I'm alive, and *you* know I'm alive," I muttered, "but let's hope they don't think about that part too hard." I was counting on my housemate's good graces, and he knew it.

"I think I'd like a special shed for Betsy Sue the Fifth," he mused.

"Done," I said.

"Deal," Dapper Dan said.

"Fine," Knuckles grumbled.

"Lenny," I prodded.

He rested his hands on his hips. "I get it. You don't call your cop buddy if we hold off on stealing." He shot me the hairy eyeball. "I waited a hundred years, so I guess I can wait a weekend."

"Then it's settled," I said.

Unless they took two seconds to think about the world of the living and realized Ellis was part of it.

"Here's what we do," Lenny said, grabbing a stick to draw in the dirt.

Knuckles and Dapper Dan gathered round.

Frankie held back. "You need to leave my urn here after this weekend."

"Frankie—" I wiped sweat from my forehead with the back of my hand.

That urn contained the only remains of him we had left. If

something happened to it or his ashes, I wouldn't be able to take him off my property anymore, not until we'd ungrounded him.

And who knew how long that would take? It had been years so far.

He held my gaze. "I know the risks."

He was willing to bet it all for a big score.

I sighed. "Find Mort's toolbox, and we'll talk about it."

Maybe by then he'd realize how crazy he sounded.

"Deal." Frankie turned to his crew. "You heard the lady. Let's get started."

"What's in it for us?" Knuckles growled.

"Practice," Frankie said. "We gotta work as a team if we're going for a legendary stash."

I opened my mouth to argue, but car doors slammed in the front drive. Multiple car doors. And this time, it was worse.

My chest tightened. I knew those voices.

The parents had arrived.

## Chapter Sixteen

I'd barely made it around the corner of the carriage house when I spotted the patrol cars. Several of them, Jackson peach logos blazed across the sides. Mom stood talking to one of the officers while his partner leaned against a cruiser, radio in hand.

"Mom." I rushed to her.

She turned to me, her long, graying blonde hair swept up in an elaborate twist held in place by chopsticks. "Verity." She enveloped me in a hug that smelled like honeysuckle. "Oh, sweetie, you look beautiful."

"You too," I said automatically. She wore a flowing coral dress with the turquoise necklace she'd found in Santa Fe. "What are you doing over here?"

"I could ask you the same question." My stepdad, Carl, drew up behind her. He stood tall and lean, with kind eyes and the perpetually sun-weathered skin of someone who'd spent his life outdoors with a hammer in his hand. "A man named Kip settled us in over at the house and told us to stay put."

Naturally, they didn't listen.

I also didn't see any sign of Brett or Honey Sue.

"We had to see what was going on," Mom said, watching the

officer she'd greeted enter the stable. "Alec's parents were more bent on following the rules."

"You sure about that?" I asked, spotting Leo and Sonya Duranja trailing my parents by about fifty yards.

I pasted on a smile and waved to them.

We were going to have some explaining to do.

"Well, we had to walk over when we saw the police cars," Mom said. "Kip from the bed and breakfast was jumpy. Melody's not answering her phone. I can see you and your sister wandering off, but Alec promised he'd be there to greet *his* parents."

I smoothed down my dress and tried to arrange my face into something that didn't scream *I just found a dead body*. I scanned the area. I didn't see Melody or Alec.

"Well," I began as Ellis emerged from the stable with a Jackson police officer, who began stringing crime scene tape. There was no getting around it. "There's been a murder."

Mom's hand flew to her chest. "At Melody's wedding?"

"Technically, that's not until tomorrow," I said, not helping a bit. "Don't worry," I added, trying a different tack. "I'm on the case. As maid of honor, I promise I'll make sure Melody's wedding goes off without a hitch."

Mom's face fell. "I daresay this is a hitch."

"Now, Tilly, you're always saying how proud you are of your detective daughter," Carl said.

"That doesn't mean she needs to be solving murders at Melody's wedding."

"Just one murder." I'd already solved the murders of the three dead gangsters. Not to mention two dead grooms. So maybe I was ahead.

Mom rubbed a smudge of dirt off my arm. "Surely you can take a break tonight and tomorrow."

"I wish I could." But this was my job. I was good at it, and Alec needed me. "Don't worry. I've got this under control." Mostly. "We're keeping Melody safe."

"Where is Melody?" she asked, her gaze darting across the stable yard.

"I don't know," I admitted.

"Well, let's find her," she said, heading to the carriage house as if she were here to save the day.

"She won't be by the horses." Or the body, I thought to myself as I trailed a half-step behind. In fact, I wondered where my sister could be if she wasn't at the house or out front of the stables.

"I sent you to school to be a graphic designer," Mom said, trekking around the far side of the barn.

"I like my new job better," I said.

Most of the time.

I could tune in to the other side and see things the police couldn't. I could learn the truth about the history of this place and the people who lived and died here. I was using Frankie's power for good. I mean, *somebody* had to. Together, we were helping people.

I only hoped I could make a difference this weekend.

We found Melody and Alec on a wrought-iron bench at the side of the stable, under a beautiful maple tree. "Mom!" she said, rushing up to her for a hug.

"Look at your dress!" Mom gushed, folding Melody into a hug. "I'm so sorry this happened," Mom added, holding her tight. "You should be worried about cake, not corpses."

Before I could assure her the cake was fine—though honestly, I had no idea at this point—Alec's dad called out, "Hello?"

Alec went pale. "Mom? Dad?" He jerked as his dad rounded the barn. "Why are my parents here?"

Perhaps I should have warned him.

Leo Duranja was just as tall as Alec but thinner, with wire-rimmed glasses and the kind of posture that suggested he'd never slouched in his life. "He's all the way back here," Leo called over his shoulder.

"The Jackson police obviously need his help," Sonya said,

bringing up the rear. It was easy to see where Alec had gotten his dark hair and sharp cheekbones.

Alec's mouth slacked open. "Why is everyone coming over here?"

"There's no one at the house," Carl said pragmatically.

"Except that nervous man, Kip," Sonya said.

"Who pretended he didn't know anything about the police cars," Mom added.

"Your mom can tell when people are lying," Carl said.

"I taught Verity," my mom said proudly.

Alec stared at the lot of them like he couldn't quite believe they'd crashed the murder scene.

Melody and I exchanged a helpless look. Leo and Sonya Duranja had moved to Memphis at least a decade ago when Leo had gotten promoted at the post office. They didn't make it to Sugarland much, but I had a feeling I'd be seeing a lot more of them now.

Alec kissed his mother on the cheek. "There's been an accident, but we're fine. Let's get everyone back to the house."

Her face softened as she took in her son. "Verity told us about the murder."

"Seriously?" Melody asked me.

"I didn't say a word. Well, except to Mom and Carl," I promised my sister, ignoring the sharp look Alec directed my way.

"Her voice carries," Sonya said, fussing with Alec's hair.

"That I believe," Alec groused.

I was a lady. It couldn't be that bad.

"How are you holding up?" Sonya asked.

"I'm good. I catch murderers for a living," he pointed out.

"I know," she said, taking his hand, "but this is your wedding, Pooches."

This was new. "Pooches?"

Alec's cheeks went red. "Seriously, Mom?"

"I'm sorry, but I've been calling you Pooches since you were a chubby baby," she said, reaching up to pat his cheek.

"That was before I could walk," Alec said, refusing to acknowledge any of us. "I'm walking now, Mom."

"Why don't we all head back to the house?" Melody suggested.

Leo took a seat on the bench. "I'd rather wait and see what happens here." He stretched his arms out. "If this were one of your cases back in Knoxville, you'd have it solved by now. Top detective in the department. Isn't that what they said when you transferred?"

"Dad—"

"Second-highest clearance rate in the county," his father continued, warming to his subject. "Remember that case with the stolen artwork? Solved it in forty-eight hours."

"This isn't my case," Alec said, his voice tight. "The local police have it handled."

"Why don't we show everyone the historic wedding chapel?" Melody suggested.

Ellis rounded the corner and sped up when he saw Leo motioning for Sonya to have a seat. "We're being asked to leave this area while they finish securing the scene."

My hero.

He greeted both sets of parents, then added, "Of course, we're not to leave the property."

"No chance of that," Melody said to Alec, and I watched the tension drain out of him.

"And, Verity," Elis added, "the Jackson police need to talk to you later."

I'd expected as much.

"Then it's settled," Melody said, ushering both sets of parents to the wide-open yard out front, bypassing the police cars and anyone else they could ask about the body.

I only hoped Frankie was on the job, looking for that toolbox.

"The chapel is from County Wicklow. Built in 1683," Melody said, slipping into librarian-tour-guide mode. "They numbered every stone before they dismantled it, over seven thousand pieces. It took two years to reassemble here."

Mom clucked her approval. "I'd love to see pictures."

"I found plenty in the Jackson Library archives." Melody linked arms with Mom as she led us to the chapel, pulling ahead of our group.

Leo let them go on a little before he cleared his throat and looked to Alec. "Did you give it to her yet?"

Alec glanced toward my sister. "Dad—"

"Your great-grandmother's necklace," Sonya pressed. "The heirloom diamonds. I don't see her wearing them. Didn't you say you were going to give them to her last night?"

"I didn't get the chance," Alec said, keeping his voice low.

"Well, you should do it soon," Leo said. "It's tradition."

"I hate to interrupt," I said, "but you can't." It was too dangerous. Both of them looked at me. Leo, surprised. Alec, well, like he was expecting the other shoe to drop. It pained me to ruin their moment, but there was no getting around it. "There's a poltergeist on the property."

Both men looked at me like I'd lost my last marble.

Alec should know better.

"Alec, you remember about..." The dead grooms. I'd rather not bring that up. So I plowed forward on a parallel track, explaining about Lady Brigid and how violent she became when her ruby earrings were threatened.

Leo gaped. "So you're telling me a ghost says my son can't give his fiancée a wedding gift?"

"Yes," Alec said. His entire body had gone rigid as he took even longer strides forward. "And I'm inclined to believe her."

Thank goodness.

"I always believe her," Ellis said.

It was one of the things I loved about him.

I had to practically jog to keep up. "Granted, Lady Brigid is mostly worried about her own stolen jewels."

Ellis nodded. "Well, we don't know what else might set her off, and there's no sense baiting her."

We were starting to catch up to Mom and Melody. "So no jewels," Alec confirmed.

"I'm not even wearing my grandma's filagree cross pendant tonight," I said, keeping my voice down this time.

"This is crazy," Leo groused.

"It's not," Sonya warned. "I feel it." She brought up the rear with me. "Did Alec ever tell you I'm psychic, too?"

Alec closed his eyes. "Mom, please."

"I get it from my mother. She was Hungarian."

"We don't need to talk about this," Alec gritted out as we neared the garden at the back of the house.

Sonya waved him off. "He's just sensitive because I told his first partner that their squad car was haunted."

"It happens." I had to agree.

Alec shot her a look.

"He also didn't want to hear it when I told him his aura's pink," she added. "It's because he's in love."

"Then my aura's pink, too," Ellis said, enjoying the show.

His eyes met mine, and I felt my chest warm.

"Ellis," I warned.

He shouldn't encourage her.

"What?" Ellis took my hand. "You can't blame a guy for falling in love with you." He gave it a squeeze. "Not when it's so easy to do."

We'd almost reached the small forest of oaks when a car pulled into the circular drive. An older man in a clerical collar climbed out of a dusty sedan, waving when he spotted us.

"Is that Reverend Grace?" Alec's father asked, squinting.

"It is." Alec's mom quickened her pace. "I haven't seen him since we moved to Memphis."

Kip greeted him and took his bag, but Reverend Grace resisted the owner's attempt to lead him into the house. Instead, the good reverend met us on the rose garden side of the circle drive.

"Leo," he said, shaking hands, "how's life in the big city?"

"Not the same as Sugarland," Leo said, stepping back for the reverend to give Sonya a kiss on the cheek.

"We were just about to stop by the chapel," she said.

"The one from Ireland," Reverend Grace finished. "I've always wanted to see it, but you know…"

"Jackson," Leo finished as if he hadn't come from a lot farther away.

"Shouldn't you at least change out of your dress?" Mom asked.

Melody looked down at her wedding gown like she'd forgotten she was wearing it. I didn't fault her a bit after everything that had happened. "You know what? It's fine." She waved it off. "I'd rather create some new memories."

We both agreed later that we should have been careful what we wished for.

∽

We arrived a few minutes later. The cemetery came into view first, the weathered headstones tilting at odd angles and the small Byrne mausoleum with its iron gate rusted shut. Beyond it rose the chapel, its limestone walls dark with age, moss creeping up from the foundation. A stone cross stood at the peak of the roof, silhouetted against the sky.

"It's gorgeous." Mom clasped her hands together. "Absolutely gorgeous."

I brushed past the camellias at the entrance, their white blooms catching on my dress.

"Wait until you see inside," Melody said, leading the way.

She pulled open one of the doors, the hinges groaning softly as we stepped into the dim interior.

And froze.

## Chapter Seventeen

A man in his mid-forties stood near the altar, his phone pressed to his ear, his voice low and urgent. He wore a crisp white chef's coat and had a solid build with a slight belly. "Yeah. Listen to me. I need three dimes on the house special. Two-fifty on the line. What's the spread on the Sharks? I don't care about the juice! I told you I'm good for it."

He turned and spotted us.

His eyes went wide. The phone nearly slipped from his hand.

"I'll call you back," he said, jabbing a button, ending the call. He shoved the phone into his pocket. "Oh my. It—it's the bride," he said, taking in Melody's dress.

She tilted her head. "Chef Duchamp?"

He recovered enough to give a swift nod, his gaze dissecting the group of parents, the reverend, all of us staring at him. "I was only...taking a private phone call."

"In the chapel?" It seemed a bit sacrilegious.

Even if I *had* been digging up the floor last night.

He edged sideways and nearly stepped on the wobbly slate tile.

We were really going to have to fix that.

"The reception in the kitchen is terrible," Chef said,

smoothing down his immaculate white coat. "And with everything happening today, I needed a quiet moment to handle some...supplier issues."

Leo's eyes narrowed. "I hope everything's on track for dinner tonight."

"We can take everyone out for dinner if it's not," Sonya added.

Chef's nostrils flared. "It's a supplier issue for another event." He grabbed the notebook he'd left on the altar. "Nothing I can't handle."

"You're serving shark?" Mom asked.

"Best in the South." He forced a laugh.

"Perhaps we should leave this for another time." Reverend Grace suggested.

"Well," Melody said, breaking the tension, "as long as the food's taken care of."

Chef seized the lifeline. "Absolutely. Now, if you'll excuse me, I must return to the kitchen. The braising waits for no one." He gave a small bow and hurried past us toward the door, his footsteps echoing on the stone floor.

"It wasn't a quick phone call," Ellis said as soon as the door had closed.

I joined him near the front. "Why do you say that?"

"His coffee's barely warm." A paper cup sat in the first pew next to the chef's forgotten hat. "He's been here at least twenty minutes."

I ran a finger along the side. He was right. "I wonder what else he's lying about." Chef Duchamp had supplied the whiskey that drugged Alec. He'd been on the property when the evidence went missing and when Mort was killed.

And he was going to feed us tonight.

"Good thing Honey Sue didn't catch him using her chapel for a phone booth," Mom said, retrieving the coffee cup.

"Or leaving a mess in the pews," Melody added, gazing up at the gallery loft above. "All those stone angels watching over us and not one of them thought to bring a trash can."

It could wait.

"We saw Honey Sue last night," Mom said, taking the cup and carrying it to the front door. "At Kira Freeman's sweet sixteen party."

"You went to the Freemans' party?" Melody asked. "I was the one who used to babysit her."

"You know how it is," she said, dumping the coffee out the door, shaking out the cup. "We went to Ed Roan's for chili, and they were all heading over to the party after dinner."

Sugarland had a the-more-the-merrier attitude when it came to family parties.

"Etta Freeman waved us inside." Carl grinned. "They had the doors wide open, music spilling out into the parking lot. I'm always glad to make it back to Sugarland."

"We grabbed a card on the way. Wrote little Kira a nice check," Mom said, stashing the empty cup in her purse. "She's taller than me now."

Carl nodded. "Half the party was in the parking lot."

"Still, you were the one who saved the day when Honey Sue's tire went flat," Mom added.

She'd told us about it. "I hear it took a while."

"Nah." Carl waved me off. "Ed and I fixed it in five minutes." He planted his hands on his hips. "Would have been harder if we'd had to find the leak, but she had a knife slash in it. Terrible to think somebody would do that. A patch, a pump, and she was good to go."

Ellis's expression mirrored my thoughts. "Why did she lie to us?" I asked Ellis.

Honey Sue had implied she couldn't make it to the estate last night because she was a mess from fixing the tire.

But according to my parents, Ed Roan had her ready to go in no time.

Ellis drew closer, his voice dropping. "What time did this happen?"

"Seven?" Mom asked Carl.

"No later than eight," he said.

Plenty early enough for her to drive to Jackson if she'd wanted to. So why had she told us she'd been stranded all night? What had she been doing instead?

And why hide it?

I'd definitely be asking Honey Sue about that.

"Look." Mom gazed up at the vaulted ceiling. The gallery wrapped around three sides of the chapel. It went all along the back wall above the entrance and down both sides to frame the front. Stone angels perched along the railing, wings spread wide, watching over all who gathered here. "It's so romantic."

"It is." Melody and Alec stood at the altar, arm in arm, while Sonya took a picture and Leo chuffed with pride.

Carl took Mom's arm. "Reminds me of our day. You looked so pretty with those daisies in your hair."

Melody turned to us, beaming. "I can't believe it's really happening tomorrow."

Reverend Grace took his place near the front of the altar. "Dearly beloved..." he began with a jovial smile when Melody cocked her head.

"You know," she said, "we could just rehearse now."

"You're wearing the dress," Alec said, earning a swat from her.

"I forgot you're not supposed to see it before the wedding," she teased.

"Too bad I'll never be able to forget how beautiful you look today," he said, taking her hand.

"That's it. We're doing this," I said, taking my place at the front near the altar.

"I mean, why not?" Ellis said, stepping up opposite me. "We're all here."

We could use the distraction.

And a bit of fun.

"This way, we'll have time for a drink before dinner," Leo said, leading his wife to the front right pew.

"As long as it's not whiskey," Alec smirked.

Melody laughed.

"Anyone up for a cigar?" Ellis joked.

"Wait. We don't have Honey Sue," Carl pointed out.

"She'd just want to fluff my hair," Melody said.

"And I'm done with being herded," Alec said, facing the preacher, who stepped forward, right onto the wobbly tile.

Oh.

"You might want to step back," I said on my way to rescue him.

"I'm more spry than I look," Reverend Grace said, holding me off. He smiled warmly at the assembled group, completely oblivious to the grave beneath his feet. And the ruby earrings that had cost three men their lives.

He'd better not fall in and touch them. We'd had enough trouble today. We didn't need Lady Brigid poltergeisting up the rehearsal. Or the wedding, for that matter.

"Now then," he said, pulling reading glasses from his pocket and settling them on his nose. "Let me just say, before we begin, how special this moment is for me personally."

The tile shifted slightly with his weight.

He didn't notice.

"I've known Alec since he was in Sunday school," Reverend Grace said, his voice taking on that misty quality that all preachers must have learned at seminary. "When he raised his hand and asked if Jesus had a dog."

"That's not going in tomorrow's ceremony, right?" Alec made a mock cringe.

"Oh, I'm just getting started." The reverend shifted his weight.

Melody stifled a giggle.

"A very serious theological question for a four-year-old," the reverend continued. "But watching him grow into the man standing before us today, preparing to marry the love of his life..."

His voice cracked.

Leo dug a finger under his collar. "No need to get emotional."

"It's what I do best," Reverend Grace said, dabbing at his eyes with a handkerchief he'd pulled from his robe. "I remember the time Alec was five and asked during children's sermon if angels had belly buttons. Then he spent the next twenty minutes explaining his reasoning to the entire congregation."

"Can we maybe not say all this tomorrow?" Alec pleaded, though he was grinning at Melody. "My boss will be here. My entire department."

"I think you invited some guys from the FBI," Ellis added.

"I'll edit," Reverend Grace promised. "But I'm keeping the dog story."

Alec groaned, but he was smiling as Melody kissed him on the cheek. Ellis couldn't stop grinning like a fool. I couldn't either.

This was what it was all about.

"Weddings are my favorite." Reverend Grace rocked forward on his heels, and I heard the scrape of loose stone beneath his feet. His eyes went wide.

My breath caught.

He stumbled backward.

Alec rushed to steady him, hand outstretched. "I've got you—"

"Watch out!" Leo shouted.

Alec turned.

A statue crashed down from the gallery wing above, the stone angel shattering on the floor.

"My God!" Carl shouted.

The impact shook the chapel, chunks of limestone exploding like shrapnel.

Melody screamed. I yanked her toward me and held on tight.

Ellis shielded both of us as a piece skittered past my feet.

Carl pulled Mom back against the wall. Leo bent over Sonya.

As the dust settled, we saw the shattered remains. The stone angel's serene face split in two, its hands still clasped in prayer. Its wings and body had crumbled, reduced to rubble scattered across the chapel floor.

Right where Alec had been standing.

If the reverend hadn't stepped back, if Alec hadn't rushed to help him...

"What in God's name—" Leo started.

"That could have killed someone!" Sonya's voice shook.

Reverend Grace stood frozen on the wobbly tile, dust coating his face. He clutched his handkerchief, taking sharp, wet breaths, his eyes locked on the destruction.

Alec let go of the reverend and crossed to us in two strides.

I released Melody. She turned straight into his arms.

"Is everyone all right?" Reverend Grace managed.

Melody trembled against Alec's chest. He buried his face in her hair.

I looked up at the gallery wing, past the dust still thick in the air, to where the last angel had stood right above us. The weathered limestone revealed a lighter patch where the angel had been.

I bolted down the aisle for the gallery stairs.

Ellis reached them first, taking them two at a time.

The narrow wood staircase spiraled upward. My shoes slipped on the worn treads as I pushed myself faster, my heart hammering against my ribs.

Ellis hit the gallery.

I was right behind him.

The narrow gallery ran down both sides of the chapel with benches tucked under the sloping roof. Ellis sprinted up the left side. I went right, my footsteps echoing on the wood floor. The angels stood sentinel along the railing, their carved robes flowing as if caught in an eternal wind, their hands clasped in prayer.

I reached the end, breathing hard.

A gaping hole showed where our angel had been. Right alongside the altar. Fresh scrape marks marred the stone pillar.

"I don't see anyone," Ellis called from the opposite side.

"Me either." The gallery ended in a wood-paneled wall. Could someone have slipped down the stairs while we were running up? No. We would have seen them.

Only there was no other exit. No windows large enough to climb through. No rope, no ladder.

I searched behind the pillar. It was too dark to see clearly. I dug the flashlight out of my bag and clicked it on. A crowbar lay wedged in the gap, along with a hammer.

Oh boy.

Just like the one I'd left behind last night.

I slammed my eyes shut. *Why, oh why had I left it behind?*

Because I'd been distracted by crazy gangsters, that was why.

*Focus.* I grabbed my phone and snapped a picture.

"Verity." Ellis's voice carried across the chapel. "You need to see this."

"I was about to tell you the same thing."

The look on his face told me I'd better get over there.

I hurried back along the U of the gallery and met him halfway down the left side, where he was locked in on a wooden roof support tucked under the eaves.

"There," he said when I reached the spot.

"Where?" I looked up and saw nothing but shadow.

"You're too short," he said, like a revelation. He pulled out his phone and snapped a photo, then showed me the screen.

There, wedged between the support and the sloping roof, sat Mort's toolbox.

My stomach dropped. "Damn it."

"Damn it, indeed," Ellis said, scanning the chapel.

This was the same person. It had to be. I'd enlisted Mort to help find out who drugged Alec's whiskey. Mort ended up dead. Now someone had used his tools to try to finish what they'd started—to kill Alec.

Someone who'd been watching us, who knew this chapel. Someone who'd seized the opportunity when we showed up early.

An attacker who'd almost succeeded. And who had escaped once more.

## Chapter Eighteen

"Are you ready?" Ellis asked. "We were supposed to be downstairs five minutes ago."

My hand went to my bare throat for the third time since I'd showered and changed for Melody's rehearsal dinner. I felt naked without my grandmother's filigree cross.

"Let's go," I said.

*Please let the dinner go better than the rehearsal.*

I smoothed my ice blue cocktail dress and took Ellis's arm as we headed downstairs. The delicate gold and silver cross had seen me through countless moments when I'd needed courage. Tonight, it sat in a velvet box along with the pearl earrings Ellis had given me for our first anniversary.

We weren't taking any chances. Not with Lady Brigid. Her jewelry obsession had caused enough damage. And frankly, with a real-life killer on the loose, it felt like the one thing we could control.

Ellis halted as we reached the top of the stairs, his gaze traveling slowly from my pink-glossed lips down to my silver shoes with the three-inch heels and the rhinestone buckles. The look he gave me made me feel like the only girl in the world.

"You look gorgeous tonight," he said, planting a sweet kiss on my cheek.

"Thanks." I'd needed to hear that. I was used to wearing dresses, but tonight's outfit was something else.

"This is all going to work out," he promised, and I knew exactly what he was talking about—the wedding, the night, the killer among us.

"We'll figure it out," I promised back.

We didn't have a choice.

And we were late.

"Showtime," I said.

He offered his arm, and we headed down.

It had taken three attempts, two blueberry bribes, and one minor wrestling match to get Lucy settled for the evening. And by "settled," I meant luring her out onto the porch for dinner and a snuggle. I'd served her a slice of apple cinnamon skunk crumble, her favorite. She'd promptly shared it with Lucky before I'd managed to snag her and park her in our room for the night.

At least she'd eaten something.

We passed through the narrow hall on the way to the ballroom. The clattering of pans echoed from the kitchen, where Chef Duchamp was tasked with creating our dinner.

If he wasn't placing bets on whether we'd all survive the wedding.

The ballroom glittered ahead of us, ready for tomorrow's reception. Champagne-colored linens draped round tables. Fairy lights twisted through the exposed beams overhead. White place card holders rested on strips of ice blue ribbon.

Ellis paused. "Your dress matches those ribbons."

He was right. "Leave it to you to notice every detail."

The owners had provided the dress. And the shoes.

"I feel like we're each playing a part in a production we're only beginning to understand," Ellis said as he led me toward a long table at the back. It sat along the wall of windows, set for ten.

The others had arrived before us.

The garden lay beyond the glass, with its riot of roses and cupid fountain, as twilight settled over the grounds. Candles flickered down the center of the table between low arrangements of white roses. The server poured champagne into fluted crystal glasses.

It would take more than champagne to forget someone had tried to kill Alec at his own wedding rehearsal.

Mom and Carl sat at the far end of the table with Leo and Sonya, still visibly shaken. Reverend Grace occupied the middle, a cocktail glass already half-empty in his hand.

Melody and Alec had retreated to the opposite side, their heads bent in urgent conversation.

I crossed to my parents first, leaning down to hug Mom, then Carl.

"You look beautiful, sweetheart," Mom said, squeezing my hand. But her heart wasn't in it.

I understood.

"We all cleaned up nice after…" Carl didn't quite want to finish the thought.

I slid into the chair Ellis held out for me on the end across from Melody. Ellis settled between me and the reverend.

That was when I heard my sister's low, urgent whisper to her fiancé, who crouched next to her. She slammed her eyes shut and said it plainly. "I think we should cancel the wedding."

I froze and looked to Ellis, who was busy greeting the reverend.

"Don't say that," Alec urged, taking her hand. "I want to marry you."

Melody leaned her forehead against his. "We can do it at the justice of the peace in Sugarland." She wrapped his hand in both of hers. "We can go tomorrow morning. Get it done. We'll be married and safe and—"

"Hey." He tilted his head. "I'm fine."

Melody's gaze found her lap. "For how long?"

"We have the preacher and the place and the dress. Look at me." He tipped her chin up. "I can handle myself."

"You can't always dodge falling angels." Her voice rose just slightly before she caught herself, dropping back to a fierce whisper. "You aren't immune to drugged whiskey. And someone is still after you."

He dropped his head. "I know."

I winced. It was true. Every last bit of it. I felt guilty for witnessing it. Guilty for wanting to look away. Melody's heart was breaking, and I wasn't sure how to fix it.

We needed to learn who was after Alec. Who had it in for this wedding. Because until we did, Alec wasn't safe, and Melody wasn't either.

"I can't—" Her cheeks went pink, and her voice broke. "I can't stand at that altar tomorrow wondering if it's the moment they'll finally succeed."

"We'll solve this," Ellis vowed. "Tonight."

"How?" Melody pleaded.

Ellis glanced to me. "I don't know."

I didn't either.

Alec's chair sat across from Ellis, with an empty seat between him and Carl. He took it and dragged it to the far end of the table, between me and Melody. "Any word on the toolbox you found?"

"Not yet." Ellis leaned back for Claire to pour him a glass of champagne. "I dropped in on the Jackson police before heading back to the house to change."

Alec nodded.

The Jackson officers were already on the property, investigating Mort's murder in the barn.

Ellis waited for Claire to fill the rest of the glasses and depart. "They sent an officer over to guard the door to the chapel. When they finish with the murder scene, they'll process the scene in the chapel."

"They have it from here?" Melody asked, taking the champagne from Alec's former place and passing it down to him.

"The Jackson police have the manpower, the resources," Ellis began.

"It's their jurisdiction," Alec added, accepting the glass.

"I hope they take it seriously," Melody said.

"They will." The town of Jackson might be deficient in a lot of ways, but even they took murder seriously. "And they might find something we missed. Fingerprints, DNA, something that tells us who left that toolbox in the rafters." I glanced down the table to where our parents were in deep conversation with the reverend. "The Jackson Police could solve this for us tonight." It really was our best shot. "Everything could turn out just fine."

Or it could be a disaster.

But I didn't say that last part out loud. I didn't need to say it.

Because we all knew the alternative. If the Jackson police came up empty, if we went into tomorrow's wedding without answers, then we'd be standing at that altar, sitting ducks for whoever wanted Alec dead.

And next time, they might not miss.

The clanking of a knife on a crystal glass stole our attention.

Kip stood with the window wall behind him, plucking a champagne flute from Claire's tray as she passed. "Welcome, everyone!" He raised his glass as Lonnie joined him. "We are thrilled to have you all here for our showcase wedding weekend."

Lonnie nodded along. "We apologize for the unfortunate incident this afternoon—"

"But we saw your pictures," Kip cut in smoothly, "and they are absolutely stunning."

"We think you'll be as pleased as we are," Lonnie added.

"So pleased," Melody gritted out.

Ellis's hand found mine under the table.

Kip gestured toward the kitchen. "Chef Duchamp has prepared something extraordinary for you tonight. Brett"—he turned to where the photographer lurked near the windows, his camera hanging heavy around his neck—"we'll need you to capture Chef presenting each course. The plating is exquisite."

Brett nodded without his usual enthusiasm.

"He hasn't been himself since we found Mort's body," I murmured to Ellis.

Melody caught my eye from across the table. "I noticed that. Does it mean he's horrified? Or does it mean he's feeling guilty?"

We'd keep a close watch.

"So please"—Lonnie spread his hands wide—"enjoy yourselves this evening. Eat, drink, celebrate."

"And remember to smile," Kip added as Brett's camera flash captured the entire table.

I blinked away the dots as Kip and Lonnie retreated out of camera range to watch while Brett set up for another wide shot.

"Brett couldn't have done it," Melody said, watching him adjust his lens. "He was taking pictures with us all afternoon."

"The blood around Mort's head was matted," I said, low under my breath, eyeing the reverend as he launched into a story about Alec that had my mom covering her mouth. "Brett could have killed him before the photo shoot."

"Oooh...that's cold," Melody said, running her fingers along the stem of her glass.

But possible.

So possible.

"He's living above the carriage house," I reminded her. "And Brett admitted Mort wanted to search his room."

Brett materialized next to Melody's shoulder, camera raised. "Looks like you're having your own little party down here."

I froze. Melody stared at me, eyes wide, as Claire glided up with a pristine white plate in hand. She set it before Melody with practiced grace, a tower of butter lettuce and microgreens artfully arranged with candied pecans, crumbled goat cheese, and paper-thin slices of pear fanned across the top. A drizzle of balsamic reduction created an elegant spiral on the rim.

"Now smile like your sister just said something hilarious." Brett's camera flash hit Melody three times in rapid succession, capturing Chef's work from different angles as Claire stood behind him, watching.

"Beautiful." Brett stepped back, mouth tight, eyes on us.

"He heard us," I said under my breath after he'd gone.

"Not necessarily," Ellis murmured as Claire retrieved a tray full of salads from a folding stand and began placing them in front of us.

"He heard us," Alec said, glancing at me. "You need to learn volume control."

Or maybe Alec just had super bat hearing.

"Did you get the salad by itself?" Kip asked, passing behind us with Brett in his wake.

"Now get the parents' reaction," Lonnie said from down the table.

Melody eyed Brett. "It doesn't matter if he heard." Still, she waited until he'd started snapping pictures of the parents before continuing, "Brett had opportunity. We know Mort suspected him or at least wanted to search his room above the carriage house."

"But what's his motive?" Alec pressed.

"Wine?" Claire asked.

I hadn't even seen her coming.

"No," all four of us said in unison.

I sipped my water and watched the waitress retreat.

Alec speared a pecan with his fork. "We need to know more about our suspects. We need those background reports. Any word on them?"

"Nothing yet." Ellis rechecked his phone before setting it face-down on the table. "It's got to arrive any minute now. Katie said she'd email it by dinner."

This was dinner.

"Well, it wasn't Chef," I said, keeping my voice low. "He walked out of the chapel before the statue fell."

"He's also as tall as I am," Ellis added.

"So he could have easily hidden the toolbox in the rafters," I concluded.

Ellis shot me a sideways glance. "I'd be willing to bet a shorter person hid that toolbox up in the rafters, thinking it was out of view."

Alec fiddled with his fork. "Brett's short."

"So's Honey Sue," I added, earning a shocked look from Melody. "Just stating the facts."

Ellis fingered the base of his champagne glass. "Lonnie's not overly tall. And he was in the carriage house right before Mort died."

"But Mort was dead when Lonnie got there," I said. The blood was matted. He'd been there a while.

"Unless Kip and Lonnie dropped by before they ever drove through that front gate," Melody said, reaching to fiddle with her earring before realizing she didn't have one.

"In that case, it could have been anyone," Melody continued. "It seems Mort was asking a lot of questions before the photo shoot."

"He was working hard," I said, feeling a twinge of guilt. I looked to Ellis. "I'll bet Brett heard us send Mort after that whiskey." For all we knew, he had pictures.

Alec ran a hand through his hair. "Okay, but why would Brett want to drug me? I don't even know the guy."

"Okay, let's consider who might have paid him—" Melody suggested, stopping short when Sonya appeared at Alec's elbow with Mom right behind her.

"Sweetheart, you need to be more social," Sonya said. "Even if Reverend Grace's stories embarrass you. You can't just huddle at the opposite end of the table."

"Sorry," Alec said reflexively, appearing as shocked to see her as I was. Even if she'd only been sitting four chairs down. He tossed the fork onto his plate with the pecan still on it. "I wasn't even listening. We got to talking down here."

"Oh, and about the processional order," she said, glancing to

Mom. "Tilly and I are thinking you should wait up front at the altar with Ellis next to you. Then Tilly will proceed down the aisle first, followed by Leo and me. Then Verity walks alone and waits up at the altar next to Ellis. And Carl walks you down for your big bridal entrance."

"That sounds great," Melody said with forced brightness.

"Unless you don't want to stand under those stone angels for long," Sonya added, her smile faltering.

"It'll be fine," Alec said quickly.

"Will it really, though?" Sonya asked, posing the question of the hour.

"Sonya!" Leo called from the other end. "They want us seated for dinner."

"Of course." She squeezed Alec's shoulder once more before returning to her seat.

"Try to relax," Mom said before following her. "Remember, this is a fun dinner."

"I'd have fun arresting somebody right about now," Alec muttered.

But who?

I leaned an elbow on the table. "What you said about money before has me thinking. Chef could have been hired by someone. I'll bet he needs money to pay off his gambling debts."

My silverware rattled as Chef slammed a pristine white plate in front of me. Pan-seared duck breast fanned over a sweet potato puree, roasted Brussels sprouts with pancetta, and a port wine reduction that gleamed like blood.

"Whatever you think you heard, you did not." He slapped the sauce spoon down on the edge like he wanted to hit me in the head with it, sending droplets of reduction onto the white tablecloth.

"No. Wrong," Kip said from behind him. "You need to look happy, and you dribble the sauce. You don't toss it."

"Superstar chef, indeed," Lonnie muttered from behind Kip as Brett moved in with his camera.

"Do it again," Kip ordered.

I allowed chef to serve me once more, the picture-perfect wedding guest. As soon as he finished, I shared a glance with Melody. She kept her expression placid as Chef served her and Brett snapped away under Kip's watchful eye.

We were conducting an investigation in a fishbowl.

With the fish watching.

I sliced into my pan-seared duck breast, not sure if I wanted a bite. The excitement of the afternoon had stolen my appetite. Not to mention the chef might be trying to kill us.

Ellis's breath tickled my ear. "Want to switch plates?"

Not unless he had takeout from the diner in Sugarland.

"It's got to be fine, right?" I buried a bit of duck under the potato.

"If it's good, we'll know Kip and Lonnie are innocent," Alec said, stealing a glance at the owners, who stood near the chef's serving station, giving orders to Brett. "They should want us upright tomorrow."

Ellis's phone buzzed against the table.

I dropped my fork. "Is it the background reports?"

We needed to know who was after Alec, who wanted to hurt him or sabotage the wedding. To this point, our investigation had produced more questions than answers.

He stared at the screen, the color draining from his face.

"What?" I leaned closer.

He read it twice. "The Jackson police never secured our evidence," he said, low, cold, and unmistakable.

"*What?*" Melody's voice rang out.

Every head turned. Mom. Carl. Leo and Sonya. Reverend Grace paused mid-sentence.

I kicked Melody under the table.

She flinched. "Oh. Sorry!" Her laugh came out too high. "Verity saw Lucy eating cake frosting in the kitchen. Can you imagine?"

That earned polite chuckles from our parents and a death glare from Chef.

Like we needed to tick him off more.

Chef Duchamp and Claire stood by a rolling cart loaded with sauce boats, wine bottles, and garnishes. He nudged Claire, and she approached the parents with a bottle of wine.

Closer to the windows, Kip and Lonnie flanked Honey Sue. All three watched our end of the table like they were afraid we'd go rogue any second. Brett's camera flashed.

My stomach dropped. "The evidence is gone?" I hissed, leaning closer. "Did someone snag Mort's toolbox?" The crowbar? The hammer our would-be killer used to drop that angel right where Alec had stood?

"It's impossible to say." Ellis slid his phone across to Alec.

Alec held it low and scanned the note. "They went home." He tossed the phone onto the table. "The Jackson police locked up the chapel and went home for the night."

What good would a lock do? For all we knew, the killer had taken Mort's keys.

That was what I would have done in their shoes.

"The Jackson PD are coming back tomorrow," Ellis said grimly.

"The Sugarland Police would never—" Melody began.

"No." Alec took her hand. "They wouldn't."

"They can't just leave it for tomorrow." I looked to Melody. "You're getting married tomorrow." Her eyes met mine, uncertain. "We are not debating that."

My sister deserved her wedding. She deserved to marry the man she loved without fear, without someone trying to kill him. Mort deserved to have his killer brought to justice. Alec deserved to see justice done to the person who'd drugged him and tried to crush him. And if the Jackson police weren't going to make that happen, then we would.

"We need to guard that chapel." Melody reached for her purse.

Alec pushed back from the table. "We'll secure the evidence."

"I've got it." Ellis stood.

I reached to unbuckle my crazy heels. Looked like the worry warts were right about us making a scene.

"Excuse me," Ellis said to the table. "Something's come up."

"What? No," Sonya's voice rang out. "You can't leave. We're about to do the toast."

Ellis held up his phone. "Police emergency. I'll be back."

When the Jackson police arrived tomorrow.

Leo pushed back his chair. "Oh now, Ellis. It's like I tell Alec. You're not the only one on the force." He raised his champagne glass. "Stay for my toast, at least."

Mom stood. "That. Means. Sit."

Ellis dropped into his chair.

"I'm picking my battles," he said under his breath.

"At least all our suspects are here," I murmured.

I scanned the room. Chef Duchamp stood by his serving station, arms crossed, watching us. Claire lingered beside him, holding a bottle of red. Kip and Lonnie whispered to each other, both keeping an eye on Ellis like he'd just tried to flee the scene of a crime.

Honey Sue stood near the door, clipboard in hand. Brett had lowered his camera but stayed put, positioned to see everyone. Even Reverend Grace was on high alert, his gaze darting between Ellis and my mom.

"I'll slip out after the toast," Ellis whispered, his eyes fixed on my mom, who tilted her head as if daring Ellis to try.

Leo cleared his throat. "I'm so glad we could all gather here this weekend to celebrate these two wonderful people—"

At least nobody could leave now. Not without being noticed.

Melody glanced at Brett, then the owners, then Honey Sue. "It's okay. They don't know we're onto them."

Kip walked over to block the garden door.

Ellis stiffened. "They know."

Alec leaned forward, hands flat on the table. "They don't realize you found the toolbox." He looked at me. "Right?"

"Of course not. At least I haven't said anything in front of anybody."

Ellis and I had been alone when we'd found the box in the rafters and the sabotage tools behind the pillar. Ellis had told Alec and Melody privately in their room. That was it.

Until Alec had mentioned it in front of Claire at the start of dinner.

The other end of the table laughed. All of them looked our way.

I lifted my champagne glass and smiled.

"Excuse me," Claire said from my left. How had she gotten there? "Are you finished?"

"Yes."

She took my plate.

"—and I remember the first time Alec brought Melody home to meet us." Leo's voice carried across the room. "She stood in that doorway, looked at all of Alec's trophies and awards, and said, 'So this is where you keep your participation ribbons.'"

Everyone laughed. Sonya beamed. Even Alec smiled.

"I knew right then she was the one. She didn't see Deputy Alec Duranja, decorated man of the law. She saw him as Alec. Just Alec. The man who will eat burned toast rather than waste it and can't fold a fitted sheet to save his life—"

More laughter. Melody took Alec's hand. Claire cleared our plates.

"—who's hard to get to know but loves with his whole heart. Melody, you've made my son happier than I've ever seen him. And Alec, you found someone who makes you laugh even when the world gets dark. That's the kind of love that lasts."

Leo raised his glass. "Here's to Melody and Alec."

We all raised our glasses.

"May nothing stand in the way of your happiness."

I drank. We all did.

Ellis's phone vibrated against the table.

I froze.

I looked at Melody over my glass. She'd turned to Alec.

Ellis grabbed his phone. "We've got the background reports."

This was it. "What does it say?"

Ellis scanned too fast for me to read.

"Kip and Lonnie are in a property dispute." He glanced to the owners by the door. "Mort Shackleton was named in the Byrne family will. He had a claim on the estate." He glanced up. "The lawsuit died with him."

"That's a motive for murder." I stared at Kip.

He didn't even blink.

Melody leaned in. "Okay, but why would Kip or Lonnie try to kill Alec?"

"Good question." I didn't have an answer.

"I'd never met them before today," Alec said.

Ellis kept reading. "And now we know why Chef Duchamp is working weddings. He's been arrested twice for theft."

Melody nearly knocked over her glass. "Cash for his gambling?"

Chef slammed a chocolate soufflé down in front of her. "Oh my," she said as it collapsed like a maiden on a fainting couch.

Brett's camera flashed.

"I do not have a gambling problem," he spat. "And I didn't get fired."

Ellis watched him storm off. "Says here he was skimming money off the top. Expensing high-cost items like truffles and then substituting farmer's market mushrooms."

"I wouldn't be able to tell the difference," I admitted.

Give me a nice, homegrown mushroom any day.

"Put that phone away and enjoy your dessert," Sonya called from the other end of the table. "I never allowed phones at the table..."

"Ellis just has to show me something," Alec said, even though she wasn't listening anymore.

I leaned in. "The pdf is so tiny."

Brett moved in, his camera hand resting on his shoulder. "Kip needs a picture of Alec enjoying his dessert. Upon pain of death."

Alec looked at his empty charger plate. "I didn't get any dessert."

Chef had abandoned us after his encounter with Melody.

"Be right back." Brett left.

"I swear this is like trying to solve a murder in the middle of a..." Ellis pressed his fingers to his temples.

"A wedding party?" Melody offered.

Ellis shot her a dry look.

"Is there anything on Brett?" I watched him glance over his shoulder as he found Chef.

Ellis squinted at the screen. "Two DUIs in Connecticut. One bankruptcy. One marriage license." He glanced at Brett, who was in a heated discussion with Chef. "Huh."

Melody followed his gaze. "What?"

"He's married to Claire."

We watched Claire slip past Chef, grab a tray full of soufflés, and head our way.

We all smiled too brightly as she set plates in front of Alec, Ellis, and me.

"Thank you," I told her. "It looks delicious."

"He's a good man," she said under her breath.

"Brett?" I asked. But she was already gone.

"Verity," Carl's voice called from the other end, "are you listening to Leo's stories about Alec as a boy? You'll appreciate this one."

I smiled. "Wouldn't miss it!"

Leo was mid-story about eight-year-old Alec trying to arrest the mailman for trespassing.

Ellis had switched to Google. "According to the local business journal in Connecticut, Brett has been working for the Pierces since shortly after his arrest. He gets free housing and a generous salary."

"So he's loyal." Melody watched him return to our end of the table.

"And he wants me to eat this." Alec stared down at his soufflé.

Brett raised his camera. "Come on now. Take a bite and look like you're enjoying yourself."

Alec raised his fork. Posed for the camera. "Hate to tell you, but I'm allergic."

Brett's mouth tightened as he took the shot. "Isn't that bad luck?"

"Yoo-hoo!" Sonya called. "Get a picture of us laughing."

I waited until Brett left. "What about Honey Sue?"

Ellis set down the phone. "Her record's clean." He looked to Alec. "But I wanted to ask you, do you remember the Abernathy case?"

"Sure," he said, pushing his plate away as if it might bite him. "Will Abernathy. I arrested him for embezzlement eight years ago." He rested his elbows on the table. "It was sad. He killed himself in prison."

Ellis looked toward Honey Sue. "He was her fiancé."

"Poor thing." Melody's voice softened.

"That's awful," I murmured.

No wonder she'd been hesitant to share engagement stories with me earlier.

Honey Sue stood near the garden door, clipboard pressed to her chest. She'd seemed so warm during our photo shoot, so genuinely excited about the wedding. Had she planned her own wedding once? Picked flowers, tasted cakes, only to have it all fall apart?

"She dodged a bullet," Alec said. "Abernathy embezzled from their church building fund. Nearly two hundred thousand dollars." He caught Honey Sue's eye from across the room. "He was a smooth operator. I could see how she got taken in."

It was still heartbreaking, I knew. I'd misjudged my old fiancé, and it still stung to think how badly I'd been duped.

At least I'd moved on. Honey Sue hadn't. Not in eight years.

"So anybody could have done it," I said.

Ellis pocketed his phone. "We thought the reports would narrow it down."

"Instead, it gave everyone a motive," Melody said.

Alec pressed his fingers to his temples. "Kip and Lonnie want the property. Honey Sue could blame me for her fiancé's death. Chef needs money, so anybody could be buying him off. Brett and Claire are loyal to the Pierces, who have a clear title to the property now that Mort's gone."

"And Claire's standing by her man," I said.

Dessert was winding down at the other end of the table. Claire cleared plates. Carl talked with Sonya and Leo. Reverend Grace had cornered Mom. Everything looked normal.

Except someone here wanted Alec dead.

"What do we do?" Melody's voice came out tight. "The wedding is tomorrow."

Alec sat, grim. "Even if we left right now, I wouldn't be safe."

He was right. Our best shot was to solve this.

I looked at Ellis. "This is our last chance with everyone together."

I scanned the room. Chef Duchamp at his station. Claire making another round with the wine. Kip and Lonnie by the door. Honey Sue with her clipboard. Brett adjusting his camera.

They all had secrets.

Then it hit me.

"I have an idea." A way to flush out the killer.

Three pairs of eyes locked on me. If I stopped to explain, I'd lose my nerve.

I stood and picked up my champagne flute. Tapped my fork against the crystal. The clear chime cut through the conversation.

"I need everyone's attention." I raised my voice and put on my best Southern-belle smile. "I have an announcement to make."

## Chapter Nineteen

Melody choked on her champagne. "What are you doing?"

"Trapping the killer," I said under my breath, keeping my smile fixed as the room quieted.

"At dinner?" Her voice cracked.

"This hasn't exactly been your typical dinner." Although I knew better than to think our killer would give themselves up so easily.

Still. There was no getting around it. If we didn't lay this trap tonight, we'd be walking into tomorrow's wedding with a target on Alec's back. And possibly Melody's. And after tonight's dinner, I'd probably earned one as well.

All our suspects had motive. Kip and Lonnie stood to gain control of the property with Mort dead. Honey Sue could blame Alec for her fiancé's suicide. Chef Duchamp needed money for his gambling debts. He could be bought off by anybody. And Brett and Claire were loyal to the Pierces, who had big plans for the estate and wouldn't let anything—or anyone—stand in their way.

Worse, every single one of them had opportunity. They'd all been on the property when the statue fell, when Mort was murdered, when someone hid that toolbox in the rafters.

Any of them could have snuck upstairs that first night to drug Alec.

But there was one thing our killer hadn't anticipated; Ellis and I had found Mort's toolbox. If they hadn't had time to hide it well, they probably hadn't wiped the evidence tying them to it, or to Mort's murder. We'd had the place under guard up until the Jackson police left.

But that was *after* everyone arrived for the rehearsal dinner.

We needed to make them think we were set to catch them come morning. Force them to make a move tonight.

And hoped to heck we were ready when they did.

I took a breath and looked out over the table. Candlelight flickered across my mother's expectant face, Carl's quizzical expression, and Claire's strained features as she topped off his wineglass.

Chef Duchamp stood at his station, fists clenched, next to Honey Sue. Kip and Lonnie stopped their quiet conversation. Brett lowered his camera, just slightly.

I cleared my throat.

"I want to let everyone know we just got word from the Jackson police. The officers guarding the chapel have left for the night, but they'll be bringing in a forensics team at dawn to process the chapel gallery."

Mom dropped her soufflé fork. "Tomorrow morning?"

Leo tossed down his napkin. "That's nuts. The wedding's tomorrow."

"Tell them *no*," Sonya snapped.

"We can't." Alec rose to his feet. "The Jackson police believe the attack on me may be connected to the murder in the carriage house."

Sonya gasped. Mom looked ready to faint, Leo fumed, and Carl appeared disinterested. Dang. If he wasn't my stepdad, I'd think he was in on it. Our suspects were another matter.

Brett went rigid. Claire lowered her silver coffee pot to the point of spilling a bit on the floor. Honey Sue drew a hand to her chest, stricken. Lonnie stood gaping, and Kip said, "Absolutely not."

"I don't think we get a choice when there's been a murder," I reminded him.

"He was an employee," Kip insisted.

"A man died," Melody said as she stood. "I don't see any harm in moving the ceremony to the garden."

Kip crossed the room, his footsteps heavy on the hardwood. "You are here for the ultimate wedding package, and we are here to make sure you get it."

"We have vendors coming," Lonnie said, bringing up the rear. "Deliveries."

Honey Sue had commandeered the coffee pot and poured herself a shaking cup. "The florist needs access at six a.m." Color rose to her cheeks. "Perhaps the police will work around Peg and Kitty. They're professionals, too."

"A murder investigation isn't going to work around your flower delivery," Alec said with a bit too much relish considering this was his wedding.

"This is a disaster." Brett slung his camera around his neck. "I need those shots of the chapel interior for the website and for the brochures we were supposed to print last week," he added, eyeing Kip.

Kip nodded. "Mort would have wanted it that way."

"Seriously?" Ellis said.

"How about some coffee?" Claire skirted the table to pour us each a cup.

Chef Duchamp stood with his back to the window wall. He hadn't said a word, but the look he aimed at me could have curdled cream at twenty paces.

Sonya stood. "Alec is right." She shot him a loving look down the table. "We need to do what the police say."

Leo tossed his napkin onto his plate and joined her. "Alec's a smart officer. We trust him. We're proud of him."

Kip threw up his hands. "What are we forgetting? I'll tell you what we're forgetting. This is my venue. My call."

Leo smirked. "You can tell that to the police when they arrive at dawn."

"Now wait—" Lonnie started.

"I think what he's trying to say—" Honey Sue insisted.

"I don't care what the lot of you think you know—" Leo was going strong.

"That went well," Ellis said to me.

"It did," I remarked, taking a sip of champagne. We'd set the trap. "The killer will have to retrieve any evidence they left behind. When they do, we'll catch them."

"It can't look like we're trying to catch them," Melody said, leaning a hip on the table.

Alec nodded. "Okay, we'll make it seem like we're having a pre-wedding party up in the honeymoon suite."

Perfect. "They'll think the chapel is empty. We'll put someone up in the gallery. When the killer goes to retrieve the toolbox, we'll catch them red-handed."

"This is why I love you," Ellis said, leaning to kiss me on the cheek. I shifted so he got my lips instead. He lingered while I reminded him exactly why he loved me.

"I feel like we're the ones who should be doing that," Melody said to her fiancé.

"Do you remember the cemetery?" he prodded.

I didn't want to know.

Ellis pulled back. "I'll take first watch."

"I'll relieve you at midnight," Alec said. When we all looked at him, he added, "Too wired to sleep anyway."

"Hate to break it to you, buddy, but you're not going anywhere," Ellis said, planting a hand on his friend's shoulder before taking a healthy sip of black coffee. "You're the target."

"I'm not a damsel in distress." Alec scowled at him. "And you need sleep too."

"I'll relieve him," I piped up.

"No, you won't," Ellis said. He loved taking first watch and then never waking anyone else up. "I've worked on no sleep before." He took another swig of black coffee.

"He has, you know," I reminded Alec.

Melody wound her hand into his. "You'd do the same for him."

"I know." Alec winced, shaking his head. "But I don't have to like it."

Ellis snagged his cup and my full one for the road. He kissed me on the head and headed out.

"Wait—" People might notice.

Melody and Alec took the cue and walked over to his parents, who were still arguing with Kip. My parents had sat back down to enjoy their wine and had somehow talked Honey Sue into joining them.

"Excuse me, everyone?" My sister's voice cut through the chaos, clear as a bell.

Honey Sue stood and quickly ditched her wineglass.

Melody tucked a strand of hair behind her ear. "Alec and I, along with Verity and Ellis, are going to head up to the honeymoon suite for a little pre-wedding celebration." Melody's smile was pure Southern grace. "Just the four of us."

Chef stiffened. "I'll see if I have *more* charcuterie."

"No, thank you," Melody said quickly. "No fanfare. No pictures," she added to Brett, who looked ready to say something. "Ellis is grabbing his bottle of Southern Spirits. That's plenty for us. We'll want to turn in early to make sure we're well rested for tomorrow."

"Perhaps some wine?" Claire ventured.

Melody waved her off. "I have a bottle." She turned to our parents. "Mom, Carl, Leo, Sonya, thank you for being here. For making this weekend so special." Her voice caught. "It means everything to us."

"Oh, sweetie." Mom dabbed at her eyes. Sonya beamed. Even Leo softened.

"Dinner was absolutely lovely," I added. "You all enjoy the rest of your evening. We'll see you bright and early."

And hopefully, with the killer behind bars.

We made our way toward the stairs as the wedding location debate started up again. We'd leave them to it. We had bigger fish to fry.

"You know, I don't even care if the wedding is in the cemetery," Melody said to Alec. "I just want to marry you."

"I prefer the garden," he said, "where there are no dead bodies."

I didn't have the heart to tell him.

We hurried up the stairs, Melody and Alec first, with me on their tail. She shot me a glance over her shoulder. "Do you think they noticed Ellis left early?"

"You covered it well. With any luck, he's halfway to the chapel by now."

"He'll beat our killer there, and that's the important thing," Alec said, hitting the landing.

Melody stopped by their room to grab the wine, I checked on Lucy, and Alec went straight to the honeymoon suite.

My skunk wasn't in her bed or in our room. And when I saw a fresh clump of mud on the floor, I knew.

She'd snuck out with that boy again.

There were too many people coming in and out of this house, and it was clear none of them were watching for sneaky skunks, one of whom should know better.

That was it. We were going to set some rules come tomorrow.

I ran into Melody in the hall. "Lucy got out again."

"I think you should ground her," Melody said.

"Stop smiling," I said, heading for the honeymoon suite.

"You're going to be a strict mom."

"I just want the best for my little girl," I said, pushing the door open.

A chilly breeze wafted from the open balcony doors. Alec stood outside with both hands on the rail, tempting fate.

"Can you not be the groom standing on the balcony the night before his wedding?" Melody asked, depositing the wine on the low table by the doors. "Grooms were killed fifty years ago and a hundred years ago on this very night. In the very spot you're standing."

Well, technically on the pointy fence below.

"The light in the chapel is off." Alec turned, resting his hands on his hips. "The Jackson police turned it off when they left."

Yikes. That meant Ellis would be forced to wait in the dark. He'd need those two cups of coffee to stay awake.

"At least he'll get a jump on the killer," I said, trying to sound more confident than I felt.

"Unless the killer gets a jump on him first." Alec's voice was flat.

"Don't say that." Melody joined him near the rail. "We're worried enough as it is."

"I'm just being realistic." He dug a hand through his hair. "It should be me out there."

"He's doing this for you like you'd do it for him," I said, stopping at the door. "It's fine."

Only it wasn't fine. Not by a longshot. Ellis was hiding in the dark in the chapel gallery, guarding the only evidence we had linking Alec's attacker to Mort's murder, waiting for a killer who'd already proven they weren't afraid to strike.

"We're supposed to sound like we're having fun," Melody said suddenly. "Like we're celebrating."

We looked at each other. Then Alec let out the most forced laugh I'd ever heard. Melody giggled nervously. "Whee..." I managed.

We sounded like three people who had never been to a party before.

Alec dug his hands into his pockets and appeared surprised when he withdrew a small jewelry box.

Melody lit up. "Is that a present?"

"Could you be any less coy?" He grinned despite himself.

"You like me this way," she said, reaching for the box.

"No jewelry." I halted that train before it got started. "It upsets the ghost."

"Verity's right. We'll do this when things calm down," Alec said, popping it back into his pocket.

"Tease." Melody went to lean against the iron rail, but Alec caught her arm before she could.

"Stop."

She startled, and the whole rail swayed. She didn't notice. "Is that Lucy down there?"

"Don't." Alec pulled her back. "The bolts are loose."

"Really?" Melody tested them.

I did too. The entire railing tipped hard.

I shared a wide-eyed stare with Melody. That wasn't normal give. And it hadn't been like that yesterday.

Oh, my word. "This thing is rigged."

"Designed to go down as soon as I put any real weight on it." Alec ushered us back inside. "Focus. Let's worry about the problems we don't see coming."

"Did you really see my skunk out there?" I asked Melody.

"Yes," she said as Alec shut the doors.

At least I could see out the window.

Dang it. There she was. Romping in the garden with Lucky.

He'd better not be *getting* lucky.

"I haven't seen anyone crossing over to the chapel yet," Alec said from the other window. "The party in the ballroom has to have broken up by now."

As if on cue, I heard our parents tromping up the stairs.

Melody let out a laugh like a dying hyena.

"What?" she asked when we both stared. "Somebody has to sound like we're partying."

I leaned against the wall. "What kind of parties does this man take you to?"

"You've known her longer," he said, crossing to the mantel.

Melody poured herself a glass of rosé wine. "You're the one marrying me." She toasted him, then took a bracing swig.

He placed the velvet box from his pocket right next to Lady Brigid's jewelry box. "I'm leaving this here for safekeeping." He eyed his fiancée. "Don't touch it."

"Why would I?" she asked.

"Because you're Melody," I answered.

Alec tried to smile, then let out a curse instead. "I've got to do something. I feel like an ass hanging out up here."

"Let Ellis work," I ordered.

"How about I go get your skunk?" he offered.

Now he was talking.

"How about you sit down?" she said to him, refusing to even look at me.

She knew my weakness.

So did Alec.

"It would give him something to do," I reasoned. *Where we could keep an eye on him.* "Just make sure that jerk doesn't try to follow her to bed again."

"Again?" Melody lowered her glass and raised her brows.

"Don't ask."

Melody turned her head. "Is he—?" she started. Then we both realized Alec had escaped into the hall.

"He's fine," I said, moving to the window. Alec was like Ellis. He needed to be doing something.

Plus, the closer he was to the ground, the better.

As if on cue, the balcony doors began to creak open.

"I hate when they do that." Melody retreated toward the fireplace.

"Just stay away from the mantel." I didn't want anyone near Lady Brigid's jewelry box.

A few minutes later, I saw Alec out on the lawn. "Oh, good."

Lucy was climbing up onto the fountain to join Lucky on the rim. "They'd better not be skinny-dipping."

Melody joined me at the window. "Let me see."

"Look at the way he swishes his tail. Like he's all that." He rubbed his nose on her nose. "He's going to give her cooties."

"Verity." Melody's voice thinned.

"Don't lecture me about being overprotective. You realize he's literally a wild animal."

"Verity." Melody dug her finger into my arm again and again and—

"Ow. What?"

"Alec is headed straight for the chapel."

"Frick." She was right. "He lied to us!"

"Are you surprised?"

"Kind of." Ellis wouldn't have done that. He'd have told me the truth.

"He's a low-down, no-good do-gooder." She spun and deposited her wine on the table. "I'm going after him."

"Not you, too."

Alec had become a shadow in the dark, heading straight for the copse of trees and the cemetery. Then I saw the glow of Frankie and his buddies.

"For heaven's sake. Frankie's out there too." Which was actually good. "He can act as a lookout. I'll go talk to him."

"We can't both go," Melody protested, tailing me toward the door.

"Exactly," I said, putting an ear to the wood, making sure the hall was clear. We didn't need anyone to see our dwindling group.

Melody planted her hand above my head. "So I'm in here partying by myself?"

"Yes." I straightened. "That's your job."

She stared me down.

"You're good at it," I added.

"Now I know you're full of horse pucky."

But she didn't protest anymore as I eased the door open. In fact, her attention was drawn to Lady Brigid's portrait staring down at her as I slipped out into the hall.

The corridor stood empty. Way too quiet for a house full of wedding guests.

I hurried toward the stairs, my footsteps muffled on the runner. And as I stepped outside, I could see Alec's silhouette disappearing into the trees.

And beyond him, in the chapel window, a flicker of light where there shouldn't have been any.

## Chapter Twenty

I burst down the front stairs and into the night, making a sharp left past the garden.

Lucy pranced along the fountain rim with Lucky in her wake. Then she dove into the water and swam a circle while he belly-flopped in after her.

"Lucy!" I hissed, not slowing down.

This was not *The Blue Lagoon*.

I didn't have time for this. Couldn't deal with teenage skunk romance when Alec was about to get himself killed.

I chucked off my heels and ran faster. Alec's shadowy figure had already disappeared into the trees, heading for the cemetery and straight for the chapel beyond.

"Alec!" I hissed, knowing better than to call out. I didn't want to give away his presence or mine.

The stubborn, reckless, self-sacrificing jerk.

He just had to be the hero instead of letting his best friend protect him for once. Never mind that he was the target and that he'd already almost been murdered once today.

Shouldn't once be enough?

Noooo. He had to rush into a dark chapel to rendezvous with his killer.

Ellis had it handled. That was the plan at least.

Although Ellis would never have turned the light on in that chapel.

I pushed past a low branch, barely feeling it scrape across my arm.

Why couldn't we all just be partying in the honeymoon suite for real? Drinking Melody's wine and Ellis's Southern Spirits and talking about nothing more dangerous than my friend Lauralee's four young boys attending a reception that involved a fountain?

Leave it to my skunk to swim in it first.

I glanced back at the house, at the warm glow of the windows.

And my heart stopped.

Melody stood on the balcony. Alone.

Seriously?

I had to think she was smart enough to stay away from the rail. That someone wouldn't sneak up and push her, even though I'd left the door unlocked.

I halted. Reached for my phone in my bag.

Only I'd left both upstairs in my room.

Damn it.

If it were Melody versus Alec, I'd choose Melody.

She picked that moment to turn and walk back into the room.

Thank heaven. I ran for the chapel.

Now Melody just needed to stay inside with those balcony doors closed. She had to lock the door to the honeymoon suite. And she had to stay away from that pretty velvet jewelry box.

Why had he even told her he was going to give her a present, much less left it on the mantel?

Melody was a terrible snoop when it came to gifts. Always had been. When we were kids, she'd find every single Christmas present Mom hid. She was a master unwrapper/rewrapper. And even if she didn't open the box on the mantel and try on the Duranja family heirloom, she might console herself by opening the other box. The one with Lady Brigid's bracelet.

That would be a nightmare.

"Watch it!" Frankie burst out from behind the Celtic cross tombstone and nearly ran me over. I dodged and leapt over a ghostly canvas bag the size of a small child. Then I about brained myself dancing past a brick of clay wrapped in a newspaper that screamed *Babe Ruth Hits 54th Home Run!*

"She's a disaster!" Dapper Dan's voice rang out to my left.

"That's my dynamite!" Knuckles materialized way too close, grabbing for the bundle.

Frankie's eyes bugged out. "We're about to execute the heist. Go away."

"You—" I stopped. They had wire running along the ground, connected to a wooden box with a plunger.

Lenny picked it up. "You didn't see this."

"No, no, no, no." They had even more dynamite stacked next to the grave by Lenny. Loads of it. "You said you were going to wait till after the wedding."

Frankie zipped up close. "The guys aren't waiting."

"We worked together, like you said." Lenny grinned.

"We figured it out," Dapper Dan added.

"The jewels are in the altar!" Knuckles held up a brick of dynamite like a trophy.

What? Wait. "Don't do this. Don't touch Lady Brigid's jewels. Don't even think about them."

"Sorry, babe." Dan winked. "It's going down now."

"I need to be there to get my share of the loot," Frankie said as if he were powerless to stop it.

"We're gonna blow the thing sky-high." Lenny rubbed his hands together.

"You think five charges are enough?" Knuckles asked.

"Better make it twelve," Frankie said.

"Frankie!"

Dapper Dan smoothed his mustache. "I'm not going to heaven anyway. Might as well make it count."

"Control them," I commanded my ghost.

He looked at me like I'd asked him to change the weather. "Are you serious?."

Oh, what was I thinking? I couldn't even control my skunk or my sister or *Alec*.

I had to get in there and stop Alec and Ellis from being killed before the gangsters blew the chapel up.

But not before I stomped a living foot right down in the middle of their detonation wire. It stung like the dickens, but I didn't care. Let them try to blow the place once that little piece disappeared.

Frankie saw me do it. His expression darkened, but he didn't rat me out.

Yes, well, it was either that or ask him to take his power back, and I didn't want to be blind in case Lady Brigid showed up.

I notched my chin. "Did you see Alec pass this way?"

"We've been busy putting together a *masterpiece*," he growled.

One that I'd just stomped on.

"Did you see anyone else?" I prodded. Like the killer. "Think."

He held out his hands. "I've been busy."

"Hey…" Knuckles pointed as part of his wire began to fade.

"I gotta go." I ran straight for the chapel, then slowed as I neared the stone building.

A shadow of a man disappeared around the corner. Alec?

Something moved behind the stained-glass window near the altar.

Ellis was supposed to be on the second floor, guarding the evidence.

I edged the heavy door open with barely a whisper and slipped inside.

No one stood near the windows by the altar. The pews sat empty. Waiting.

The light flickered, then held steady.

Above me, a floorboard creaked.

## Chapter Twenty-One

I hurried up the spiral staircase, my bare feet light on the wood.

When I reached the gallery, I turned left, to the wing where Ellis should be.

*Would* be.

I saw him halfway down, slumped on the floor, his back against a roof support beam. His head tilted to one side, his legs stretched out in front of him.

Oh no.

"Ellis," I whispered, dropping to my knees beside him. "Hon." I cupped his chin, tilted his head up.

He was out cold.

I checked the back of his head for blood. Nothing. Thank goodness I didn't see any injuries. His skin was warm, his breathing steady. "Come on." I patted his cheek. "Please."

He didn't even flinch.

I sat back, not sure what to think. Then I saw a coffee cup from dinner lying on its side under the church pew, a dark stain spreading across the wooden floorboards.

The coffee.

Someone had drugged the coffee.

*Did I drink any?* My heart caught. No. Ellis had taken both cups, mine and his.

I scanned the gallery, peering into the shadows at both ends. The benches. The pillars. The sloping roof.

We were alone up here.

For now.

I pushed to my feet and climbed onto the pew. I stood on it, using the pillar for cover as I peeked between the roof support and the sloping eaves.

The toolbox was gone!

Voices drifted up from below.

No. Wait. They weren't coming from the main chapel.

I scrambled off the pew and followed the sound to the wood-paneled wall at the end of the gallery.

That didn't make sense. Until I realized it wasn't a solid wall.

Up close, I could see the gap along one edge. A seam in the wood where there shouldn't be one.

It was a door.

That was how the killer had escaped.

I had to go down. But first, I hurried back to Ellis. "Sorry, babe," I murmured, reaching for the back of his belt, for the holster where he kept his service revolver.

It was empty.

He hadn't brought his gun.

That...wasn't like Ellis. Only he'd come here straight from the rehearsal dinner.

I wiped a stray hair out of my eyes. That was okay. I could handle this. I hoped.

I eased the door open, holding my breath as the hinges creaked.

Alec's voice drifted up, strained. "Put the gun down."

Now I really, *really* wished I had Ellis's service revolver. I slipped through the opening and found myself on a narrow staircase leading down into darkness, stone walls on both sides.

I pulled the door closed behind me and descended as quietly as I could, one hand against the wall for balance.

"You destroyed him!" Honey Sue's voice cracked with rage, and I nearly tripped down the rest of the flight.

Honey Sue?

No. It couldn't be.

Not Honey Sue, who'd coordinated nearly every funeral reception and church bazaar in Sugarland. Not Honey Sue, who'd wanted to plan my wedding, who'd been so excited about Melody's big day.

The person who'd handed Melody the opportunity to be here this weekend. The perfect venue. The perfect wedding.

*The perfect setup.*

Oh, my God.

"Your fiancé destroyed himself," Alec said, his voice cold, matter-of-fact.

"You were the one." Her voice shook. "You were the one who sent him to prison."

I ventured another step down. Alec had been the arresting officer. He'd testified against Will in court.

"You shamed him!" Honey Sue's voice rose, raw and broken. "You paraded him out of the church potluck in handcuffs. You made sure everyone saw. The people at church, his neighbors, his own mother. And when he couldn't take the humiliation, he killed himself in his cell." Her voice cracked. "You didn't even care."

"He stole from those exact same people," Alec gritted out. "He should have felt ashamed."

"You never cared about those people. You cared about being right. About following your precious rules no matter whom it destroyed." A hollow sob escaped her. "Hands back up," she demanded.

"Take it easy," Alec said as I neared the bottom.

The staircase opened into a small reception area, a servants' entrance, where the help could slip into the chapel and reach the gallery without disturbing the family. An empty coat rack sat against one wall, and a cardboard box huddled in the corner, stuffed with programs for tomorrow's wedding.

Honey Sue stood between me and Alec, her back to me, the gun leveled at his chest. The archway leading into the church loomed behind him, and the altar lay beyond.

"You arrested a good man. A decent man who never hurt a soul."

His eyes went hard. "Tell that to the congregation who lost their building fund for the free preschool and Sunday school addition. Tell that to the people counting on the food pantry they had to shut down to fix the roof."

His gaze found me, but he didn't react.

"No one's coming," she said, leveling the gun at him. "I made sure of that. They're all back at the house, drugged, fast asleep. We have all the time in the world."

Could I jump her? I wasn't sure how without causing her to shoot him.

Alec stared her down. "William would be ashamed of you. You're a murderer."

I closed my eyes. For the love of—*Shut it, Alec. Please. Just once.*

"You're the killer," she ground out. "I need you to admit it," she hissed. "I need you to say you were wrong. Say that Will Abernathy was a good man and you destroyed him for nothing. I won't let you go to your grave thinking you were right. Thinking you were some righteous hero when all you did was ruin everything."

I took a few steps closer to Honey Sue.

Alec glared at me. *Don't.*

He retreated into the church.

"Look at you. Ready to collapse on the altar like a damned martyr," Honey Sue spat.

I followed them as quietly as I could. I turned the corner and got a crystal-clear view of what was happening behind Alec at the altar.

Lenny and Knuckles crouched low, working fast. Frankie appeared to be supervising. Dapper Dan hovered behind. "I still say you could have spliced the wires back together."

"This is better." Duct tape screeched as Lenny wrapped it from the floor all the way up and over a block of dynamite Knuckles pressed against the base of the altar. Then around again. "More dramatic."

They were wiring the altar to blow.

"You missed a spot." Frankie pulled a cake of explosives out of his suit pocket and stuffed it between two loaded charges.

He was going to kill himself.

Again.

"Say it!" Honey Sue screeched. "Say you were wrong!"

She steadied her aim.

"I wasn't wrong, and you know it." The corner of Alec's mouth tilted up. "That's what drives you crazy."

That mouth was going to get him shot.

I knew because I'd wanted to shoot him plenty of times myself.

But what could I do? Hit her with the coat rack? Throw a box of wedding programs at her? She was armed, and she'd already killed once.

"I think that'll do her." Knuckles stepped back like a proud papa. And as his buddies admired his work, I saw the true horror of the situation. If those explosives were in *our* world, they'd have taken down the entire church. "Let's blow this thing."

"Say it!" Honey Sue pulled the trigger.

A bullet whizzed past Alec's shoulder.

For the first time, he looked scared.

And I had hope. Knuckles backed up, his hand on the detonator. Dapper Dan put his fingers in his ears. Lenny rubbed his hands together.

An explosion on the other side could be enough. Traumatic ghostly events could bleed over. It might offer a distraction, something to pull Honey Sue's attention away just enough to give me an opening.

If Alec could keep his mouth shut long enough not to get shot.

"Stop." Frankie put his hand between Knuckles's open palm and the detonator.

*What?*

I nearly said it out loud.

My housemate locked eyes with me. "There's living people too close by. I got your back, Verity."

Noooo.

I shook my head at him, motioning frantically. *Go. Go. Do it. Smash it. Explode it.*

I made the motions. I mimed the actions. I practically got out the hand puppets.

"Stop?" Knuckles looked at Frankie like he'd lost his mind.

"Yes. Stop." Frankie threw his hands up. "I owe this to my loyal sidekick."

The one time he listened to me and didn't act like a selfish, self-involved, insane gangster was the one time I actually wanted him to blow it all up.

And I wasn't his sidekick.

"Sorry, kid." Knuckles slammed his hand down on the button.

The explosion ripped through the ghostly side in a brilliant flash of light and fire. I dove behind the archway. Stone chunks flew in all directions on their side. Frankie hit the deck. Dapper Dan skidded behind a pew. Lenny threw his arms over his head. And Knuckles watched it all and laughed like a maniac.

The altar in our world shook violently.

The floor beneath my feet bucked and rolled. The coat rack crashed over. Wedding programs spilled across the floor. Dust rained down from the ceiling.

Alec stumbled against the altar.

Honey Sue lost her balance and shot wild, the bullet firing straight through Knuckles, who let out a curse and glared at her.

The chandelier above the nave swayed wildly, its crystals chiming like mad church bells.

A stone angel toppled from the gallery above.

It crashed down right beside Honey Sue, exploding into chunks on the floor.

She screamed and held her hands up to protect her face.

Alec lunged at her. He got behind her, grabbed her wrist, and twisted. Her revolver clattered to the floor.

On the ghostly side, Knuckles stared at the mangled altar, smoke still rising from where he'd laid the charges. "What the hey? Where are the jewels?"

The altar on our side had a long crack running down one side, but it was still standing.

You had to hand it to old-world craftsmanship.

On the ghostly side, their altar looked about the same—splintered but not destroyed.

Lenny stuck his head into the stone. "I can see them!" he called, voice muffled.

"Then take them," Dapper Dan huffed.

"They're wedged in tight." Lenny pulled his head back out. "We need to blow the altar again."

Knuckles let out a strangled curse. "I used all twelve charges."

Dapper Dan ran a hand down his face. "This is a disaster."

"You said you could blow stuff up!" Frankie hollered.

"What do you call this?" Knuckles gestured at the cracked-but-standing altar.

Lenny pulled out his revolver and fired at the ghostly altar.

The bullet ricocheted off the stone on his side. I heard the high-pitched whine as his ghostly bullet screamed past my ear.

"Watch it!" I stumbled from behind the archway, my hand flying to my ear. It was still there. Both of them, thank goodness. My head rang like I'd been standing inside a church bell.

Alec's head snapped toward me. "Verity," he warned, "let me handle this."

That was when I saw it. Honey Sue had a second gun—Ellis's service revolver. She must have taken it from him upstairs after he'd passed out.

She jammed it against Alec's ribs. "Shut up." Her hair had come loose from its perfect curls. Mascara streaked down her cheeks. "I'm done with you."

Her finger whitened on the trigger.

I stood frozen in the archway.

I needed to do something. *Now*. But I had nothing. No weapon. No plan. No way to get her to lower that gun before she pulled the trigger.

Unless... I looked at the broken altar. At Lenny's head stuck halfway into the ghostly stone, staring at the jewels he could see but couldn't reach.

I had one choice. One way to save Alec.

And it probably wouldn't work, but I was out of options.

I took off at a dead run.

Past Honey Sue and Alec. Past the startled gangsters. Straight for the altar.

"Stop or I'll shoot!" Honey Sue screamed.

"Verity, no!" Alec shouted.

I didn't stop.

I lowered my shoulder and slammed into the cracked stone with everything I had.

Pain exploded through my arm and shoulder. The impact knocked the breath from my lungs, and I bounced backward onto my butt.

The crack splintered wider with a sound like thunder.

Dapper Dan piled on. Knuckles joined him. Frankie landed on top with a whoop.

"What the hell?" Lenny yanked his head out.

He stumbled back as the altar shuddered. Tilted.

And began to collapse.

The crack gaped open. Jewels poured out—diamond brooches, emerald rings and necklaces, diamond-studded pearl chokers and loose sapphires—a glittering waterfall of precious stones and jewelry cascading across the floor in both worlds.

Necklaces tangled with bracelets. Rings bounced and rolled. A tiara clattered down the aisle.

It was a massive haul. Enough to buy the town of Sugarland twice over.

"Thank you, Jesus!" Knuckles pumped his fist in the air.

"Now you find religion," Dapper Dan said, trying on a ring.

Lenny scooped up handfuls of ghostly jewels, letting them run through his fingers. "We're rich! We're filthy stinking rich!"

Frankie looked at me, eyes shining with pride. "I knew you had it in you, kid." He turned to the guys. "I trained her. That's me!"

Honey Sue stared at the fortune spilling across the floor, her mouth hanging open. She dug the gun into Alec's side. "You're as crazy as he is mean," she said to me.

A ruby ring set in gold rolled across the floor toward them.

Honey Sue's eyes tracked it, and for just a moment, I saw her face soften with longing for the ring Will would have given her. The life they'd never have. Then her grief twisted into something raw and ragged.

"You denied me my wedding ring," she said, her voice breaking. She crouched down, keeping the gun on Alec as she lifted the ring, turning it side to side. "I deserved a ring. I deserved a happy marriage."

The air turned ice cold, and a shriek tore through the chapel —inhuman, seething with rage and grief.

Lady Brigid flew down from the ceiling like a vengeful angel of death. Her white gown trailed out like smoke, tattered and stained. Black hair streamed behind her. Her face was a skull, her empty eye sockets black, her jaw hanging open in an eternal scream.

She descended on Honey Sue with terrifying speed.

Honey Sue looked up just as the ghost's hand came down.

The blow caught her on the back of the head.

Honey Sue crumpled to the floor, the gun clattering from her hand, the ring rolling away from her fingers.

She didn't get up.

# Chapter Twenty-Two

I knocked on the door of the honeymoon suite, balancing a cup of coffee in the other hand.

"Come in!" Melody's voice rang out.

I pushed open the door to find the room transformed by morning light. Sunshine poured through the wide-open balcony doors, the white curtains billowing in the warm breeze. A chorus of birds sang in the garden below.

Melody stood in front of a full-length mirror next to the fireplace, radiant in her wedding gown. The white silk hugged her figure before flowing out in elegant lines, her hair cascading down her back, studded with clips tipped with pearls.

I placed a hand over my chest, on the gold and silver filagree cross our grandmother had left to me. "You look gorgeous."

"Look what Alec gave me." She turned, her hand pressed to the sweetheart neckline of her gown.

The diamond necklace was a work of art. A single strand of perfectly matched stones, each set in delicate platinum filigree. The center diamond was larger than the rest, an old European cut, with the depth and fire modern diamonds never quite achieved.

"It belonged to his great-grandmother," Melody said softly,

her fingers tracing the stones. "She wore it on her wedding day in 1947. And her mother wore it before that and smuggled it out of Poland in 1939. It was pretty much all she took when they left for America." Her eyes grew misty. "Alec said his grandmother always told him to save it for someone who made him believe in good things. Who made him believe in forever."

My throat tightened. "You made his happy ever after come true."

She smiled, pure and sweet. "And he did the same for me."

Melody looked to Brigid's portrait above the bed. The painted lady of the manor gazed down at us, serene in her burgundy silk and emeralds. "When he put it on me, I swear I saw her smile."

I studied the proud set of her shoulders, the subtle curve of her lips. "She'd be the one to appreciate a nice necklace."

Melody turned to me. "I called a researcher I know at the Smithsonian, Dr. Patrick Kilbeggan. He specializes in British and Irish decorative arts of the Edwardian period. I asked him to come verify the Irish Crown Jewels." She paused, breaking into a smile. "He's catching the first flight from DC."

I stared at her. "You called in a Smithsonian expert on the morning of your wedding?"

"More like eleven o'clock last night," Melody said. "He should be here soon. I called him right after you and Alec got back with Ellis." She crinkled her face. "How is Ellis feeling, by the way?"

"Hungover," Ellis answered from the doorway. He stepped into the honeymoon suite, one hand pressed to his temple, the other loosening his bow tie. He looked like a modern James Bond in his black tux if you didn't count the fact that his face was pale and his eyes a bit bloodshot. The jacket fit perfectly across his shoulders, and his shoes were polished to a shine. "I feel like someone stuffed cotton in my head and set it on fire." He rested an elbow on the doorjamb. "And I didn't even get to have any fun doing it."

"I'm just glad you're okay," I said, kissing him on the cheek. "That Alec is in one piece. That we're all here, healthy and happy and ready to celebrate Melody and Alec's big day." I leaned into him as he wrapped an arm around my waist. "Where is Alec?"

"He's seeing to Honey Sue." Melody crossed to the low table by the balcony. "She's in custody, but she needs help." She poured a glass of water from a crystal pitcher. "Alec knows he was right to arrest Will, that he was guilty. But he didn't realize how it would impact Honey Sue." She handed the glass to Ellis. "Alec said he'd never been in love before, but now that he knows what it's like to want to spend the rest of your life with someone... Well, he wants her to get the help she needs to work through things. To see if she can make peace with what Will did to himself in prison."

He had been listening last night. He'd wanted to help. Perhaps he really did deserve my sister.

"Excuse us," Sonya called from the doorway behind Ellis.

"Mission accomplished," Mom said, squeezing past us.

We let Sonya through after her.

Mom held up a delicate lace handkerchief, yellowed with age. "I found your something borrowed. Kip is lending us Lady Brigid's handkerchief."

Sonya produced a small velvet box. "And I found something blue." She opened it to reveal a pair of sapphire earrings. "Alec's grandmother brought them. She's been saving them for today."

Melody's eyes glazed, and she held out her hand. "I think I'm going to need that handkerchief."

A few minutes later, I watched as Sonya helped her fasten the earrings in place and tuck the folded handkerchief into the bodice of her gown. "Now do you think you're ready to get married?"

Melody was the picture of a beaming bride. "I do."

Melody walked down the aisle of the historic stone chapel shortly after noon, escorted by Carl. Sunlight streamed through the stained-glass window, pooling across the weathered slate floor, painting the aisle in shades of gold and rose.

Every pew was packed. The whole town of Sugarland had turned out, filling the ancient wooden benches until people stood shoulder to shoulder along the back wall and packed the gallery above.

Police Chief Pete Marshall sat in the second row, his arm draped across the back of the pew behind his wife, Beatrice. She'd worn her best Sunday hat, the one with the silk flowers. Alec's fellow officers from the department filled the row next to them—Deputy Laurens adjusting his tie, Officer Chen trying to keep his toddler from climbing over the pew, Sergeant Williams digging a finger under his necktie.

Virginia Wydell sat behind them with the Sugarland social crowd. And across the aisle, Kay Roan from the hardware store dabbed at her eyes with a tissue. Maisie Hatcher sat in her Sunday best, and Nancy Tarkington, who'd checked out mystery novels from the library every Thursday for the past thirty years, sat bright-eyed near the center aisle.

Bert MacDonald sat tall in his VFW hat, his wife, Ellie, fussing with the program in her lap. Across the aisle, Ovis Dupre had claimed an entire pew for his family—his son Malcolm and Malcolm's wife, Sheree, who ran the craft classes at the community center, corralling their two boys as they swung their legs and poked at each other's shoulders.

Melody's good friend Julie from the New For You resale shop squeezed her boyfriend Todd's hand, both of them beaming. Lee Treadwell, my very first ghost-hunting client, caught my eye and gave me a thumbs-up.

The library staff had taken over a middle section—Jean, Ellen, Sheila, and the rest of Melody's coworkers whispering and smiling, clearly delighted to see their colleague getting married in such style.

In the back corner, Frankie sat with Lenny, Dapper Dan, and Knuckles. They'd straightened their suits and slicked back their hair and were passing a flask between them, celebrating the best way they knew how.

My best friend, Lauralee, waved at me from her spot near the back, somehow managing to keep all four of her boys in line while her husband, Tom, distributed crayons and paper to keep them occupied during the ceremony.

The children from Melody's after-school reading program sat in the third row, scrubbed and dressed so nice. Little Emma Dwyer clutched a handful of wildflowers she'd picked that morning. Seven-year-old Marcus Johnson fidgeted with his clip-on tie.

As Melody passed, five-year-old Lily Chen stood up on the pew. "Miss Melody, you look like a princess!"

The whole congregation laughed. Melody paused to blow her a kiss, and Lily's mother gently pulled her back down, smiling through happy tears.

At the altar, Alec stood waiting. His black tuxedo fit him like it was made for this moment, the bow tie perfectly knotted, a single white rose at his lapel. But it was his expression that made my breath catch, the way he looked at Melody like she was the only person in the world. Like every step she took toward him was a miracle he couldn't quite believe.

Ellis stood beside him, hands clasped, grinning like a fool. He caught my eye, and I smiled back, feeling a warm flutter in my chest. We'd made it. Through murder and mystery, through dark times and doubt, we were here. Watching two people we loved promise each other forever.

In the front pew on the left, Mom pressed a handkerchief to her cheek. On the side closer to where Ellis stood, Alec's parents leaned into each other. His mother's hand rested on his father's arm, her expression soft with joy. Leo dabbed at his eyes with the back of his hand while Sonya whispered something that made him smile.

Reverend Grace stood in front of the crumbled altar, and we'd laid a wreath over the wobbly tile. A crisp white cloth was draped over the broken altar, festooned with arrangements of white roses and hydrangeas.

Carl handed Melody off to Alec, and she took his hand.

He leaned close as his fingers closed around hers. "Hi," he whispered.

"Hi," she whispered back, her eyes alight.

Reverend Grace opened his book of prayers. "Dearly beloved, we are gathered here today..."

His voice filled the chapel, warm and steady. The remaining stone angels looked down from the gallery, their wings spread wide as if in blessing.

When it came time for the vows, Alec's voice cracked on, "for better or worse." Melody squeezed his hands and smiled.

"I now pronounce you husband and wife."

Alec pulled Melody close and kissed her as the chapel erupted in applause. The sound echoed off the ancient stone walls, pure joy in life, friendship, and love.

I smiled at Ellis, then looked back at my sister, radiant in Alec's arms, surrounded by everyone who loved them.

This was what mattered. Love and trust and people who showed up for each other. For better or for worse. Today and always.

The reception was so large it spilled out of the ballroom and into the garden, where outdoor lights crisscrossed overhead and event staff hurried to set up more tables and chairs among the roses. Chef Duchamp, barking orders like a general, arranged a second buffet near the fountain, the scent of honey-glazed ham and buttermilk fried chicken drifting through the evening air.

Everybody was there, laughing and talking, plates piled high with collard greens and sweet potato casserole. The party was going strong, music floating out through the open ballroom doors.

Little Marcus Johnson tore past me, Emma Dwyer and Lily Chen hot on his heels, all three of them shrieking with laughter. Adults lifted their champagne flutes and plates out of the way, grinning as the children wove between the tables like honeybees among flowers.

Brett threaded through the crowd with his camera, snapping photos of Pete twirling Beatrice past the fountain, of old neighbors laughing together, of Mom crying happy tears while Carl tried to feed her a bite of wedding cake.

Melody spotted me from across the garden and waved me over to where she stood with a distinguished-looking man in his sixties, silver hair neatly combed, wearing a tweed jacket despite the warm evening.

"Verity, I'd like you to meet Dr. Kilbeggan from the Smithsonian."

I shook his hand warmly. "I can't believe you made it so fast."

"Congratulations on recovering the lost Irish Crown Jewels, along with so many other priceless treasures that were stolen from my home country."

"You're most welcome." I was touched and still a little shocked. "So the jewels in the altar were the real deal."

He tilted his head. "We still have to examine and catalog everything you've recovered here. But I've confirmed the authenticity of the badge and star of the Order of St. Patrick. Those were the biggest, most heartbreaking loss." His voice softened. "And I never thought we'd lay eyes on the queen's rubies ever again."

As long as he didn't lay a finger on them.

But he must have. I shifted my wineglass to my other hand. "Did you touch them? The jewels?"

Dr. Kilbeggan shot me a puzzled look. "Of course. Why do you ask?"

"Hm." How to explain. "I just would have expected..." I trailed off. Ghostly retribution? Was that even a proper wedding reception topic?

"I measured and matched them to their original pictures," he said.

Maybe Brigid realized he wasn't there to take them for himself.

Melody smiled proudly. "Dr. Kilbeggan has been in contact with the Dublin Castle Trust and the Irish National Museum."

He nodded. "We're working with them to see the jewels are returned to Ireland, where they belong."

*Home.* The word echoed in my mind. Lady Brigid had been so connected to those jewels, tied to them the same way Frankie was bound to his urn. She'd never wanted to be here. Never really belonged here, had she?

She'd been exiled, lost, trapped in a foreign land, clutching onto the only pieces of home she had left.

Maybe she could go home too.

Brett snapped a picture, and behind him, I spotted Kip and Lonnie near the buffet table.

I excused myself and started toward them, but before I could reach them, a flustered Chef rushed up to Lonnie.

His cheeks were red, his tall hat askew. "I didn't make enough food."

Lonnie handed him a champagne from a passing tray. "That's okay. Can you believe it? Everybody brought casseroles."

Sure enough, three long side tables were laden with Pyrex dishes and covered platters. There were green bean casseroles, cornbread dressing, ambrosia salad in cut crystal bowls. I saw smoked brisket, pulled pork, deer sausage with red gravy, wild turkey and dumplings, and at least six tomato pies.

"People love this place," Kip said, grinning at his husband. "Our place."

"Did you see it?" Lonnie asked. "There's an entire party going on in the cemetery. When I saw people heading out there, I had a few of the waiters string some lights. That's a hit, too."

"We're keeping that cemetery," Kip said decisively. He snapped his fingers. "Maybe we should even expand it."

"I'm not sure how I feel about that," Lonnie said, running a hand down Kip's back as if he'd heard this sort of whackadoodle idea before. "Mamas are booking this place like mad. Even without Honey Sue." He pulled a weathered notepad from his back pocket and scanned it. "We're already booked for the rest of the year."

"I'm not surprised at all," I told him. "This is such a special place."

Lonnie shot me a grateful grin. "Nobody in Jackson is interested, what with it being haunted. And it's been harder than I thought to get people to fly out from back East. But Sugarland loves it."

I smiled and took a sip of wine. "Sugarland folks are used to hauntings. It's part of the charm."

For better or worse, these two had inadvertently picked Melody for their promotional wedding. My sister, who was beloved by the entire town of Sugarland. And the townspeople who had come to support her had fallen in love with this venue, too.

Kip shook his head. "I still can't believe our wedding planner was a killer."

"Poor Mort." Lonnie sighed, tossing the dregs of his wine. "He was a good guy."

He was. I tilted my head. "I thought you two were at odds with him."

"Not at all," Kip said. "Mort helped us so much when we first got here. Introduced us around town, showed us the best places to shop, explained all the Southern customs we didn't know about."

"He even brought us a welcome casserole our first week," Lonnie said, grabbing a fresh wine from a passing tray. "Mort taught me how to make proper sweet tea."

Well, of course he would. That should be common knowledge. "But I thought you and Mort were in the middle of a property dispute."

"I suppose you could call it that," Kip said.

"But could you really?" Lonnie asked his partner.

Kip shrugged a shoulder. "Mort was left the caretaker's cottage in the will. We didn't have a problem with that. He'd grown up in that house."

"We did have to have the place rezoned for our business, though," Lonnie said to me. "So it was a legal issue. We paid for his legal fees."

"He didn't have the money," Kip said.

"And he also wasn't the one who needed it rezoned," Lonnie pointed out. "We offered to renovate the outside of the house, free and clear, but he liked it as it was."

Kip looked thoughtful. "We really should fix it up now."

"That's what I've been saying!" Lonnie said. "We'll renovate it and give it over to Brett and Claire. They'll have a nice place to live rent-free for as long as they want to stay here. I mean, the carriage house is fine, but this would be better if they want to start a family."

Brett lowered his camera. "You mean it?"

I turned to find both Brett and Claire standing right behind me. Claire's eyes were teary, a wine bottle dangling from one hand.

"It's what Mort would have wanted." Lonnie clapped Brett on the shoulder.

"Thank you," Claire managed. "That's... thank you so much."

I left them to it.

Frankie was holding court near the fountain with Lenny, Dapper Dan, and Knuckles. They'd commandeered a table and were passing the flask around, laughing uproariously at something Knuckles had said.

I walked over. "Enjoying yourselves?"

"Best party since the Cicero Boys threw that shindig in '22," Frankie declared, raising the flask.

"That one ended with a police raid," Lenny pointed out.

"As all the best ones do." Frankie poured some into a glass Dan held out. "Now can you believe it? We're drinking *with* the fuzz!"

He was right. Chief Marshall stood not six feet away, raising his own glass to his wife.

Dapper Dan smoothed his lapel. "I gotta tell you. That tomato pie is a tease."

"I'll make you one." Frankie's girlfriend, Molly, stood up from her seat on the edge of the fountain.

"It's wonderful to see you," I said as Frankie slung an arm around her and kissed her on the cheek.

"Someone has to keep these boys in line," she said, ruffling Frankie's hat.

"Tell me something," I said, sizing up the guys. "How did you know the jewels were in the altar?"

The four of them exchanged glances.

"You already stole it," I pointed out. "I can't steal it again."

Dapper Dan shot me a grin. "Well," he said, "I knew they had to be in the chapel. What better place for a hidey-hole?"

"My ma told me they was encased in stone," Lenny added. "She overheard it from Lady Brigid herself when she was arranging her hair combs."

Knuckles looked me up and down. "I heard Lord Thomas say the old priest watched over 'em every day. What's in a church, made of stone, and watched over by a man of God?"

"The altar," I finished.

Knuckles smiled. "I always wanted to blow something up."

"Good for you." I supposed. Although there was one thing I had to point out. "You know you can't keep the jewels, right? They'll disappear eventually since you didn't die with them."

Frankie looked at me like I'd missed the point entirely. "But we stole 'em."

"And we did it first." Dapper Dan nodded sagely. "That means they'll always be ours."

As long as they were happy.

Lauralee's youngest, Ambrose, came flying up to me and pulled on my dress. "Miss Verity! Come look!"

I left the gangsters to it and followed the five-year-old over to where Lucy and Lucky faced each other in the grass. Lucky reared up on his hind legs and twirled for the crowd. Lucy mirrored him, her tail fanning out like a feather boa.

"Now she's teaching him tricks?" My mouth dropped open. That was Lucy's trick.

I'd taught her.

Lauralee's other three boys had formed a circle around them, clapping and laughing.

"I think he's fabulously talented," Lauralee said. "Lucy, too. Of course."

Of course.

I felt compelled to point out the obvious. "You realize that's a wild animal."

Lauralee passed me a bit of cheese on a cracker. "Oh, he is not. This skunk is someone's pet. Look at him."

As if on cue, Lucky rolled onto his back while Tommy Junior gently petted his belly. The skunk's little paws waved in the air, setting the boys off in another fit of giggles.

"He did have a friend," I said, "but that man recently passed away."

Lauralee brought a finger to her lip. "You're saying he needs a home."

That was not at all what I was saying. "He has a home. Here."

"But does he really?" She squinched her nose.

Was she even listening to me? "You can't be serious."

"Lucy loves him."

No denying that. "Lucy is out of her mind."

Lauralee gasped. "They could be friends." She slapped a hand on my arm. "I could bring him to visit you."

What? No. "Lucy has enough friends."

"I think she could use one more." Lauralee grinned as she watched Lucky waddle over to Hiram and plant himself in the boy's lap. "Tom?" she called across the garden.

"Wait." We were getting spouses involved? "Don't you think this is a little sudden?"

Now Lucky was in Hiram's lap, snuggling in tight.

Lauralee sighed. "Not when it's true love."

Big Tom walked over with a plate piled high with pulled pork and cornbread dressing. "What's up, buttercup?"

"You know how the boys always wanted a skunk like Lucy?" Lauralee said sweetly. "Well, this little fellow needs a good home."

Big Tom watched as Lucky leapt from lap to lap. He ended it by climbing up George's shoulder and curling up on his head like a furry hat. "Looks like he can handle the boys."

"So it's settled!" Lauralee clapped her hands together. "Boys, we can take him home!"

The kids cheered. Lucky did a little hop-dance. Lucy fluffed her tail out and ran circles around them all.

And I thought, *Well, if Lauralee can control those four boys, she might just have a shot with Lucky the skunk.*

Then I heard a familiar voice behind me. "May I have this dance?"

I turned to find Ellis, his hand extended. The music from inside the ballroom drifted out through the open doors, something slow and sweet.

"I'd love to, but—" I glanced toward the packed ballroom where couples swayed shoulder to shoulder. "I don't think we could squeeze me in there if you greased me."

Ellis smiled big. "Who said anything about the ballroom?"

He took my hand and led me away from the house and the garden and toward the cemetery gates. The trees were strung with party lights, and I could hear music there too.

Someone had set up speakers under the tall oak trees, and several couples danced on the smooth stone pathway between the graves.

Moonlight filtered through a magnificent old magnolia, casting dappled shadows across the dancers. It was beautiful. Romantic in a Sugarland sort of way.

Ellis pulled me close, one hand at my waist, the other holding mine. We swayed together, and I realized how perfectly we fit.

"You know," he said softly, "when I moved back to Sugarland, I thought I was looking for a quieter life. A place to slow down."

"And instead you found gangsters, ghosts, and murder."

"I got you." His thumb brushed across my knuckles. "Everything else is just...atmosphere."

I laughed, resting my head against his shoulder. "That's one way to put it."

"I mean it, Verity." He pulled back just enough to look at me. "This place, this life—it's chaotic and strange and nothing like what I planned. But I wouldn't change it. I wouldn't change you."

My throat tightened. "Even when I tend to attract trouble?"

"Especially then." He brushed a finger along my shoulder. "Though maybe we could aim for slightly less attempted murder in the future."

"I'll see what I can do."

We danced, the music wrapping around us like a dream. Nearby, Bert waltzed with his wife, Ellie, next to Steve and Kay Roan, next to a glowing gray couple dressed in their Edwardian finest. And somewhere not too far, Lucy was probably teaching Lucky another trick. This strange, wonderful, small-town, haunted life was mine.

And so was this man.

"Ellis?"

"Hmm?"

"I love you too."

He kissed me softly. Sweetly. "That's all I need to know."

## Chapter Twenty-Three

A few weeks later...

It felt so good to be back in Sugarland.

"Two scoops of butter pecan," I told Krissy, who worked the counter at Lickety Split Ice Cream.

"And I'll do chocolate," Ellis said.

We stepped out into the perfect fall afternoon, the kind that made it easy to forget about the rain that had soaked Sugarland for the past week. The sidewalks were still damp, puddles collecting in the low spots, but the sun had finally broken through.

Lucy pranced at the end of her leash, inspecting every interesting leaf, rock, and crack along Main Street.

Ellis took my hand as we strolled past Sweetbrew coffee. "I talked to the DA's office today. Honey Sue's being charged with second-degree murder, attempted murder, and assault with a deadly weapon."

I edged closer to him. Even knowing she was guilty, it was hard to think about. "How is she?"

"In the mental health unit at Methodist University Hospital in Memphis." He squeezed my hand. "She's getting the help she needs."

I nodded. That was something at least. Honey Sue had been consumed by grief and rage for so long. It was too bad no one had recognized how bad things had gotten until she'd killed a man.

She'd seen her opportunity when Kip and Lonnie were having trouble booking their new venue. She'd suggested hiring models to re-create the ultimate wedding weekend, and then a "better idea," Melody—spontaneous, budget-conscious Melody—who had been the ideal mark.

The 100th anniversary of the original groom's death was approaching. It had been too perfect.

I lifted my cone and greeted Peggy Wilson from the post office as she passed.

Honey Sue had admitted to loosening the balcony rail on the honeymoon suite the day we'd arrived. Kip and Lonnie hadn't made it to town yet. Chef had been busy in the kitchen. Brett and Claire had been enjoying a day off. And Mort had been out buying party lights for the garden.

Honey Sue had orchestrated our entire first evening on the property as an alibi for herself—the misdirected flowers, the flat tire at the sweet sixteen party. She'd seen to every detail, like the master planner she was. But instead of spending all night handling emergencies as she'd claimed, she'd driven to Jackson and hidden her car in the woods beyond the carriage house.

Lucy stopped to investigate a particularly interesting puddle near a parking meter. I leaned against the meter and let her have her fun.

"Honey Sue slipped into the kitchen while Chef was holed up in the foyer, placing bookie bets," I said, piecing it together aloud. "That's when she drugged the whiskey with crushed Ambien, her own prescription." She'd known just how much it would take.

Ellis stroked Lucy. "We were right there, completely unaware."

I shuddered. "The plan was simple. Wait for you and Alec to pass out, drag Alec's chair onto the balcony, and tip him over the loosened rail." She'd even nailed chair wheels under the legs. We'd missed them entirely.

She'd figured Alec's body weight would do the rest. And it would have, sending him down onto the deadly pointed tips of the iron fence below.

Impaled like the dead grooms decades ago.

"She'd hidden in the room above, her ear to the floor, waiting," he said.

"Only you didn't pass out." Thank heaven. "You escorted Alec from the suite before the drugs fully took hold."

Panicked, Honey Sue had rushed to the second floor and took the laced whiskey, dumping it in the garden. She realized she'd grabbed the cigars as well and tossed them into a rosebush.

"But she kept the crystal decanter," he said, "hiding it under some clothes in her drawer until she could figure out a way to get rid of it for good."

I lifted Lucy up when she looked ready to start playing in the puddle, and gave her a bit of ice cream as compensation.

She did not complain.

"Honey Sue thought she was in the clear," Ellis said once we started walking again. "No one could connect her to anything. Until Mort searched her room—"

And found the decanter.

"That had to be illegal." I hadn't realized he'd be so...enthusiastic.

"It's completely illegal and inadmissible in court." Ellis finished his ice cream and started in on the cone. "But it wasn't her only crime."

"If only she'd have stopped there."

When Mort confronted her with the decanter, she'd asked to speak to him privately. She found a quiet spot, then grabbed it from him and bashed him over the head with it.

Poor Mort. Sweet, nosy, well-meaning Mort.

We passed Tina Louise with her golden retriever and waved while Lucy tried to follow them.

"This way," I coaxed. Lucy aspired to be more of a direction giver than a direction taker.

"She stole his toolbox afterward," Ellis continued. "Hid it in the chapel while she figured out a way to execute plan B—the angel statue. She made the videographer excuse to get away. She tried Mort's chisel first, but it broke. Then she found your discarded crowbar."

"I never should have left that behind," I said.

"You were only trying to help." Ellis shook his head. "In any event, Honey Sue barely had time to hammer that angel loose before Chef arrived to make his phone call; then everyone showed up early for the rehearsal. She waited until she had a clear shot at Alec, gave it one final whack, and escaped down the servants' entrance."

We turned the corner and crossed Main onto Sassafras Street.

"She had to know she'd left her fingerprints all over the tools." They'd found mine along with hers on the crowbar.

Luckily, I'd already confessed my part.

"She didn't want to be seen fleeing with the crowbar or the toolbox. It would tie her directly to Mort's murder. Some of the tools were splattered with his blood." Mick Roan stopped his pickup to let us cross, and Ellis waved his thanks. "Her fingerprints were also all over the toolbox. I saw the Jackson police tests. It was ridiculous. She tried to go back for it, but by then Jackson PD was guarding the chapel."

"Then when I announced they wouldn't be searching until the next day, she suspected it was a trap." I'd done my best, but Honey Sue was smart. "She drugged the rehearsal dinner coffee with the same baggie of crushed Ambien she'd used the first night."

Everyone had drunk it. Everyone except Melody, Alec, and me.

Lucy saw a squirrel and decided to make friends.

I coaxed her back.

"I'm surprised Honey Sue got past Claire." That girl was everywhere.

"I suppose she wasn't looking for someone to lace the coffee."

True.

We walked in companionable silence for a moment, finishing our cones. I felt lighter, talking it through. Like naming it, understanding it, helped put it behind us.

"I did some of my own research on Lady Brigid," I said, tossing my napkin in a trash can as we passed. "With the help of Kip and Lonnie. Remember how Mort was having trouble with that generator downstairs?"

Ellis laughed. "How could I forget?"

That had been the night he'd distracted Mort for me any way he could.

"The generator was new, yet it was causing him all that trouble. And then Knuckles said something that struck me. He said it was Lady Brigid banging around. I wondered why, so I asked Kip and Lonnie to see if there was anything under it." I smiled. Kip hadn't been a fan of the idea, but Lonnie agreed and called in a handyman to move it. "They found a box with Lady Brigid's personal effects stashed in the foundation and forgotten about. Letters from home, her mother's locket, her diary, a pressed four-leaf clover from Ireland. Later generations paved over it."

"And stuck the generator on top."

"Yep. Lonnie emailed me photos of some of the diary pages. Apparently, Brigid had been forced to leave everything she loved when her husband fled Ireland. They brought his estate with them—brick by brick—but none of her things. She struggled with the bugs, the drastic climate change. She died less than a year later."

"And when the opportunity was right, her husband decided to remarry," Ellis said quietly.

"He tried to give her royal jewels to a young Southern woman who wasn't even a lady." It was no excuse. It wasn't right of Thomas to steal those rubies, or for Brigid to wear them in the first place. But still. "I can't deny that she paid dearly for her mistake. I read in her diaries how she'd regretted it. She'd been forced to give up her entire life. Had it taken apart and reassembled across an ocean. All she had left were her pride and those jewels. And then they were gone too."

"I'm glad she's back home," Ellis said.

"Me too." Kip and Lonnie had carefully packed up the box and returned it to Ireland, to Brigid's family estate. It felt right.

Lucy swished her tail as we passed Sarah Beth McClary and her daughter, Meg.

"Did you see Alec yet?" I asked. Melody and Alec had gotten back from their honeymoon the day before, and I'd heard all about it when I'd dropped by with groceries.

I knew she'd be too exhausted to shop.

"Not yet." Ellis grinned. "I can't believe they went glamping in Gatlinburg."

I could. It was so perfectly them. Alec with his love of the outdoors, and Melody, who made sure they had a mini-fridge and running water.

They'd stayed in one of those fancy safari tents with a king-size bed, a woodstove, and a porch overlooking the mountains. "They spent their days hiking, then came back to s'mores and stargazing."

"Alec reserved a tent with a skylight over the bed," Ellis said with a smirk.

"I wouldn't be opposed," I teased.

Ellis laughed, the sound warm and easy. We continued north toward the town square.

"Meanwhile Frankie's been out in his shed for a week straight."

He raised a brow. "Planning their next heist?"

"I'm afraid to ask."

Frankie had been on cloud nine since the wedding. He'd spent every day with Molly, and every evening in the shed with Lenny, Dapper Dan, and Knuckles. Plotting.

"At least he's having fun," Ellis said.

Yes, well, with Frankie, that wasn't always a good sign.

"Lucy's starting to run out of juice," I said as she gave me some slack on her leash.

"I never thought I'd see the day."

"She's been at Lauralee's all day, playing with Lucky."

"How's the new arrangement working out?"

I smiled. "Better than I expected, actually. George has been teaching them to play fetch. He found this little rubber ball, and Lucky brings it back every single time. Lucy only brings it back when she feels like it."

"How very Lucy."

Indeed.

"Tom Junior and Hiram built Lucky a fort out of couch cushions. He sleeps in there during naptime." I grinned. "And Ambrose has been sharing his snacks. Lauralee caught him trying to feed the skunks a peanut butter sandwich yesterday."

"The height of gourmet skunk food," Ellis drawled.

"It wasn't a cinnamon skunk crumble, but Lucky loved it. Lauralee was less thrilled about the peanut butter paw prints all over her kitchen floor."

Ellis took my hand, lacing our fingers together. "Sounds like Lucky found the perfect home."

"He really did." I watched Lucy's tail swish as she was overtaken with a new burst of energy. "Lucy's never been happier. When Lauralee brings him over, the two of them take off like two peas in a pod."

Although she'd gained a bit of weight in her belly lately. Perhaps we ought to start watching how many treats she had over at Lauralee's.

Ellis smiled at her. "I'm glad she found a friend."

Me too.

As long as he behaved.

We'd reached the edge of the town square and saw a couple

picnicking on the courthouse stairs, just past the First Bank of Sugarland.

I began heading that way, when Ellis gently steered me on. That was different.

I figured we could stop by and see how the library restoration was going or maybe sit and talk under the statue of our town founder, Colonel Ramsey Larimore.

"Where are we going?"

He squeezed my hand. "I thought we'd take a walk through Larimore Park."

My heart did a little skip. I hardly ever went to Larimore Park. Sure, it wasn't more than a stone's throw past the square, but the only thing there was the proposal tree.

I tried to keep my voice casual. "That sounds nice."

But inside, my pulse kicked up a notch. The proposal tree was a two-hundred-year-old oak where generations of Sugarland couples had gotten engaged. Where my mom had said yes to my dad. Where it was tradition to carve your initials into the bark afterward. Decades of faded hearts and intertwined letters, each one a promise, a beginning.

Was this... Could he be?

I snuck a glance at Ellis. He looked calm, relaxed, but there was something in the set of his shoulders, the way he held my hand just a little tighter.

Lucy plowed ahead, speeding up as I slowed.

I wanted to remember every moment of this.

I had to fight to keep from holding my breath as we walked through the iron gates into the park. It was small, barely more than a quarter acre, and people who weren't from here often missed it, what with the hedges all around. It didn't even have a bench. But it was one of the most cherished spots in Sugarland.

The massive oak stood at the center, its thick trunk wider than three men lined shoulder to shoulder. The branches spread out in a glorious canopy of deep red leaves.

Beneath that tree was the final resting place of our town

founder, Colonel Ramsey Larimore. Only good luck finding his tombstone. The oak had grown up around it over the centuries, the granite marker embedded deep into the trunk, all but the angel at the top swallowed up by bark and time.

This was a place of tradition. Of permanency. Of roots that ran deep.

I'd walked past this park and this tree a thousand times. I'd admired the carvings, imagined what it must feel like to stand here with the person you loved and know—just know—that this was it. This was forever.

And now I was here. With Ellis.

The wind picked up, sending leaves skittering across the ground.

Lucy broke free and ran to the far edge of the park, where a paper wrapper had gotten caught in a bush. Instant toy.

I left her to it.

The old tree swayed slightly, its branches creaking. I looked up at the arching canopy, the way it bent and curved. It was beautiful. Romantic in a way that made my chest ache.

Ellis led me closer, right up to the base of the trunk where dozens, no, hundreds of initials spoke of love.

*JM + RP 1987*

*Thomas & Betty, forever*

*JG hearts AF*

Some were fresh. Others had darkened with age, but they were all there, all those promises stretching back through time.

"Verity," Ellis said softly.

He was looking at me the way he had that night in the cemetery, when we'd danced under the magnolia tree. Like I hung the moon.

"This life, with you," he said, his voice steady and sure, "it's everything to me."

My throat tightened in the best way. "Me too. I've never been so happy."

Ellis took both my hands in his.

Then he went down on one knee.

My hand flew to my mouth.

This was happening. This was really happening.

He reached into his pocket—

A sharp *crack* echoed through the park.

I started.

The massive oak groaned, a sound so deep and primal it seemed to come from the earth itself.

"Ellis—" I started.

The wind whipped harder.

Another crack, louder this time. The tree swayed, no longer romantic, no longer gentle. The trunk tilted, slowly at first, then faster.

It was falling.

Directly toward us.

"Move!" Ellis yanked me sideways, his arms wrapping around me as we hit the ground hard. I felt the rush of air, heard the deafening crash. I buried my face in his shirt as the impact shook the earth. Branches snapped. Leaves exploded into the air. Dirt and debris rained down on us.

Then silence.

Ellis's weight pressed against me, his body shielding mine. "You okay?" His voice was rough, urgent.

"Yes." I coughed, fighting off the dust. "I think so."

The proposal tree lay on its side, its massive mud-caked roots exposed, its branches littering the park.

Lucy ran to us and buried her face in the crook of my neck. She was shaking.

So was I. "It's okay, baby," I said, holding her tight.

Only it wasn't. The tree had gone down hard, ripping

through layers of soil and stone. A crater gaped where it had stood.

Ellis helped me up. I held Lucy tight and peered down into the hole.

The roots had dragged up more than earth.

Four feet down lay a coffin, the old wood splintered and cracked open.

And inside—

Mercy me and save the gravy. "That's not Colonel Larimore."

And when I saw what else was buried there, I realized our town's most treasured story might have been its biggest lie.

# Note from Angie Fox

Thanks so much for celebrating Melody's wedding with Verity and the gang! I hope you snagged a slice of wedding cake and a plate of Sugarland's yummiest home-cooked casseroles.

Can we talk about Lucy for a second? Because watching her fall for a rough-and-tumble Jackson boy with blue eyes and a shared passion for rose bushes was hands-down my favorite part of writing this book. Those two are ridiculous and I love them.

And speaking of romance...poor Ellis. The man had such a lovely proposal going until the tree fell down. In the next book, A Spirited Scandal, he's determined to do it right and create the perfect proposal for Verity. But between a centuries-old secret turning Sugarland upside down, a brand-new murder, and some big news from Lucy and Lucky, nothing is going according to plan.

A Spirited Scandal releases next spring. I don't have an exact date yet, but sign up for my newsletter at www.angiefox.com and I'll send you updates and behind-the-scenes peeks as we get closer. I promise I only email when there's something exciting to share.

Thanks for reading!
Angie

**Don't miss the next
Southern Ghost Hunter mystery
A Spirited Scandal**

*Ellis is determined to give Verity the perfect proposal. But when a centuries-old secret turns Sugarland upside down and a brand-new murder lands in her lap, nothing is going according to plan.*

*And Lucy's big news isn't helping.*

*New York Times* and *USA Today* bestselling author Angie Fox writes sweet, fun, action-packed mysteries. Her characters are clever and fearless, but in real life, Angie is afraid of basements, bees, and going up stairs when it's dark behind her. Let's face it: Angie wouldn't last five minutes in one of her books.

Angie earned a journalism degree from the University of Missouri. During that time, she also skipped class for an entire week so she could read Anne Rice's vampire series straight through. Angie has always loved books and is shocked, honored and tickled pink that she now gets to write books for a living. Although, she did skip writing for a few weeks this past winter so she could read Charlaine Harris's Southern Vampire mysteries straight through.

Angie makes her home in St. Louis, Missouri with a football-addicted husband, two kids, and Moxie the dog.

Sign up to receive an email each time Angie releases a new book. Go to www.angiefox.com for the link.

www.ingramcontent.com/pod-product-compliance
Lightning Source LLC
LaVergne TN
LVHW040043080526
838202LV00045B/3471